SOUL
FIRE

D1336011

C800491738

Also by Kate Harrison

Soul Beach

SOUL FIRE

Kate Harrison

Indigo

First published in Great Britain in 2012
by Indigo
a division of the Orion Publishing Group Ltd
Orion House
5 Upper St Martin's Lane
London WC2H 9EA

An Hachette UK Company

1 3 5 7 9 10 8 6 4 2

A catalogue record for this book
is available from the British Library.

ISBN 978 1 78062 023 7

Typeset by Input Data Services, Bridgwater, Somerset

Printed and bound by CPI Group (UK) Ltd, Croydon, CRO 4YY

The Orion Publishing Group's policy is to use papers
that are natural, renewable and recyclable products and
made from wood grown in sustainable forests. The logging
and manufacturing processes are expected to conform to
the environmental regulations of the country of origin.

www.orionbooks.co.uk

To Rich, my Barcelona beach buddy

Another death is coming, I can feel it.

Maybe I gained a sixth sense when I decided I would be the last person to hold Meggie Forster. The last person to touch her skin. The last to brush her hair.

It wasn't murder. I was protecting her from the others, the ones who wanted to exploit her face, her name, her soul.

Yet the news headlines talked of slaughter. No! She left the world so gently, under that feather pillow. I made sure of that.

Those unjust stories make me burn with rage, though I try to stay calm. Alice calms me. She is every bit as radiant as her elder sister, but unlike Meggie, Alice doesn't see how special she is. Which, of course, makes her even more precious.

But her obsession with truth endangers us both. An innocent like Alice doesn't realise that in this ugly world, there are a billion versions of the truth. If she cannot accept my version, then another death is inevitable.

I

1

Happiness is simple. All you need are the people you love.

After Meggie died, I thought I'd never be happy again. Yet here I am on the Beach, where life is absolute heaven. I can hear my sister humming softly as she draws patterns in the sand. I feel the warmth of the sun on my skin, and the touch of Danny's body against mine, and the sway of the hammock as the sea breeze rocks us.

How many people get a second chance like this?

'Are you daydreaming again, Alice?'

I hesitate before I open my eyes, because there's always the fear that one day this could all disappear.

But Danny's still there, his face so close to mine that I can't decide whether to touch him or just admire him: eyes as green as a tropical lagoon, blond hair that's curly after swimming (he hates that, I love it), lips that fit mine so well it'd be a crime not to kiss them again . . .

'Why would I need to daydream?' I whisper. 'Everything I want is within reach.' And to prove it, I reach out to take his hand.

'Right answer.' He leans in to kiss me.

'Come on! Guys! Can you not leave each other alone for a minute? I will have to throw a bucket of water over you, like they do with dogs!'

Javier is the grit in the pearl of paradise: sarcastic, occasionally cruel. But I can't imagine Soul Beach without him. Every group needs a comedian. Some of his jokes are on the dark side, but he *is* dead. That could give anyone a strange sense of humour.

Danny and I smile at each other. Maybe we should make an effort to be more sociable.

We whisper, 'Three, two, one ...' then tumble out of the hammock onto the soft bed of pillows below. However hard we try to do it gracefully, it never works. Maybe it's because we can't resist hanging onto each other till the last possible moment.

'Such elegance!' Javier scoffs, and my sister giggles. Beach life seems to suit her more and more. Her hair is blonder, her million-dollar smile now worth at least a billion. When she was alive, the TV production people kept telling her to lose weight – 'the camera adds five kilos and the audience only votes for thin girls' – but now she's happy in herself and has the perfect figure again.

Danny and I check out Meggie's drawing. It's a bird-of-paradise flower, with spiky petals sprouting like wings. 'You've got hidden talents, big sis.'

She laughs. 'I'm inspired by how beautiful the Beach is now, thanks to a certain Very Important Person.'

I blush. When I first arrived here, it was beautiful but barren. There were no exotic flowers springing up from the sand, no jewelled birds swooping across the blue sky, or diving towards the ocean where metallic fish ripple through the warm water.

Then I helped a desperate girl called Triti to escape, and the Beach became more bewitching for those left behind – almost like I'd unlocked a new level of experiences by doing the right thing.

And since then ... I can't get used to the hushed tones the Guests on Soul Beach use when they talk about me. Especially not the way *Meggie* talks about me. When she was alive, she was the star: the prettier, smarter, more talented sister.

4

But now I'm the one who stands out. Everyone wants a Visitor, but I'm the only one anyone can remember. In my real life, I'm just sixteen. I can't even drive.

Here, I can change lives – and afterlives, too. Sure, the Beach seems like paradise, but there's no way out. Unless I can solve the mystery of a Guest's death, as I did with Triti. *Then* they can find peace. Or at least, disappear. No one knows where they go.

It's my sister's death that brought me here, of course. Her killer's still out there, and finding who murdered Meggie is my top priority. Even though if I do that, I'm terrified I might lose her for good, and the Beach too.

'You're the best, Alice Florence Forster. You know that?' Meggie says. 'Don't you dare leave me, right? Not ever?'

I smile at her, but I don't say anything, because I can't promise her that, and she knows I can't. Anything could happen.

Out in the bay, some Guests are wading out to neck height, catching fish. There's talk of barbecuing the catch later, when the sun's gone down. I'll probably leave, then, because the one thing I can't do here is taste. Sometimes I forget, and reach out for a slice of mango, or an ice-cold beer, and as I raise it to my lips, it tastes of ashes ...

Or worse, of nothing. And that breaks the spell of the Beach, and brings me back to earth in my dingy bedroom, where I'm hunched over my laptop. And that starts the doubts off again: is soulbeach.org a hoax, or even some kind of mirage I've invented because I can't bear the thought of Meggie being dead?

But her hugs and Danny's kisses and even Javier's insults seem so much more real than homework, chores and bitter April gales.

'You daydreaming again?'

I blink. 'I told you, I'm not day—'

5

But then I realise I *must* have been, because something's changed. Meggie and Javier have disappeared, and the Guests are rushing towards the water's edge and in the far distance there's a single figure, the head only just above the waves.

The swimmer seems to be struggling, even though it's impossible to drown off Soul Beach. You can't die twice.

'It's someone new,' Danny says.

I turn towards him. 'A new Guest?'

He tries to smile. 'Must be. Poor bastard. This is how we all arrive, as a castaway. I still remember washing up here, coughing, blinking. None of it made sense. Where was I? Was I alive? Who were all these people?' He shivers, then stands up. 'Come on. You want to understand the Beach? Then you'd better see how it all begins.'

2

The walk towards the water's edge takes effort, our feet sinking into the hot, dry sand. Ahead of us, more Guests than I've ever seen appear from nowhere. A hundred, maybe more. The chatter gets louder, *shriller*.

'It's a guy.'

'Are you sure?'

'I can't see him. Is he cute?'

'Is that all you girls ever think about?' Javier's voice rises above the hubbub. 'The guy's just died. He's about to discover the so-called gift of eternal life. Show some humanity, please.'

It *is* a man, tripping and staggering as the waves sweep him ashore. He struggles to stay upright, arms held up, reaching out for something or someone to steady him.

My lungs won't work. I gasp for air but nothing comes. I feel his *terror*. His breathlessness. The sensation of Danny's hand gripping mine becomes more distant, and I'm floating above everyone and everything.

Is this what *dying* feels like?

'Alice. What's up?'

Danny's voice is so far away, soft above the uglier sound of Guests gossiping.

'*Where do you think he's from? He has auburn hair. Quite Celtic looking.*'

'*Ugh, but he's too short. When are they going to send someone taller? Plus, he's a mess.*'

'*Be fair on the guy. I bet you didn't look so hot when you'd just died, did you?*'

7

I lean against Danny. My vision is blurred, my breath short. 'I'm ... OK. But this feels so intrusive.'

No one else seems to care. I'm shivering. What's that phrase? It's like someone walking over my grave. Even though I'm the only one on the Beach who doesn't *have* a grave.

Danny nods towards the bar, which is deserted. 'Now could be a good time for a drink.'

I'm about to agree when something makes me stop. 'Where's my sister? We should find her first.'

I scan the faces, looking for Meggie. I hate the idea that she's alone in the crowd. In spite of the fierce sunshine and the azure sky, the Beach feels a dark, raw place right now.

Then I see her. She's almost at the water's edge, her long hair blowing in the breeze. I'm about to call out to her, beg her to stay away because it's bound to remind her of her own first hours on the Beach ...

But then I see *him* and I can't call out. Can't even breathe.

My eyes lock onto the shipwrecked man.

No.

Impossible.

It can't be.

But even as my mind fights it, my heart knows it *is* him. Red-gold curls, freckles, that bewildered expression. It's a face I haven't seen for eleven months, yet I could draw it from memory.

It's Tim.

The first – the only – boy my sister's ever fallen in love with.

And the chief suspect in her murder.

3

Random thoughts fire as fast as bullets from a machine gun.

Tim is on the Beach.

Everyone on the Beach is dead.

Except Visitors.

But everyone says I'm the only Visitor to show up in a very long time ...

Tim's eyes are wide with panic.

If Tim's not a visitor, he must be dead.

A tightness spreads from my chest up to my throat, as though I'm being choked. Danny is frowning at me.

'You look terrible. What's up?'

I want to tell him everything: how Tim was the love of Meggie's life. *And* the police's number one suspect. How in my last phone conversation with him, Tim promised me he didn't kill her. Told me his own life meant nothing with her gone.

But I daren't say any of it. As a Visitor I must watch every word. Nothing can upset a Guest, or remind them of how they came to be on the Beach. Break that rule, and I'll be banned forever from the site.

I made that mistake once, when I'd just found this place: I dared to ask my sister who she thought might have murdered her. The Beach disappeared before she could answer, and with it, all my hopes. I was only allowed back because I was new, and unfamiliar with the rules. Second time round, there'd be no mercy.

I'd lose the Beach, lose *everything*.

'Later, Danny,' I say. My voice sounds like a stranger's, hoarse with dread.

The Guests are moving forward, packed together so tightly that we're being pulled along with them.

Tim is dead. But how did he die? *Was he murdered too?*

I watch him scrambling ashore, as though he's climbing the summit of a mountain, rather than simply stepping out of the water onto the sand. He's come a long way, so he must be exhausted. My instinct is to run to him, hold him, help him ashore. Tell him everything will be all right.

But that would be a lie.

He's blinking constantly, as though if he does it often enough, he'll see something different.

Already the Beach has changed him. In real life, he barely noticed what he wore, sticking to jeans and t-shirt whatever the weather or the occasion. I remember him at Meggie's first outdoor gig, his face turning ice blue because he'd not realised everyone else was wrapped up for a winter's night. He hadn't even remembered his coat. His mind was always on higher things.

Now he's in 'Beach uniform' – surfer shorts, linen shirt in flame red – and even though it's dripping wet, it makes him look like every other Guest here. He never had those muscles in his arms before, and I don't think I ever saw him clean-shaven, as he is now.

He's a Guest. No doubt. A too beautiful version of his living self: transformed by death into a phoenix Tim, bearing no sign of how he died.

Danny takes my hand. 'You're frozen.'

'It's the shock of seeing Tim.' Then I realise what I've said. Perhaps even speaking his name is a breach of the rules.

But Danny doesn't disappear. He stares at me. 'Tim? Meggie's *boyfriend?*'

I nod. It must be safer than speaking.

'Jeez, Alice.' Danny shakes his head. 'Does that mean … the person who killed Meggie might have killed Tim? Why is he here, else?' Danny doesn't have to be careful what he says, because he won't be banished from the Beach, even if he wanted to be. Paradise is forever.

Even as I nod, I realise there's another, darker possible reason for Tim being here. Maybe he *did* smother my sister. And he's here now because he couldn't live with the guilt …

'Danny, we need to find Meggie before—'

But then I see her myself, three rows of Guests away from me. I shout out, but my voice is lost in the chatter as Tim finally makes it onto the shore.

Too late.

'Tim?' Her voice trembles as she pushes towards him. I try to reach her but too many Guests are in the way. They're not moving. They're too gripped by the drama.

'*Tim*,' Meggie whispers. It's not a question anymore. He's gawping back at her.

Meggie stops a couple of steps away from him. She's shaking her head, but there's something in the way she's gazing at him that tells me nothing has changed for her, that she still loves him.

The Beach holds its breath.

And then I hear knocking. It's coming from such a long way away.

'Alice?' My father's voice, his breaking-bad-news voice, the one I've heard too many times in the last few months.

Shit. Not now.

Meggie takes another step towards Tim.

'Alice, if you're online again, I promise I won't tell your mother. But I do need you to open the door *now*.'

I shut the laptop lid as gently as possible. 'Dad? I'm not online. I'm asleep. It's one in the morning.'

'I'm sorry, sweetheart. I wouldn't wake you if it wasn't urgent. It's just ... we have a visitor. And he wants to talk to all of us together.'

4

The policeman is sitting at our dining-room table, his backside too big for the chair. Usually they send the family liaison woman. She knows us so well now that she always puts the right number of sugars in Dad's tea and offers Mum a tissue before she even begins to cry.

Either Mrs Family Liaison has got the night off, or the fat guy is here because the news is too serious for her to break.

I think about Tim, on the Beach. *Of course it's serious.*

We sit round the table as though we're about to have Sunday lunch, even though the sky is midnight blue, and we're all in our dressing gowns except for the policeman. He puts his chubby fists together, and I half expect him to say grace.

Instead he says, 'I'm afraid I have some shocking news.' His breath condenses like smoke in the cold air.

Mum reaches for my hand and my dad's. Perhaps she thinks that we're safe, so long as we're all together. She's wrong.

'Timothy Ashley was found dead tonight. Well, last night. A little over four hours ago.'

Mum's hand flies to her mouth. Dad closes his eyes. And even though I knew already, the words are still shocking.

'Suicide!' my mother cries out. 'I'm right, aren't I?' Her eyes have a crazy glint, the one they always get when she's thinking about Tim.

The policeman's face doesn't change. 'At this stage we are awaiting the results of the post mortem examination.'

Dad shakes his head. 'Come on. Surely you can give us more than that? We are ... involved, after all.'

The policeman sighs. 'The circumstances are that Mr Ashley's flatmate,' he checks his notes, '... Adrian Black, returned home last night just after nine o'clock, and discovered the deceased's body in the kitchen.'

Ade found him.

'How did he die?' I ask.

The policeman looks at me for the first time. 'He appears to have died from asphyxiation.'

That means suffocation. *Meggie was suffocated.* Someone held a pillow over her face until all her breath was gone.

'Someone *smothered* Tim?' Dad whispers.

The policeman shakes his head. 'No. A plastic bag ... It's a method suicides sometimes use. He was slumped over the kitchen table. Alcohol was found alongside his body, too.'

Acid fills my throat as I picture him drinking alone, then deciding he couldn't face the world anymore. *She lit up my world ... and now the world feels so dark without her.*

It's one of the last things he said to me.

'And a note?' Dad asks.

Dad's question helps me focus. I need to know more before I go back to the Beach, before I talk to him. If it *was* Tim who killed Meggie and then himself, I am certain he'd have left a note to explain what he did, and why. He'd know that he owed us that.

'As I understand it, nothing in the nature of a note has been found.'

The Tim I know wouldn't have left this unfinished. So any doubts I had about his guilt disappear, in an instant. I feel I can breathe again.

Until I remember: if he didn't kill himself, someone must have killed *him*.

'However, the circumstances do point strongly towards Mr Ashley having taken his own life,' the officer says.

'But you're keeping an open mind? While you investigate?'

The policeman looks cross with me, almost. 'The details have been passed to the coroner. It's not our remit anymore.'

'You've already decided it's not suspicious! Even though it's possible he could have been killed by the same person that killed Meggie. Did you think of that?'

Mum stands up and puts her hands on my shoulders. 'Alice, love, it's over. I know you thought Tim was innocent, but you must see this changes things.'

Dad's still thinking it through. 'You understand why emotions are running high, officer. I know you can't talk on the record, but does this effectively mean the inquiry into Meggie's murder will be closed?'

The policeman examines his neatly clipped fingernails. 'Uh, I'd say that's a fair assumption. We reached certain conclusions about Mr Ashley many months ago. This pretty much confirms them. I'm sorry. This must all be very distressing.'

A flash of anger passes across Mum's face and I think she's about to launch into a rant: that *she*'s not sorry, that Tim deserves all he got. But then Dad squeezes her hand and tears cascade down her face.

'It's over,' she whispers, then she stares over my shoulder, as though she's seen someone behind me. 'Meggie. My darling. It's over, at long last. You can sleep soundly now, darling, wherever you are.'

My blood turns to ice. I'm ninety-nine per cent sure that Meggie's killer is still on the loose.

But the one per cent doubt is enough to terrify me. If it's

really over, then my sister will be leaving the Beach, forever. Before sunrise.

Please, *no*. I'm not ready to lose her for a second time.

5

I need to get back online *now*.

'I think I'll go back to bed,' I say. Mum kisses me on the forehead and Dad hugs me and I go into the kitchen to pour myself a glass of water.

Dad walks into the hallway with the policeman, who is trying to whisper but can't control his bossy, booming voice.

'... obviously the work of a lunatic fringe, but I wanted to warn you, in case they try to get in touch with you or your family.'

'And you're certain this Burning Truths website is connected to Meggie's case?' Dad asks. 'But there are hundreds of tribute sites, aren't there? We discovered that after she died.'

'Yes, except this isn't really a tribute site. This one focuses on trying to convince the world that Tim Ashley didn't kill your daughter.'

'What?'

Someone else believes he's innocent! It's enough to make my heart stop pounding, to make the fear that Meggie's gone disappear. This must mean I'm not the only person who realises Tim's death is not the end of the story.

'One of our detectives found it by accident a fortnight ago. It's a hysterical hotchpotch of wild statements with no evidence to back them up. We were pretty convinced that Tim was behind it except it's been updated tonight. Since ...'

'Since he was found dead?'

'Exactly. So we think he must have had help from a friend.'

'Didn't he pretty much lose all his mates after the stuff in the papers?'

'You'd be surprised, Mr Forster. The smarter the killer, the more able they are to manipulate people. Especially females. You might want to keep an eye on that daughter of yours. They're very vulnerable, teenage girls.'

As if my dad needs reminding of *that* after losing his eldest daughter.

I hear them say goodnight, and the front door opens, then closes. I peer into the hallway to see if the coast is clear for me to go upstairs. This Burning Truths website could change *everything*.

But my father hasn't moved. He's leaning his head against the wall, as though he's about to fall over.

And when I turn towards the kitchen window, I see Mum step through the patio doors, onto the decking. Something's changed. It takes me a few seconds to realise what. It's snowing. Snow, in April. This has been the longest winter.

White flakes land on Mum's hair as she reaches out to touch Meggie's tree, a spindly olive we bought last autumn. In the moonlight it looks so fragile. I doubt it'll survive this snow.

As I watch, my father joins her. He's standing close to Mum, but he doesn't touch her. She was always so warm and affectionate before Meggie died, but now she often can't bear to be held.

I close my eyes, make a wish. We can't go back in time, but I wish my parents could comfort each other, the way the Beach comforts me.

When I open my eyes again, my father is brushing snow-flakes off Mum's dressing gown sleeve. Mum looks up, then lets her body lean into his.

Despite the cold, watching them makes me feel a tiny bit warmer inside. If only I could join them.

But I *need* to be back on the Beach. I'm no longer terrified that Meggie's gone, yet if anything, that makes it even more urgent.

Because if Meggie's killer is still out there, and has murdered Tim too, then I cannot waste another second.

6

I wedge two cushions against the gap under my bedroom door so Mum won't be able to see the glow from the computer. Lately, she's been nagging me more and more about how much time I spend online.

You'd think she'd be grateful that I'm at home, out of harm's way. Not out *there* where Meggie and Tim's killer could still be free ...

For the first time, I realise the murderer could come after me. It's like someone's dropped an ice cube down my back. My fingers tremble as I type *Burning Truths* into my browser.

> PLEASE ONLY CLICK THROUGH IF YOU ARE
> PREPARED FOR AN INJUSTICE SO TERRIBLE IT WILL
> MAKE YOU BURN WITH RAGE.

I hesitate. If I'd never clicked on the invitation to Soul Beach, I'd have seen the world differently. I might even be beginning to get on with my 'real' life.

But then I'd never have found my sister.

I click through. The screen turns black, before red and yellow lick across the screen like a flame, revealing the site behind.

> BURNING TRUTHS
> TIMOTHY ASHLEY IS INNOCENT
> BELIEVE IT

The lettering is the Goth kind they use on vampire books.

The whole design is like a Halloween piss-take. Except this is not funny at all.

BURNING TRUTHS IS ALL ABOUT JUSTICE FOR MEGAN FORSTER AND TIM ASHLEY.

I've seen some strange things online since Meggie died. First, her Facebook page filled up overnight with badly spelled messages, and videos of people sobbing into their webcams as though they'd known her personally.

When we closed her account down, fans moved to sickly tribute sites where virtual candles burned, and virtual angels with her face on them floated up to heaven.

But this is the strangest site yet.

WE ARE BURNING TO PROTECT THE INNOCENTS: ONE MURDERED, ONE PERSECUTED.

I scroll down ...

'Oh, Tim.'

His picture fills the screen. Not a snatched newspaper shot, or the airbrushed version I just glimpsed on the Beach. This photo was taken in a park, and makes him look hopeful and normal and bursting with, well, with *life*. His chestnut hair glows in the sunlight, and his hazel eyes look directly at the camera with no trace of guilt.

I'd forgotten all about *that* Tim. All the newspaper photos showed a haunted man who looked forty, not twenty.

I realise I'm crying.

I scrub my eyes with my fingers. No time for emotion. I fight to drag my gaze away from his photo, to read what's below in even bigger, blood-red lettering.

URGENT UPDATE, 19 APRIL TIM ASHLEY IS DEAD!

Suddenly it hits me: the news isn't out there yet. Apart

from Ade and the police and us, no one should know what's happened to Tim.

And yet it's all here, on the screen.

> TIMOTHY DAVID ASHLEY WAS FOUND DEAD AT HIS HOME ON 19 APRIL, LESS THAN THREE WEEKS AFTER HIS TWENTY-FIRST BIRTHDAY.
>
> THERE ARE NO MORE DETAILS YET, BUT BE ASSURED, THIS IS NOT THE END OF BURNING TRUTHS.
>
> TWO LIVES HAVE BEEN LOST. WHATEVER HAS HAPPENED TO TIM, HE WAS AN INNOCENT, AND A VICTIM OF THE WORST KIND OF INJUSTICE.
>
> THE BATTLE TO CLEAR TIM'S NAME WILL CONTINUE RIGHT HERE – IF YOU CARE, STAY WITH US, WEEP WITH US, BUT ALSO JOIN THE FIGHT. WE MUST USE ALL THE WEAPONS AT OUR DISPOSAL: TRUTH, JUSTICE, REVENGE.

The language is more aggressive than anything I've read on a tribute site. The people – or person – behind Burning Truths sound unbalanced ... but perhaps it's anger that's changed them. I know what that does to people.

I scroll down past the news update.

> BACKGROUND: TIM ASHLEY, A STUDENT OF HISTORY AT GREENWICH UNIVERSITY, HIT PUBLIC ATTENTION AFTER HIS GIRLFRIEND, MEGAN LONDON FORSTER, APPEARED IN THE SING FOR YOUR SUPPER TV REALITY/TALENT SHOW. HE APPEARED UNCOMFORTABLE IN THE LIMELIGHT WHEN HE ACCOMPANIED HIS GIRLFRIEND TO PREMIERES AND A-LIST PARTIES.
>
> BUT FORSTER'S MURDER (21 MAY 2009) BROUGHT EVEN MORE UNWELCOME ATTENTION. THE MEDIA,

APPARENTLY ACTING ON POLICE TIP-OFFS, MADE
ASHLEY PRIME SUSPECT. HOWEVER, REPEATED
QUESTIONING BY DETECTIVES DID NOT RESULT IN
ANY CHARGE, AND ASHLEY HIMSELF MAINTAINED
A DIGNIFIED SILENCE.

I'm not crying anymore. It's as though someone has read my mind. Does the person behind this site have inside information? The policeman was right: this is obviously written by someone who knew Tim.

ON THIS SITE, WE'RE KEEPING THE FAITH. WE HAVE
EVIDENCE – REAL EVIDENCE – THAT CASTS DOUBT
ON THE LEGITIMACY OF THE WITCH HUNT THAT
TIM HAS ENDURED. OVER TIME, WE WILL POST
THAT EVIDENCE. THE REAL KILLER MUST BE
BROUGHT TO JUSTICE SO THAT TIM'S NAME CAN
BE CLEARED – AND NO ONE ELSE WILL DIE.

The only person I know who shared my doubts about Tim's guilt is his flatmate. Yet this doesn't sound like Ade. He was always calm and logical, helping me to speak to Tim on the phone about my suspicions, and helping Tim to stay sane.

And Ade was the one who found Tim's body just a few hours ago. He must be in pieces. I can't imagine that the first thing he'd do would be to post an announcement on a website.

At the bottom of the page, there's a comment button:

BURNING TRUTHS BELIEVES THAT TIM ASHLEY IS
INNOCENT. HELP US PROVE THAT! IF YOU KNOW
ANYTHING AT ALL THAT MIGHT CONTRIBUTE TO
THAT OBJECTIVE, PLEASE POST BELOW. EVEN IF
YOU SIMPLY BELIEVE, LIKE US, THAT HE WOULD
NEVER HAVE HARMED ANYONE, ADD YOUR VOICE
TO OUR CAMPAIGN. WE NEED YOUR HELP. REST
ASSURED, YOUR CONTRIBUTION WILL BE

ANONYMOUS: MEGAN'S KILLER IS STILL OUT THERE AND WE WILL PROTECT YOUR IDENTITY AT ALL COSTS.

I've never considered leaving a message on one of these sites, but no one has added a single comment about Tim. It seems like the ultimate insult to his memory. I scroll back up to the picture. His eyes seem to follow mine.

There's so much I could say about him: the way he was the only one of Meggie's boyfriends who ever showed an interest in me as a *real* person, the way he looked after her, the way he sounded so lost without her when I spoke to him that last time.

I click on **ADD YOUR COMMENT**, but the page takes an age to refresh, and when it does, I gasp.

Someone got there before me.

7

There's one comment.

> REST IN PEACE, TIM.
> MORE PEACE THAN YOU FOUND HERE ON
> EARTH. THE BASTARDS WHO HOUNDED YOU WILL
> KNOW THE TRUTH ONE DAY. WHAT HAPPENED TO
> MEGGIE WASN'T YOUR FAULT.
> WHATEVER PEOPLE THINK, IT WASN'T GUILT
> THAT MADE YOU END IT, BUT GRIEF.
> YOUR FRIEND
> JUSTICESEEKER#1 LEFT THIS MESSAGE AT 02.07

The comment was left just one minute ago. I re-read it three times. Whoever wrote this sounds so certain they're right. Although the conspiracy theorists who blamed Meggie's death on reality TV rivals or government plots also sounded convincing, in their own freakish ways.

I'm shivering, even though the radiator by my feet is blasting out heat. The only light comes from the laptop screen, and the black and red colours make the walls of my room look like a furnace. Yet I'm colder than I would be in the blizzard outside.

I look back at the screen and notice something new. There are two flashing icons at the top of the screen – I lean closer and realise they're tiny black skulls. Next to them, a message says ...

JUSTICESEEKERS ON THIS PAGE: 2

Which must mean whoever posted the message is still online.

I click on them and a window pops up.

**JUSTICESEEKER#1 AND JUSTICESEEKER#2 ARE
READY TO TALK.**

It's a chat app. Now what? I have no idea what to type.

'Who *are* you?' I whisper out loud. My typing is clumsy, my fingers ice cold as I key in *What do you know?*

I hit return and wait. My skull icon has turned blood red, and my question is in the same colour. JusticeSeeker#1's black skull blinks back once.

And then disappears . . .

JUSTICESEEKER#1 HAS LEFT BURNINGTRUTHS.COM

No! I click wildly, but the chat window closes. I'm alone on the site.

Who is JusticeSeeker#1? Is it the same person who set up the site? But surely that person wouldn't be leaving comments . . . So that could mean there are *two* other people out there who don't think Tim killed my sister.

I'm not alone. After so many months of doubting myself, it feels good. I should leave a comment, too, so we can draw strength from each other.

But then I remember: I should have been on the Beach by now. I no longer believe my sister's death has been resolved by Tim's, so she shouldn't have gone. Yet I still need to be there, to discover as much as I can about what happened last night before Ade found Tim dead.

In my inbox, I find the email that changed my life. The invitation Meggie sent me after she died is still my only way onto the Soul Beach website. You sure as hell can't access it via Google.

'Alice?'

It's not the voice I wanted to hear, and I'm not where I want to be, either. I'm in the beach bar. Candles flicker on the tables. A ferocious drumming sound pulses through the open sides of the bamboo building.

I only ever come to the bar when there's something wrong, or when Sam – the bartender – has to warn me of danger.

'Sam. What is it?'

But before she can answer, my door bursts open.

Mum's rushing towards me, wild-eyed, and Dad's behind her.

I don't have a chance to do anything – not even to click away from the Beach – before Mum's ripping the laptop cable from the wall. She smashes the lid shut so hard that she's probably shattered the screen.

'What the hell do you think you're doing, Alice?'

I'm about to say *homework*, but then I realise that's not going to help.

'It's two o'clock in the bloody morning. We've just found out your sister's killer is dead. And where are you? Bloody well online, like you always are!' Her voice is getting louder. OK, we live in a detached house, but half the close must have heard her by now. 'It's an obsession! You're an *addict*, Alice!'

Dad puts a hand on hers. 'Bea, do we have to do this now?'

She shakes him off. 'Yes, we do! Alice, that's it. Over. You've been lying to us for months, haven't you?' She spins round. 'Look, she's even been putting pillows by the door so we can't see she's still awake.'

Dad frowns.

'No wonder you look like a ghost. You probably spend half the bloody night online. You're making yourself ill.'

I wish I could tell her I'm not ill, but happy. That being with Meggie is better than anything real life can offer.

'Alice? Is your mum right?' Dad asks.

27

He's the only one who ever listens to me. I can't lie to him. I say nothing.

'See, Glen? Well, that's enough, Alice. No more warnings. As of now, you're offline. No more living on the bloody internet. We should have done this *months* ago.'

I stare at her. She's joking. Or *drunk*. But then I see her eyes, which are scarily sober. 'But ... my schoolwork. I need to be online for my schoolwork,' I plead.

Mum laughs, but not in a nice way. 'Your dad and I managed to get through school before they even invented computers, so you'll survive. There's more to life than schoolwork, Alice. Like friends. You've broken Cara's heart the way you've treated her.'

I close my eyes. I've tried to stay friends with Cara, but if it's a choice between her and Meggie, well, my sister needs me more. There aren't enough hours in the day to look after both of them.

Dad looks shifty. 'Alice might have a point about school, though, Bea. It's not like it was for us. They even send their coursework online these days, don't they?'

I say nothing, hoping Mum will listen to him.

She scowls. 'We can't let her carry on like this. We've cut her too much slack because of Meggie, but it's almost a year now and ...' Mum stops, as though she can't believe it's been that long.

I seize my chance. 'Which also means I'm almost seventeen. You can't do this.'

We glare at each other.

Dad sighs. 'How about we move the laptop downstairs? That way, we can control her access to the web. Keep an eye on what she's doing.'

'Don't talk about me like I'm not here!' I scream. 'I'm not some little kid who needs monitoring to make sure she's not being stalked by the Big Bad Wolf.'

'That's exactly what you are. A little kid. We're still your parents, Alice, and until you can learn to exercise some self-control, we'll have to exercise it for you.'

'But, Mum—'

She turns her back on me, grabs my laptop and almost trips over the cable trailing behind her. Dad won't look at me. I've hurt him. I wish I could explain that I wouldn't have lied if it wasn't necessary. But I reckon they'd throw the laptop out of the window and send me to live with the Amish if I even mentioned Soul Beach.

Mum sticks her head back round the door. 'Oh, and before you get any ideas, I'm sleeping with the laptop under my pillow. So I suggest you get some sleep and prepare for tomorrow – when we help you get your life back. It's for your own good, Alice. We're not losing another daughter.'

8

I don't sleep at all, of course.

My head's too full of evil: of a shadowy killer overpowering Tim and watching the life drain from him. That same faceless figure combing my dead sister's hair to remove knots. She was immaculate when she was found by another student from her corridor. It's one of the many things the press feasted on: the description of my sister as a Sleeping Beauty.

Is Meggie wondering where I am tonight? And what did Sam need to warn me about? The rules of the Beach are murky and ever-changing. Perhaps Tim will take my sister's place on the shore. Perhaps she *has* left at dawn, as Triti did before her.

It might have been my last chance to see my sister.

I turn over in bed for the millionth time, trying to force myself to think rationally. Tim's death can't be the end. If he'd chosen to die, he would never have left us in the dark. There would have been a note, a message . . .

I sit bolt upright. What if he tried to leave a message for *me*? It would make sense. I'm the only one in my family who believed in him. Surely he owed me that.

I scrabble round for my mobile in my rucksack. My crappy phone doesn't even have the internet. I hardly use it anymore. It's not like Danny and Meggie can text me from where they are . . .

But *Tim* could have done, in his last hours.

Battery's dead.

I put the phone on charge and wait for the prehistoric thing to respond.

Finally it comes to life with the loudest beep. I hold my breath in case it's woken my parents. But the rest of the house is quieter than a mortuary.

In the corner of the screen there's an unopened envelope. *Click.*

From: Sahara

Alice, I have terrible news. Ade found Tim dead. Killed self. Must have been guilt. This will be huge shock 4 u. 4 me 2. Sorry to tell u like this. Yr phone was off. Call me any time. Sxxx

Sahara. Was she there with Ade when he found Tim's body? She hardly ever went to Ade's place, disgusted by the thought that her boyfriend lived with a suspected killer. News like this could knock her sideways. Yet occasionally I wonder if Sahara gets a kick out of all the drama. She's always telling people she was Meggie's best friend, even though I know Meggie fell out with her about something before she died.

And now this . . . It was sent at nine thirty, well before the police arrived, and even before I saw Tim struggle ashore.

If my phone had been switched on, it would have been Sahara who broke the news. Why doesn't that surprise me?

There's nothing from Tim. But that's good news, because it's the last bit of proof that I'm right. I'm not crazy. And he's not a killer.

Which also confirms, of course, that someone else out there has murdered two people I was close to.

I put the phone on my bed, wondering how my life has become so warped. Because the truth is, knowing there might be a serial murderer out there actually makes me feel better.

I would like to say I told you so. That I knew another death was coming.

But who would I say it to? Murder is a lonely business, and, anyway, people would say, 'Of course you saw it coming. You were the killer.'

Yet I swear it wasn't premeditated. Can anyone but a hitman or a psychopath say with certainty when they will take a life?

It would be like waking in the morning and saying, 'At nine ten a.m. I will kill a fly,' when you might not even see a fly all day, or even feel the need to open the window that could let one in.

Actions come from random encounters with opportunity. Those who obsess about motive are missing the point. One might as well argue that victims have motives, too. That they know when their moment will come.

Really, the line that separates killer from killed is thinner than any of us would like to admit.

9

Wet earth falls onto my face. My hands are tied behind my back. I choke on the soil as I try to breathe.

'Help me!'

When I wake up, I'm clawing at my face, gasping for breath.

This is the same nightmare my sister used to have. She told me about it once, when she was a bit drunk. It's as though I've inherited it from her.

I'm groggy and headachy. And – I check my watch – due in school in four minutes.

'Mum?'

I bang on my parents' bedroom door and when she doesn't answer, I push it open. 'Mum, it's almost nine.'

She doesn't stir and I notice how young she looks when she's asleep. Her skin is slightly puffy, from drinking a bit too much last night. I don't blame her.

'Alice?' Mum sits up, her face wrinkled with worry again.

'We've overslept. And I had a terrible night. And it's still snowing. I was wondering ... would it be all right for me to stay at home today? After what happened.'

'After what?' she says, scowling. Then she remembers and sinks back onto the pillow. 'Tim. Oh, God.'

'I don't want to have to see people today. It'll be all over the news. I can't face it, Mum.'

She sighs. 'We can't run away from this, Alice. If you don't go in today, it'll be twice as tough tomorrow ...'

But I can tell she's close to saying yes. 'I'm not talking about forever. Just today. *Please.*'

She holds her hand up. 'OK. I give in. Stay home with me. We can watch a movie. Order in a takeaway for lunch. Eat cake.'

I stare at my mother. She suddenly seems hyperactive. 'Are you *pleased* that this has happened to Tim?'

'No, of course not.' Then she blinks. 'But ... but I was haunted by the idea he'd go on to live a normal life. Have a family of his own. While your sister ...'

'Mum—'

'I didn't want it to happen like *this*, Alice, honestly. But I did want justice.'

So do I. And so do at least two other *JusticeSeekers*. I want to go online to check if there are other messages and scour the site for evidence: not only about Tim's death, but also my sister's. Finding *her* killer is still the most important thing to me.

OK, so Mum banned me last night. But she didn't mean it. She'll have calmed down this morning – I hope.

She leans forward and fiddles with my hair. 'Got to focus on the future. On you, my gorgeous Alice. But let's save the movies and the big lunch for when we're both feeling jollier. Take it easy today.'

'Thanks, Mum. You're great, you know that?'

She smiles. 'Do I sense you're about to ask another favour?'

I look round the room, and spot my laptop on her book-shelf. 'I just thought ... maybe I could take the computer. Do some school research. I'll even use it downstairs, if you want – so you can keep an eye on me.'

Her face hardens again. 'Alice, for pity's sake, can't you manage a single day without bloody well going online? Go for a walk. Go to the shops. I don't know. Buy some drugs or *something*.' Then she smiles weakly. 'That last bit was a joke.'

But then she reaches for her purse and passes me twenty pounds. When I go to take it, she hangs on to my hand. Her skin is warm. 'Spend it on something fun, eh, darling? We can start again now, can't we? Not forget Meggie, but move forward, knowing it's all over.'

I don't say anything. I can't lie about *this*.

She doesn't notice, though. She just closes her eyes. 'Close the door behind you, Alice. I don't think I'll bother to get up today. Then tomorrow, well. Tomorrow is the first day of the rest of our lives.'

I've got myself a day off, but with the Beach and Burning Truths off limits, I don't know what the hell to do.

I could go to Greenwich, of course, if the trains are still running through the snow. It's where Meggie died, and now Tim, too. I'm sure Sahara would meet me, and Ade. I could use today to find out more about what happened in his flat.

And yet ... something stops me calling Sahara. It's not as though I suspect her, exactly, but at the same time, if Tim didn't kill Meggie, someone must have. Once upon a time, I thought murderers were crazy strangers, the kind of stalkers Meggie gained as soon as she appeared on *Sing for Your Supper*.

But everything I've read since she died insists you're more likely to be killed by the people closest to you. I shiver. The chances are Meggie knew her murderer. And so it's possible ... no, *likely*, that I do too.

Sahara? Ade? Zoe, the girl who found Meggie's body? One of the other friends they hung around with?

I remember the language on Burning Truths. All about arming yourself with information, fighting fire with fire. Perhaps it's better if I don't talk to anyone who knew Meggie until I've read every word of Burning Truths.

But there is someone I can to talk to, someone I can trust. Someone who also happens to have a computer set-up to rival NASA.

'Hello, stranger,' Lewis answers on the first ring.

'It hasn't been *that* long,' I say, even though it probably has. 'I've been busy with revision, sorry.'

'Oh, right. I know how seriously you take your exams, Alice!' He's teasing me. He's the only person who still does; everyone else treats me like an invalid, even now.

'Something's happened. I wondered if I could come over.'

'On a school day? Don't forget those important exams of yours.'

'Ha, ha. Mum's let me stay off because ... Well, can I explain when I get there?'

There's a pause. 'All right, Ali. I'm stuck in the flat all day, anyway, doing some testing.'

'The flat?'

Lewis laughs. 'Mmm. I was finally moving out of home, remember? You were going to help me with the packing.'

Shit. 'Oh, Lewis. I'm sorry. After all the stuff you've done for me ... I'm a rubbish friend, aren't I?'

'Your heart's in the right place, though. I could pick you up in the car in half an hour if that suits you? And if you really want to help, bring your rubber gloves. The flat could do with a woman's touch.'

As soon as he rings off, I race out the door, almost slipping on frozen snow. At least I have money to spend, thanks to Mum's twenty quid and a bit extra I've put aside. But what do you buy for the guy who has everything – or, at least, can afford everything he wants? Lewis is well on the way to being the next Bill Gates, even though he never boasts about it. He has a brain the size of a very large planet, and set up his first tech company from his bedroom before his GCSEs. Four years on, the only signs that he's doing pretty well are the designer shoes and manbags, which really don't match his dragged-through-a-hedge-backwards hair and clothes.

Well, I definitely can't afford designer, and all the gift shops round here are packed with pink cupcake-themed tat. If you hung around our suburb for long enough, you'd think feminism never happened.

No wonder Meggie got away to Greenwich. This place was too small for her.

I can't buy booze, because all the shopkeepers know me. And even though it's his favourite, a crate of Diet Coke doesn't quite cut it as a house-warming present. This has to be a *good* present, to make up for neglecting him.

Lewis started off as a kind of surrogate big brother, drafted in by my mates to try to get to the bottom of the weird emails I was sent just after Meggie's funeral. By the time Lewis showed up, I'd discovered that the 'weird' emails actually came from my sister, so I've never told him about Soul Beach. But he's helped me out of a few scrapes, and more than that, he's become a real friend. And I can't wait to see him.

I'm passing the greengrocer's when I see it – a huge chilli plant with the tiniest, reddest peppers emerging from the flowers. The label says they're among the fieriest on earth, and can irritate if not handled carefully.

I don't know why I think that's just right, but I do. It seems to suit Lewis; he likes to get under people's skin.

10

'Welcome to Tomlinson Towers,' Lewis says, opening the door to his flat.

'So this is where you're plotting world domination these days?'

'Well, I couldn't stay at my mum's forever, could I? Living with Mummy does rather reinforce the stereotype of the anti-social computer nerd. I'm lucky the FBI didn't break down my door, taser me senseless and cart me off to Guantanamo.'

I'm still trying to hide the badly wrapped chilli plant that Lewis has chivalrously pretended not to notice. The flat is in the basement of a Victorian house, close to the river, and as I step inside, I half-expect it to be damp, but instead it smells green and woody, like a forest.

'Have you overdone the air fresheners, Lewis? Oh!'

The place is small, with a giant sofa, an old tiled fireplace, and an open-plan kitchen. But where the far wall should be, there's a set of arched patio doors, a giant glass desk, topped with three wide-screen monitors, and beyond that ... what looks like a mini rainforest! Glossy jungle leaves, delicate ferns, over-sized bamboos: a wild wall of colour in a glass-house.

'Are you growing drugs, Lewis?'

He laughs. 'Nothing as cool as that. No, I like plants. See, I am a geek after all!'

A neglected cactus might seem geeky, but this doesn't. 'Did you grow them?'

'Some of the seedlings are mine,' he says, still guarded in

case I take the piss. 'The rest I bought, or "adopted" from Freecycle since I moved in here. It's amazing how many people want to give up on their unruly plants.'

I smile. Lewis is pretty unruly himself, like a gangly tree growing up towards the sun. 'So you're their last hope? St Francis of the Foliage?'

'To be fair, they're working for me too. There's a theory that they help soak up electromagnetic radiation from computers. But before you ask, I don't talk to them. Or stroke them. It's a purely platonic relationship.'

That's when it hits me: the weirdness of being in his flat. I turn away from the wall of plants. The fireplace is filled with half-burned candles, and the chocolate brown L-shaped sofa seems designed for two. How many girls has he entertained here since he moved in? He was lying about it needing a woman's touch – the flat's already super-stylish, like a laid-back bar where you'd hang out all weekend with your mates.

I remember my plant. 'Oh. I, uh, got you something. It's going to look a bit pathetic next to all your trees, though.'

He takes the package, and opens it carefully. 'Habanero chilli. Wow! Perfect, Ali. I don't have a chilli in my collection yet. You read my mind. Thanks so much.'

He leans forward, as though he's going to hug me, but at the last minute he stops, puts the plant down, runs his fingers through his already messy hair. 'Right. So, can I get you a coffee?' He points proudly at the new espresso maker. Then he sees my face. 'Or would you rather just tell me what's happened straight away?'

I nod, and perch on the edge of the sofa, so it doesn't swallow me up. He sits at the other end, and, for a moment, I almost wish I had asked for a coffee because I don't want to say the words out loud.

'Tim's dead.'

Lewis stares at me. 'Bloody hell. How?'

'Suffocated.'

'Was he smothered? Like Meggie?'

I knew Lewis would make the connection straight away. 'He had a plastic bag over his head. But it's still asphyxiation. So it has to be the same person, doesn't it?'

'Hold on, Ali. A plastic bag . . . That could be suicide, right?'

'If you think that, then you're as blinded by the press as the rest of them!' I snap back. 'I thought you were different, Lewis. Aren't you meant to be a scientist? If you won't listen to the evidence, I might as well go.' I stand up.

'Calm down. I'm on your side. But you haven't given me the evidence yet. Sit down and take me through it.'

I do sit again, reluctantly, as I realise there is actually *no one else* I can confide in. 'OK. Well, Tim was found by his flatmate, Ade. I told you about him before. Sahara's boyfriend. He came back to their place and found Tim there. There was a bottle at his side, and the bag, but no note.'

'Go on.'

'That's the most important fact of all, Lewis. If he didn't leave a note, that proves he didn't kill himself.'

Lewis massages his head, like he can stimulate his brain cells through his scalp. 'Alice . . . I see what you're getting at, but not everyone leaves a note. And if he'd been drinking, maybe it got too much for him, suddenly? He might not have planned it.'

'Yes, but . . .' If only I could tell Lewis about the Beach, about the look on my sister's face when she saw Tim. That was all the proof I needed that Meggie *knew* deep down that Tim was her soul mate, not her killer.

Of course, I can't explain that to Lewis – but I *can* tell him about Burning Truths.

'OK. Say Tim didn't do it himself, then who do you think did?' Lewis asks.

'Someone who knew both of them. From Greenwich.'

'Like who? Sahara? This Ade? Some other random person?'

'I don't know. But I'm not the only one who thinks Tim was innocent. There's a website.'

He leans forward. For the first time, he doesn't look like he's humouring me. 'Those hoax emails you had hassle with when Meggie first died?'

I shake my head, perhaps too vigorously. Those 'hoax emails' were what led me to Soul Beach. 'No, that finished ages ago. *This* is something the police mentioned. It's called Burning Truths and . . .'

Lewis is already at his computer. Or, one of them. The site loads instantly, in all its gothic crudeness.

'Blimey, that's not subtle, is it? I'll bet whoever did this also loves nineties heavy metal, and is planning to get a secret skull tattoo when he's sixteen.'

I try to smile but I can't. 'It's not a joke. The design isn't important. It's what it says.'

He looks up at me and his expression changes. 'You're right. Sorry. Attack of the dangerously socially inept.'

This time I do manage to smile. 'I know it looks like one of those awful tribute sites, but it's not. Whoever wrote this is convinced Tim is innocent.'

'*You* think he's innocent, Ali.'

'That site isn't *mine*,' I say. 'Apart from anything else, I don't have the computer skills. The thing is, whoever it is might know something important. Read it yourself. The person behind this *knew* both of them, you can tell by the way it's written. So they might be the final piece in the jigsaw.'

'Or they might just be another conspiracy theorist who has become fixated on their stories the way stalkers do.' He turns his chair round to face me. 'Is it not time to let it go, Alice? Tim's death could be a full stop instead of a question mark. A chance to move on.'

I say nothing.

Lewis sighs. 'OK. OK. That's not an option. Silly suggestion, obviously.'

'Could you find out who built the site for me?'

'Probably. Anyone putting together something this ugly is unlikely to have the know-how to keep their identity a secret. I'll make a start, shall I? I should have known this was more than a social call.' But he's smiling as he says it.

Within seconds, lines of numbers and letters are streaming across the screen, and he's gazing at the code with the adoration men usually save for supermodels. I guess it's good news that Lewis doesn't have a girlfriend because then I'd have to try to get to the bottom of this on my own.

The thought of being without my only real-world ally makes me feel cold.

'What?' he says, catching me staring.

'Just wondering how you can make sense of that stuff.'

'By looking for patterns. People mystify me, but, with patterns, I can make *some* sense of the world. Isn't that what we're here for?'

'Is it?' I whisper. 'After Meggie died, any ideas I had about life making sense kind of went out of the window. I've given up trying to make sense of anything.'

Lewis's eyebrows go up.

'What?'

He shakes his head. 'Nothing.'

'Come on, Professor. If there's something you want to say, come out with it.'

'Just that if you've really given up trying to make sense of stuff, Ali, why are you asking me to do all *this*?'

I don't have an answer to that one: not one that I can tell Lewis, anyhow.

11

Almost an hour goes by. Lewis types away and makes the odd growling noise while I read yesterday's paper. Finally I get up and walk over to him. On the screen, there's a map of the world, with dozens, no, *hundreds* of orange dots on the screen.

He growls again.

'Is everything OK, Lewis? You sound a bit ... like a wild bear.'

'I might have been slightly ... overconfident about how easy it would be. Look at this.'

'Are these where the site visitors come from?'

Lewis looks at me. 'Decent guess. But, no. These are the locations of the person who made this site. According to the IP addresses.'

'Wow! They must have collected a few Air Miles.'

'Their locations for the last twenty-four hours.'

'But ...' The locations range from the west coast of the States to southern Africa, to New Zealand. Even the North Pole. 'That's impossible.'

'Yes. Even with a private jet, you'd never do it. And I suspect the person behind this hasn't actually shifted a millimetre from their beanbag. They've been masking their true location. He or she is smarter than I thought.'

'He or she? I thought you were convinced it was a man.'

'It's very, *very* painstaking work, this coding. The kind of stuff females are good at, like embroidery or crochet or ironing.'

'You're winding me up, right?'

He grins. 'Me? I wouldn't dare.'

'But a woman?' It makes the site feel even more unsettling somehow. Tim was never a ladies' man, he only ever had eyes for Meggie. And the only other girl I know he hung out with was Sahara, who thought he was guilty.

'Just a hunch. It's definitely one person, though. The design, the infrastructure, it's the work of a single brain. I almost admire it. Apart from the hideous colours and warped obsession with death, this could be my kinda gal.'

He's trying to lighten the mood, but it's not working.

'Are you saying it's a dead end, Professor?'

'No. Definitely not. I love a challenge. But I need to run a longer diagnostic. Plus there's a virus infecting half of south London's dental practices that I promised I'd sort out today. I can run you home, on my way out – or to wherever you want to go.'

He begins to pack a briefcase, coiling cables and putting one laptop into a case lined with foam that's cut to exactly the right size.

'Um ... I know I might be pushing my luck, Lewis, but could I ask another favour?'

'You know I'm putty in your hands, Ali.'

He's taking the piss, but I blush anyway. 'I wondered if you'd let me stay here on my own for a bit? It's so intense at home; Mum's watching me the whole time.' That bit's true, of course, but it's not just the peace I want here. It's the broadband.

He frowns. 'I'm not sure ...'

'I won't steal the family silver.' The joke seems to fall flat. I hate lying. 'Look, Mum's banned me from the net.'

'Woah.' Only Lewis would understand how painful *that* is.

'She thinks I'm obsessed. Which might be true but going

cold turkey right now, with everything else going on, it's too much. I'll only stay an hour ... *Please?*'

He looks torn. Then he smiles. 'I am putty in your hands, Miss Forster. Putty.' He takes a spare key out of his desk drawer and waves at his chair. 'Double lock when you leave, right?'

'Thanks. You're a mate,' I say, and sit myself down in front of the three screens. I've never logged in away from home before. It might not even work ... but if it does, the Beach will look the best it's ever looked.

So how come I suddenly want Lewis to stay here, with me, instead of leaving me alone while I go online?

'Do you have to go now?' I ask.

Lewis pulls out his gloves. 'Why? Is there anything else you want to tell me, Ali? Anything else you know?'

Apart from the fact that there's an entire other universe where dead kids go? And the fact that Lewis has already helped me to set one girl free from the eternal 'paradise' of the Beach, even though he doesn't realise it?

'It's just ...'

I break off. My friendship with Lewis works because we keep away from emotional stuff. If I want to be comforted, I go to the Beach, to be held by Danny or to hear Meggie's voice.

But what happens if I do keep going and manage to solve her murder? I'd lose her, and Danny. Will I cope when the real world is the only one I can access?

'Alice. An hour, right? Promise! You've got exams coming up, haven't you?'

I pull a face. 'It's hard to take the exams seriously.'

Lewis gives me a long look. 'Will failing your exams bring your sister back?'

'Guess not.'

He nods. 'Keep smiling, kiddo. And don't worry about

Burning Truths. I'll get the weirdo behind it. Apart from anything else, I can't stand the idea of being defeated by someone who uses Copperplate Gothic as their font of choice.'

12

After he's gone, I hesitate.

What if I'm wrong? What if my sister *has* gone since I logged in last, and Tim with her?

I focus on what I'm doing, trying to ignore the fear. I do what I've done a hundred times before: log into my email, find the one with the link, click. *Hope.*

I'm there. In the bar. The detail on Lewis's screens is breathtaking. The whorled knots on the bamboo struts, the tiny red bug climbing up the stem of a flower on the table.

Even though I hate being here – it means I'm about to be lectured, or worse – I am momentarily stunned by how real it feels.

Sam sits down next to me, loosening her grubby apron. Her tattoos look almost raw, and there's a livid reddening around her eyebrow piercing. I wonder if she ever minds being the only one on the Beach who doesn't glow with inner beauty. She's neither a Guest like them, nor a Visitor like me. Who knows what she is? Angel? Prison guard?

'How's tricks, sunshine?' She's smiling. Does that mean everything's OK?

'I . . . I don't know. You tell me. Do you have some news? *Bad* news?' I can't bring myself to say the words, to ask if Meggie's gone.

As Sam shakes her head, her dreadlocks thump against her skinny shoulders. 'Nothing bad that I know of. What's rattled your cage?'

'Your new . . . Guest.'

'Ah! Ah ...' She lights a cigarette with dirty fingers and I smell the nicotine: the only nasty thing I've ever smelled on the Beach, where everything else is as fragrant as a designer perfume. 'He's the one they arrested, isn't he? The one everyone but you thinks killed Meggie.'

'Tim. Yes, he is.' Sam's the only one on the Beach I can talk to about the forbidden stuff.

'Topped himself, did he?' In her Liverpool accent, everything sounds like a joke, even when it's not.

I look at her. 'Aren't you meant to know that?'

Sam sniffs. 'Come on, Alice. You know the Management like to keep everyone in the dark. Even me.'

'In the dark. You said it. Nothing's making sense, Sam.'

'When you're lost, stick to what you can be sure of, Alice. Your sister needs you, especially now. She needs to know you love her, so tell her.'

'She's going to disappear, isn't she? You *do* know something. Tell me.'

'I don't know anything. I promise. But, yes, she might go. It used to be rare, but since you arrived on the Beach, things seem more ... unpredictable.'

'Did none of the other Visitors manage what I did, then? To set anyone free?'

Sam stubs out her cigarette. 'There's no point looking backwards, mate. Make the most of what you've got, while it's still here.'

It's still morning here on the Beach. The sky is a soft baby blue and the sun isn't fierce yet. The shore is quiet, too, as the Guests stay in their bamboo huts, dozing or making love.

There are no deadlines here. Nothing much to get up for.

As I walk along the sand, the Guests who are out already wave or smile at me. Most of the faces are familiar now, though I've lost track of who was famous in the 'real' world and who I've only seen here. The guy over there made the news as a freedom campaigner who was gunned down during protests in Burma; the girl lying with her head in his lap drowned off a Greek island after the ferry she was travelling on was sabotaged. Knowing there is happiness to be had on the Beach makes their short lives feel a little less pointless.

'Alice!' I hear a whisper behind me.

'Javier?'

'Over here.'

I don't see him at first, but then I notice something move under one of the palm trees. A boy and a girl, their backs leaning against the trunk, playing cards.

I walk across the hot sand. Javier grins at me – that's not like him – and the girl smiles shyly. She looks younger than many of the Guests. Still pretty, of course, but the dusting of freckles over her cheeks makes her seem like a schoolgirl, rather than a supermodel.

'Good day, Alice.' Javier says, kissing me on both cheeks. 'If you're looking for your big sister, she's with the new guy.'

I hold my breath. 'You've seen her? Today?'

He nods. 'They appear to be *inseparable*. So sweet!'

She's still here. I feel my eyes blurring with tears of relief. Though the relief is mixed with anxiety; her killer is still free too.

I blink hard. On the sand, I see piles of pink and white shells on top of the cards.

'Gambling, Javier?'

'To make it more interesting. Obviously we Guests are like royalty. We do not carry cash, so I had to improvise. But it was Gretchen who invented the currency. The whites are worth five, the pinks ten and the ones with the ... *madreperla* ...' he picks one up and I see the shimmering inside.

'Mother of pearl,' I say.

'The same as Spanish! The ones with the mother of pearl inside, are worth fifty.'

'In German, is the same too. Perlmutt,' Gretchen says. She holds out her hand. 'Hello, Alice. It is *very* nice to meet you properly, at last. You are very popular, here, since . . .'

'Nice to meet you too, Gretchen.' I interrupt her, to stop her mentioning Triti's name. Triti and Javier were so close, and I can't bear to remind Javier of what he's lost.

Though perhaps that's less of an issue since he's found Gretchen. I recognised her vaguely when I first arrived here, remembered something about a kidnapping that went wrong. Then, after I noticed Javier hanging out with her a few days ago, I Googled her. The details of what the kidnappers did to her were too painful to read.

Javier sniggers as I shake hands with Gretchen. 'So English. And so Germanic. Now that you two have been formally introduced, would you like to play, Alice? Or we can see if Sam will rustle us up some tea and scones and cucumber sandwiches for you.'

I should be finding Meggie and Tim, but if Gretchen is going to be the newest member of the gang, it'd be rude to rush off this minute. 'I'm useless at cards, but I'll sit down for a bit. So, are you keeping this boy under control, Gretchen? He can be quite a handful.'

'I had a baby brother,' she says. 'I know how to handle any tantrums.'

She sounds serious, but her eyes are smiling. I can imagine her as a head girl when she was alive. Serious on the surface, but with a wicked sense of humour once you got to know her.

'What you cold-blooded northern Europeans see as tantrums, we Latinos know as being passionate,' Javier says. He's teasing, yes, but he sounds so much less savage than he did immediately after Triti died. And I wonder if Gretchen is a better match: poor Triti was so full of anguish, while Gretchen seems grounded.

They're chattering away in Spanish now – so, Gretchen is multi-lingual as well as funny. I don't understand the words, but I hear the unfamiliar lightness in Javier's voice. Yes. She is going to be good for him. And he could be good for her too. He's a sweet guy, once you can get past the sarcasm. And it's so rare to find a Guest who says he *doesn't* want to escape.

Javier's hinted at the truth a few times: Soul Beach is way, way better than his real life ever was. Occasionally he tells sweet stories about his mother, his little sisters, but never his father. His death seems particularly pointless: he fell from an unfenced roof during a festival. There was a suggestion he might have taken drugs, but no evidence. Of course there must have been more to it, or he wouldn't be here. But as long as he has friends to while away the hours with, Javier is adamant that he adores his afterlife. Though just occasionally I've wondered whether he protests *too* much. Whether he's repeating the same line over and over because he's desperate to convince himself it's true.

Every Guest here died before their time. Can there honestly be such a thing as *no regrets?*

I let my eyes wander along the Beach. It's so beautiful. If you could live in the moment, and be certain you'd never be lonely, maybe eternity could be bearable.

Then I see them: Meggie and Tim.

They're not touching, they're not even speaking, but their faces are turned to each other and they seem unaware of anything else. Exactly how I feel when I'm with Danny.

Enraptured.

I can't take my eyes off them. I don't see the violence, the waste of life that their deaths involved. I see peace and contentment and tenderness. My instincts were right: Tim couldn't have killed Meggie. This is how they'll while away their eternity. Together. The scene is perfect, too perfect to spoil.

But I know I have to. I get up and wave a goodbye to Javier and Gretchen.

I take a few steps towards my sister and Tim, but they don't stir. Have I become invisible? Perhaps the Beach is playing tricks again. Another step. And another.

My sister sees me at last, and she acknowledges me with the briefest of nods, which I take as permission to interrupt.

Now I'm so close that Tim should have noticed me, but still he gazes at Meggie.

'Tim, I know this will come as a shock ...' I whisper, and it strikes me that I sound exactly like my sister. He stares, as though he's trying to work out how she spoke without moving her lips. Then he turns his head towards me, and his jaw drops.

Meggie reaches out to grab his hand. 'It's OK, Tim. Alice isn't dead. She's ... not really here. Or, she is, but ...' The complications of the Beach are too much for her.

'I'm a Visitor,' I say, trying to keep my voice reassuring. 'I am still alive in the real world but I can come here, too. Because of the bond between me and Meggie. I know it sounds weird, but ... well, it is weird, actually. But wonderful, too.'

That's probably enough. I'll leave my sister to explain the rest when she thinks he's ready. If anyone can ever be ready for that.

The struggle to understand shows on Tim's face, but after a few seconds, he shakes his head. 'I can't make sense of any of this.'

Meggie laughs gently. 'It's hardly surprising, my love. Don't try to reason. Just be glad we're together.'

When she says that, I feel like someone's kicked me. She means the two of them. Don't I matter to her anymore?

But then Meggie turns. 'Tim, me and my baby sister Florrie. Like the old days.'

I'm about to tell her off for giving away her awful nickname for me, when I realise Tim is too shocked to have heard. She budges up so there's room for me on the blanket. As I sit down, I brush against Tim's arm, and we both jump. He feels too real.

There's so much I want to ask him.

His eyes meet mine and I can tell he's waiting for those questions. There's a steadiness in his gaze, as though he *wants* me to know the truth.

Meggie sees it too. 'Alice can't ask you anything about ... well, what happened to you or me, Tim. If she does, she'll be banned. I will never see her again. So we need to be careful. But you can tell her things, when you're ready.'

'I didn't ...' he begins. 'I didn't kill her, Alice. I didn't. And I don't know what the hell I'm doing here, either. I shouldn't be here, I shouldn't—' But then he breaks down. Tears roll down his cheeks, but he looks angry, not sad.

Meggie leans forward, and holds him. 'Shh. Don't try to explain now, baby. We have so much time. So much. I promise you. The three of us. We'll talk when the moment is right.'

I try not to cry out with frustration. They might have forever, but I don't. And I desperately need answers. But Meggie's right, I won't get them now.

I pull away from the screen. I'd forgotten I was at Lewis's place. Mum will be sending out a search party if I don't get home soon. I scramble up from the sand, kiss my sister lightly on the cheek – her breath a whisper on my skin – and she thanks me with her eyes.

Tim doesn't even notice me go.

13

When I get home, Mum's been baking; the whole house is steamy with condensation.

'Good day, Alice?' she says, wiping sweat from her forehead. She bakes when she wants to Make Everything Better. 'What did you get up to?'

'Hung out with Lewis. He's got a new flat so we ... went shopping for cushions, houseplants, that kind of thing. He's a boy, you know – no idea which colours go with which.' I lie so she won't think we spent the whole day in front of the computer.

She nods, satisfied. 'Just like your dad! Now, take a look in the dining room.'

I open the door. She's set up my laptop and keyboard on the table, so that the screen faces towards the living room; she can check up on me instantly.

Next to the laptop, there's a plate of lopsided cookies, a DVD box and an application form.

'For your provisional driving licence,' she says. 'If you apply now, you can take the theory test as soon as you're seventeen. And the DVD is driving software, to help you prepare.'

'Great. Thanks. And the cookies look delicious.'

She gives me a quick, nervous hug. 'You do understand about the online thing, don't you, Alice? I want what's best for you. New friends. New horizons. And you won't get those sitting hunched over your laptop, will you?'

If only she knew.

*

I take the cookies upstairs with me, and the space where the laptop was taunts me. I try to read a school book, but the words don't stick. I pick up a magazine, but the pages are full of 'celebrities' with less than a thousandth of Meggie's talent, and I throw it across the room in disgust, knocking over a perfume bottle. I laugh. I haven't worn perfume in months. No point on the Beach where everything smells of ozone and lilies.

I doze on my bed, wondering how long Mum can keep up this stupid bloody ban. And then I start thinking about Burning Truths ...

My phone wakes me up. Sahara's name flashes on the screen. I almost let it go to voicemail, but that's the coward's way out. And, anyway, she might *know* something.

'Hello Sahara.'

'Oh, God, Alice. I'm so glad I caught you, you poor thing. How are you feeling? It's *so* awful, but, even so, there's a kind of justice to it, don't you think? Not that I wanted Tim to die, of course, but it's the end, isn't it? Finally. The end of this whole awful, horrible business.'

She stops. I think she's out of breath. I can picture her: her long pale face slightly flushed as she waits for my answer.

'I'm not quite sure how I feel, Sahara.'

'Oh.' She sounds shocked that I'm not emoting enough. 'Well, I know you weren't convinced Tim was the, um, killer. But surely now you can see. It *must* have been him.'

There's no point trying to explain why I can't see. 'How's Ade?'

'In pieces. You know, I'm sure he feels responsible in some way. Because he'd gone out. He thinks he should have spotted the state that Tim was in. I mean, *hello*? Tim fooled us into thinking he was a nice guy. So of course he could hide suicidal thoughts, no problem. I've told Ade. The guilt stops here.'

'You're right. He shouldn't feel bad.'

Unless he killed Tim?

I don't know where that thought came from. I brush it aside.

'We're all upset, Alice. I'm trying not to let him see how devastated I am.'

'You hated Tim.'

'It's not black and white like that. I was very close to him before Meggie died.'

'We all were,' I snap.

I hear a choking sound at the end of the line. I've made her cry. Shit. If anyone should know that everyone grieves in a different way, I should.

She gulps. 'Anyway, Alice. This isn't about the past. It's about the future. The one good thing that could still come out of all this is that tragedy can bring people closer.'

We never were close. 'Right.'

'It's Ade's birthday next week. Originally we were planning a party. Now no one feels much like celebrating, of course, but I feel it's important he knows he's got friends supporting him. He'd love you to be there.'

Love? I didn't even know Ade before Meggie died. 'Are you sure? I mean, I'm not even old enough to drink, officially.'

She laughs. 'I remember saying the same to you when I bumped into you in Greenwich that time.'

That was the afternoon she showed me my sister's bedroom. She wasn't supposed to have the key, but she took a strange pride in getting in, showing me how the police had gutted the place, removed carpets, furniture, even the wash basin. The only thing that was left was *that* fear I had. The feeling that pure evil had seeped into the four walls and would never be cleaned away.

Sahara's still talking. 'Please come, Alice. I promise it'll help. We knew Meggie. We understand what a difference she made to all our lives.'

Dinner is awkward. Mum and Dad have turned into lovesick kids. The idea that they're closer now because Tim is dead makes me feel queasy.

I excuse myself as soon as I can, and I hear them stacking the dishwasher *together*, like some TV commercial couple. I go to my bedroom but I forget about my laptop again till I open the door and see my empty desk. For a moment, I feel like I've been burgled.

I half wish I'd stayed downstairs, but the thought of them holding hands while they watch *Coronation Street* is too much.

It's only when they creep past my door giggling – *giggling?* – that I have an idea. How come it's taken me this long to realise they can't watch me twenty-four seven?

I can still hear them whispering as I set my alarm. I hope they're drunk enough to sleep all through the night.

14

Four a.m. is the loneliest time. I feel like I'm the only person awake, or even alive.

I've never been on the Beach at this hour. Beach time seems fluid, but most of the Guests are asleep and the moon is ghostly.

I feel a hand on my shoulder. Spin round.

'Danny! Bloody hell, you nearly scared the life out—'

He silences me with a kiss, and my anger fades as his lips cast their spell on me. But . . .

He pulls away before I do. 'What is it?'

'What's what?'

'Alice, even a kiss when your heart's not in it is still the best kiss ever, but a guy gets insecure. Is it the new Guest who's distracted you?'

I look over his shoulder. Meggie and Tim are lying next to each other. In her sleep, Meggie loses her coolness and they look like children. Babes in the wood.

'There. You're staring at him. You don't think he's cuter than me, do you?'

I laugh, despite myself.

'That's funny?' he asks.

'It's funny because in the real world . . .' I tail off. I was going to tell him how everyone thought I had a crush on Tim when Meggie first started dating him. But maybe it's not funny anymore. 'Forget it. There's no one I fancy except you.'

'Right answer,' he says, and this time, when he kisses

me, I let myself forget everything else, just for a while. The darkness offers something so rare on the Beach – privacy.

Ever since Triti escaped, I'm always being watched. So many Guests want to leave, and they know I am their best chance. I sense them looking at me, and I feel the burden of their hopes, their dreams, their fears. If I could, I'd help every one of them, but Meggie has to come first.

Tonight, though, the dark hides me. Danny and I kiss as the water laps around our ankles. I store it up in my memory: the cool breeze, the touch of his lips on mine, the ticklish whisper of his voice in my ear.

'So what shall we do, lovely Alice?' he asks.

'Nothing. I want a night of doing nothing except being with you. Being . . . well, normal.'

'Normal has never sounded so wonderful.'

We kiss. We talk. We watch the sea, and the birds silhouetted against the moon. Whenever my eyes droop, Danny wakes me by whispering in my ear. He never falls asleep himself.

'I can sleep while you're far away from me, Alice. I'd rather be awake while you're here.'

And as we relax, we talk. Not about the big stuff, but first-date small talk. All the little things we never knew about each other.

'Favourite food, Danny?'

'Carbonara. And my grandma's apple pie. You?'

'Chicken tikka masala. And the little Greek honey pastries we had on our last holiday with Meggie.'

'I've never been to Greece. Or even Europe. I was supposed to go before college. The Grand Tour . . .'

I don't want him to dwell on what he's missing. 'What languages do you speak?'

'A little Spanish. We had a Mexican maid.'

'She taught you?'

'No. I taught myself. I was twelve. She was cute, so I tried to talk to her. My friend taught me.'

'What did you say to her?'

His forehead wrinkles. 'Um ... *Vaca guapa. Quiero la leche,*' he whispers.

'That sounds really good. What does it mean?'

'I *thought* it meant, *you're cute, girl. I want you.* But then my buddy admitted it meant *cute cow, I want your milk.* Or something like that.' He laughs. 'And what about you? What do you speak?'

'French.'

'Tell me something in French.'

'Um ... *je voudrais du lait, ma jolie vâche.*'

'Sexy. What did you say?'

I giggle. 'I'd like some milk, my pretty cow.'

'You're mocking me.'

'Never, Danny.'

We kiss more, talk more. Share first memories, most embarrassing moments. Mine was a skirt tucked into my knickers in my first week at high school. His involved a bout of vodka-fuelled seasickness on a yacht belonging to the father of a billionaire school friend.

'Was that a *female* school friend?' I ask.

'Does it matter?'

'To me it does. Is it the brunette you went to a barbecue with?'

He leans back. 'Wow. Do you have supernatural powers?'

'Only the internet,' I say. 'She was in the video they show of you ...' I stop because I daren't mention the news coverage of his death, '... well, the video of you that's online.'

Danny scowls. 'Hope they got my best side,' he says, trying to sound amused.

'You don't have a worst side.'

He laughs sadly. 'My friends would disagree.'

'What do you mean?'

'Ah, Alice, I was spoiled. The life I had, I wanted for nothing. It's not the best thing for a kid, getting everything they ask for. I was a brat.'

'You're a reformed character, now, though,' I say, holding him tighter.

'*You* changed me, Alice.'

I think I must have fallen asleep because suddenly the sky is lighter, and I'm shivering. He holds me closer but it doesn't warm me through. 'It's time.'

The spell of our magical night together is broken. I remember where I am: not a tropical beach, but a freezing cold dining room.

I kiss him once more but I hardly feel anything. Then I click out of the site. Reality is so colourless. I check the clock on the mantelpiece. Quarter past six. Bloody hell. I could have had another ten precious minutes with Danny before I had to go back to bed. But it's too late to go back, too painful to drag myself away from his arms twice in one morning.

Instead I click onto Burning Truths. It's not exactly a site I can check out while Mum's watching me. I go straight onto Tim's page, but when I look for the skull icons in the corner of the screen, I realise I'm the only person online.

I scroll down anyway. There's nothing new in the comments section, but there is an update at the bottom of Tim's profile.

TIM ASHLEY – LATEST NEWS 17 APRIL:
INQUEST OPENS TOMORROW (18 APRIL), 10AM,
SOUTH EAST THAMES CORONER'S COURT.

Inquest? Instinctively I know I need to be there, not only because I owe it to Tim.

But also beause I feel certain that whoever is behind this site won't be able to keep away either.

15

I was expecting somewhere ... scarier. A Gothic courtroom, with turrets and soot-stained black stonework. Gargoyles.

But the coroner's court is a modern brick building with huge glass windows and cheerful yellow blinds. It's too bland to be a place where the end of a life is examined.

No one knows I'm here. I texted Cara to ask her to cover for me at school till lunch, but didn't say why. Luckily, Mum's sick note from yesterday is vague enough for me to get away with it.

There are two cameramen and a huddle of reporters outside the court, their breath condensing in the cold air like dragons' smoke. I pull my scarf up around my face so they don't recognise me. For a time last summer, I was almost famous.

I check my disguise in the ladies' toilets. My school uniform's in my rucksack, and I'm wearing a shapeless shirt and jeans, my hair in a scraped-back ponytail, plus an old hooded duffel coat on top. This is pretty much the dress code for freaks – I found *that* out at my sister's funeral.

But I'm no freak. Am I? I'm here for a reason, doing the police's job for them. I feed coins into the vending machine. Espresso? Cappuccino? Soup ...

That's when I sense I'm being watched.

I spin around, but the only person near me is a thin policeman with droopy eyes.

'Hello. Are you press or family?'

'Er. Neither. I was ... studying with him. With Tim.'

'Right. You want the public gallery, at the back. You know

nothing will happen today, don't you? It's a formality.'

I nod. 'I wanted to be here anyway.'

'I hope it helps you.' He has an understanding face. Perhaps it comes of living with death every day.

He'd never believe I know how he feels.

I choose hot chocolate, then sit down in the waiting area as more people arrive. The journos come in: two men, one woman, joking like mates on a day out. The woman catches my eye and I freeze. But when she looks away, I feel safer. Obviously I don't look like me anymore.

More people come in: two policemen, a woman in a boxy suit . . .

And that . . . that must be Tim's father.

Meggie never met his family. Tim's mum died in a car crash when he was thirteen, and within a year his dad had moved another woman and her kids into the house. Tim began sleeping on friends' sofas. He once told me he had to leave home when he started feeling jealous of a three-year-old. 'I knew *why* Dad paid them attention,' he said. 'They were cute. I wasn't. So it made sense for me to go.'

Poor Tim. Not much of a life: unwanted by his father, then wanted as a murderer. Perhaps he deserves the paradise of Meggie and the Beach. If eternal life with little hope of escape really does count as paradise . . .

His father has redder hair than his son, and taut, dry skin. His eyes dart around, as though he's expecting someone to question his right to be here. It's a shame he didn't show he cared about Tim that bit sooner.

He turns towards me, and for a moment, I feel a horrible chill; those are *Tim's* eyes meeting mine, yet icier.

'Mr Ashley?' The policeman escorts him towards a side room, but I'm still shivering, even though the hall is boiler-room hot.

The clock ticks towards ten, when we're finally allowed in.

I wait until everyone else is seated, then take a seat in the empty public gallery.

'Good morning, everyone. I am the South East Thames coroner and we are here today to open the inquest into the death of Timothy David Ashley . . .'

The coroner reminds me of Dad's colleagues at the solicitors' office: grey men in grey suits.

The policewoman who answered Ade's 999 call reads a statement. 'The deceased was discovered seated at the kitchen table. A torn plastic bag was tied around his neck. We noted bottles of what appeared to be alcohol on the table. These have been removed for analysis.'

'Had the body been touched?'

She nods. 'The deceased's flatmate, Adrian Black, had come home to find Mr Ashley slumped on the table, but with the bag intact. It had been secured at the neck, to restrict air flow. Mr Black tore through it, but it appears Mr Ashley was already dead. Death was confirmed at twenty-one thirteen hours, by the police surgeon.'

'Thank you, officer.' The coroner leafs through some papers on his desk. 'An initial autopsy shows that the cause of death is asphyxiation. The pathologist is still waiting for toxicology reports on alcohol levels and so on.'

Tim's dad is motionless.

'Mr Ashley? I'm sorry for your loss. Today's hearing will be brief, I'm afraid. There will be the opportunity to ask questions when the hearing resumes once I believe I have sufficient evidence to proceed.'

'All I want to know is *why*.' His soft accent is the same as Tim's. I was too hard on him, earlier. The poor guy is totally lost.

'We will do our best to find out, Mr Ashley, you have my word.'

That's when I feel it again: the certainty that someone's

watching me. I look behind me, half expecting to see Ade waving, but there's still no one sitting in the gallery except me. I turn back. Tim's father is staring bleakly into space. I wonder if he's thinking what I'm thinking – that this *procedure* in this stuffy sanitised room seems so wrong.

'So, Mr Ashley, you understand that I am adjourning this inquest until a future date, to be confirmed, when investigations are complete.'

But Mr Ashley is understanding nothing. And neither am I.

I wait until everyone else has left. Back in the entrance hall, the journalists say noisy goodbyes before rushing off to write their stories. After a few words with the coroner's officer, Mr Ashley half steps, half stumbles outside and the cameras flash briefly and he ignores shouted questions. If he even hears them.

Then everyone's gone except him and me.

He lights a cigarette. His son hated smoking, but when Mr Ashley's lips tighten around the cigarette, his expression of concentration reminds me so much of Tim that I want to scream.

Should I try to talk to him? I could comfort him ... but then what? Tell him that his son has been reunited with Meggie in the afterlife? Yeah. That'd help. Mr Ashley throws his cigarette to the floor after a few breaths, then stubs it out under his shoe. He looks up at the court building once, before walking into the street.

Something's moving. I catch a change in the light, out of the corner of my eye. I twist to my right, and focus on the graffiti-covered entrance to a multi-storey car park. The movement definitely came from that direction.

Nothing seems to be moving now, yet I'm sure I didn't imagine it.

Tim's father's shoulders rise and fall. Sighing, or crying? I can't tell. He walks. I wait. If there *is* someone in the car park, then it's as likely that they're following him as me, surely?

But as he walks away, no one emerges from the car park. The coroner's officer glances at me as he locks the metal gate.

The car park has five storeys. There's a barrier, but no signs of life. Round here, the streets are lined with derelict warehouses. All I can see as I look up are the dead black reflections of the panes.

No one knows I'm here.

The thought makes me shudder, but I try to stay calm by thinking it through. The car park is well lit. It's not even eleven in the morning. If there's no one in there, then I'm not in danger, and even if there is someone lurking, nothing bad can happen. It's not even eleven in the morning.

I try to tune into my instinct. My heart's racing, yes, but I don't feel *terror*, that paralysing force of evil I felt in Meggie's room.

I cross the road, which is gritty with salt and melted ice. That car park smell of petrol and pee gets stronger as I climb over a low wall. Now I'm closer to where I saw something – no, it has to be *someone* – move.

Should I text someone so they know where I am? Lewis, maybe?

No. If there's someone hiding in the car park, I don't want to let them get away. They must be connected to Tim, to Meggie, to Burning Truths.

It could be the killer.

The thought makes a pulse throb in my neck. I climb over the wall. From here, I can see the whole ground floor. There are only two cars parked on this level, so there's nowhere to hide.

What was that?

I turn my head, towards the stairwell and the lift lobby. What's different?

The lift light's come on. *Someone must be inside – or calling it from a floor above me.*

I try to move silently towards the lobby, but my boots echo against the concrete. Everything's loud. The whine of the lift. My breathing.

There's an indicator light which shows that the lift is now on the second floor and still moving up.

My finger hovers over the button. Should I call it back? I don't know what the hell to do. My knowledge of surveillance techniques comes from 24. And I didn't watch how Jack Bauer operated nearly closely enough.

The lift light goes out.

I try to stay calm. It could be anyone. A driver, someone from the coroner's court.

I can hear the machinery as the lift moves again. *Down.* Towards me. I should run. But I don't. I'm frozen. With fear, yes. But with something else.

Anticipation . . .

This could end here. Whoever is in that lift might know everything: who killed Tim, who killed Meggie.

A trickle of cold sweat drips down my back as I realise that only the person who committed both murders could know for sure.

The lift brakes squeal like cats fighting at midnight. I flatten myself against the wall. *Don't think.* Just be ready.

Louder. Louder. Then the lift motor stops. Silence. And then it drops into place and I wait for the doors to open.

This is madness.

The metal doors groan open. I wait. And wait.

What are *they* waiting for?

Finally, I dare to twist my head to look to the side.

The lift light that shines back at me is bright and unforgiving. I take a step. Then another step.

No.

I look up, around, down, unable to believe it.

There's a strong smell of vomit. A crushed can of Red Bull. A cover ripped from a magazine.

But apart from that, the lift is empty.

16

I run, and run. Tearing through deserted streets. Down the escalators in the tube station. Along the empty platform.

I change carriage each stop. It probably makes me *more* obvious, but it's the kind of thing they do in the movies. Staying on the move makes me feel less vulnerable.

Even at Waterloo, I assess the passengers on my train with the wariness of a fugitive. I walk right the way through till I settle on a compartment with an old guy with double hearing aids and a mother with a crease-faced new baby in a sling.

There *was* someone in that car park, I'm sure of it. Someone connected to all that's happened. So why did they let me get away?

After the running, I'm pale and sweaty enough for everyone at school to believe I've been *properly* ill. Even Cara's fooled.

'Shit, I hope it's not catching, Alice.'

'I'm better than I was yesterday.'

She shakes her head. 'You must be so shocked about Tim. I know you thought he was innocent all along.'

For once, I don't stick up for him. Convincing Cara isn't important, even though it feels like betraying Tim not to argue. 'It was pretty devastating, yes.'

'People our age shouldn't kill themselves, should they? It's unnatural.'

'You never know what someone's going through.'

'No.' She gives me a nervous look. 'Do you want lunch, or ...'

'*Or* sounds good to me.'

We leave the common room, and head towards the sports store. Cara has the keys, thanks to the captain of the hockey team renting it out at break. It costs serious money, but Cara says it's worth it to be able to have a smoke in the warm. Last week, her mum took away her nicotine patches because she thought she was getting addicted, so Cara's pretty desperate.

We settle in a corner, on top of a string bag of netballs, which shifts under us like a beanbag. 'I'm cutting down, Alice. Honest,' Cara says, when she catches me staring at her as she makes a roll-up. 'It's only a little one. And I'll have given up by this time next week.'

'Like I haven't heard that before, Miss Ashtray Mouth. You know I only nag because I care.'

'Hey, I got my driving test date through,' she says, changing the subject. 'My date with fate is 27 June! After that, I'm taking you on a road trip.'

I laugh. 'Will you take your piercings out for the test? Examiners are very judgemental.'

Cara went to Brighton on Easter Monday and came back with rings through her nose and upper lip. 'They don't affect my ability to drive, do they?' She opens her eyes again and lights the roll-up. 'Actually, I might take them out anyway. They keep catching on stuff.'

'So they lasted, what, a month?'

'Longer than most of my boyfriends,' she says, and we collapse into giggles because it's true.

When we stop laughing, she gives me a *look*. 'You didn't read the job description for being a teenager, did you, Ali?'

'No. Never got the email.'

'OK. Let me run you through it. We're meant to get point-less piercings. Go out with pointless men. Have bad dye jobs.' She pulls at her split ends, which are showing the effects of five colours in as many weeks. 'Wind up our parents. Live dangerously.'

I think of my close encounter in the car park. 'Maybe my sister had enough danger for both of us.'

Cara blows out smoke in a steady stream and I wonder if she's going to give me the same lecture Mum gives me, about not letting my life be blighted by Meggie's death. 'Perhaps you were born square, Alice.'

'Come on. That's not fair. Just because I don't smoke—'

'You also don't date bad boys, don't bunk off school, don't lie to your folks – I could go on for hours.'

Apart from the smoking, she's wrong on every count. But I just say, 'Maybe I'll be responsible now, and wild when I'm older.'

She shakes her head. 'No you won't. It takes practice to be bad, Alice. Or ...' she smiles, 'maybe just a very good teacher.'

'Uh, oh.'

'Maybe I should teach you to live a bit.'

'What do you have in mind? I definitely don't want a piercing.'

'Nothing painful, or permanent. Just ... averagely dangerous stuff. Limited rebellion. Small-scale misbehaviour. Probably quite a lot of drink. What do you say?'

We start to laugh and I realise I've really, really missed hanging out with her. The fact that *she* still wants to hang out with *me* after I've ignored her for so long makes me feel so lucky.

'You're on.'

She leans forward and gives me a big sloppy kiss on the cheek. 'Welcome back to wonderland, Alice. Fasten your seatbelt; it's going to be a bumpy ride!'

A bumpier ride than today?

Yet despite my terror, nothing actually *happened* at the car park. Except I waited for a lift that was empty. I ran through the streets even though there might have been nothing behind me but shadows.

Perhaps a crash course in normality from my best friend is exactly what I need to cure my paranoia.

Alice is the very prettiest prey.

But she needs to exercise more care to avoid her predators. Anyone might have seen her today, despite that dowdy coat and the horrible hair. There are people out there who are less concerned for her welfare than me.

I don't think she realises how closely she is coming to resemble Meggie. Her face has lost some of that chubbiness – from the grief, I suppose – and as her eyes darken, her hair seems to lighten. It is almost as blonde now as her sister's was, spread out on that pillow.

Though Alice's hair still tangles. She should brush it more.

Is it also in the Forster DNA to be a heartbreaker? Meggie liked to play with people's emotions.

I don't believe Alice does it on purpose. It is just a fact that, sometimes, we cannot help ourselves.

17

It's amazing how little sleep you need when you're living a double life.

I grab an hour after school. Then another five between eleven p.m. and four a.m. OK, the first couple of days, I really struggled to get up, but now I wake up before the alarm even goes off. I can't wait to get onto the Beach.

I love it here at night. The rise and fall of Danny's chest as I lie next to him. The secrets and confessions that darkness teases out. The silly things – first pets, first crushes – and the important stuff about happiness and love and even whether God exists.

You'd have thought that dead people would have some pretty strong opinions on that last topic, yet the Guests have no idea if they're in heaven, in hell ... or even just in my imagination.

'So this friend of yours, Cara?' Danny says. He pronounces it *Kerr-uh*, but that's not what's strange. What's strange – and wonderful – is talking to him about everyday stuff. It makes us seem like ... well, like an ordinary boyfriend and girlfriend.

'Hmm?'

'These plans she has to make you go wild? They don't include introducing you to guys, do they?'

'They might.'

'But I get so jealous, Alice.' Those big green eyes are completely focused on me. He's doing a very convincing impersonation of total adoration.

'I don't get jealous of all the gorgeous girls you hang out with here.' It's a lie. I do, a bit.

'That's different.' He reaches over to take my hand. 'I have to face it. Other guys have what I don't have.'

'Body odour?'

Danny smiles sadly. 'A future.'

I don't know how to answer that, so I kiss him instead. But afterwards, reality still lingers like a nasty smell. 'Let's go and see the others.'

There's a group sitting on the end of the rickety wooden pier. Meggie and Tim are there.

'Hello, gorgeous little sister,' Meggie says, hugging me tight.

'Hi, Alice.' Tim gives me a little wave but he reaches for my sister's hand again, as though he can't bear not to be touching her for more than a few seconds.

Next to them, Javier and Gretchen are dangling their feet in the moonlit water.

'Hey, guys. How's life?' I ask them.

'Life after death is excellent,' says Javier. 'So good I think I might just stay here forever.'

I'm about to say something sarcastic back, until I realise they're both giggling.

Gretchen shakes her head at him, then smiles at me. 'Alice, he can't help himself. Do you have this phrase in English? So sharp he will cut himself.'

'That's the perfect description of Javier,' I laugh.

But then I stop laughing. Gretchen's face is changing before my eyes. Her skin is livid red, and so swollen you can barely make out where her eyes are. As I watch, she begins to shake, as though she's fitting, and I hear an awful noise from her throat, as though she's so puffed up that she can't breathe anymore.

I blink, and when I open my eyes again, she's back to

normal. And no one else seems to have noticed.

'I am sharp no longer,' Javier insists. 'Instead, I am a big fluffy ball of softness. Now that Miss Gretchen keeps reminding me of how lucky we are to be here, I would not dare complain about my existence.'

I sit down next to him. 'You *are* feeling better, then? I was so worried about you. After Triti went . . .'

He looks down. 'It was a dark time. So many times I wished I could have gone with her. But now . . .' he looks up again, smiling at Gretchen, 'I forget all the many bad things I can do nothing about. Triti, of course, but also the past.'

I say nothing. He's never complained about ending up here, never even hinted that he wishes things could be different. *What happened to you, Javier?* I can't ask outright, but I try to tell him with my eyes that it's OK to tell me his troubles, if it would help.

But the moment passes. 'Enough self-pity. Gretchen has cured me. She is like medicine. No. Not like medicine. Like cava, you know, the sparkling wine of Cataluña, where I am from. Full of happy bubbles. With her, I am a reformed pessimist. In fact, an optimist!' And he reaches out to take her hand.

'Optimistic is the only way to be.' Gretchen's feet splash in the sea. 'The water is wonderful tonight, Alice. Like a Jacuzzi.'

I stretch my legs down, and the warm water does seem to fizz and foam around my skin. Meggie is humming a melody I don't recognise.

If cameras existed on the Beach, this would make the perfect photo. Six friends in a line late on a balmy summer's night. No need for words. It feels even more precious, now that my time on the Beach has to be snatched and secretive.

I try to fix the moment in my mind, every detail from the warmth of the water against the soles of my feet, to the jokes

Javier is whispering to Gretchen, the touch of Danny's hand as he strokes my hair, and the faraway smile on my sister's face as she gazes at the dark horizon.

Memories are made of this.

18

The weekend. Usually it's when I spend both days hanging out on the Beach with Danny and my sister. But now that's impossible, and I realise how little else there is in my life.

Today Cara's seeing her father, Lewis is at a geeks' conference in Edinburgh, my mum is at her therapy group's 'Saturday social' and Dad's watching golf on TV. I'm lying low in my bedroom with a plate of beans on toast, counting down the hours till my parents are in bed, and trying to motivate myself to make a start on the History essay that was due in last week.

I tried to persuade Dad to let me bring my laptop upstairs but since he got back into Mum's good books, he won't risk annoying her by breaking the rules.

To what extent were totalitarian states influenced by ideology?

I've read and re-read the question so many times now that the words don't even look right. My textbook lists all the usual suspects: Hitler, Stalin, Mussolini.

The usual suspects . . .

I stare at the blank page in my notebook. I've never written out a list of people who might have murdered my sister. It seemed too much like playing detective.

But when the detectives can't be bothered to do it themselves . . .

I write:

SAHARA

The block capitals look more certain than I feel.

Sahara? *Really?* She is the most intense person I have ever met. But there's a huge difference between clingy and homicidal.

TIM

OK, so I don't believe it, but it feels like cheating to rule out the police's number one suspect.

ADE

Because ... well, he was part of the circle, wasn't he? He spent time with Sahara, which meant he must have been friendly with Meggie too, even though she never mentioned him.

So he had the opportunity, but what could have been his *motive?* Or Sahara's for that matter? I know my sister and Sahara argued before she died, but I argue with Cara and next day we're best mates again.

I rattle the pen between my teeth, trying to focus. Then I add:

PERIPHERAL FRIEND

MYSTERY FAN

RANDOM STALKER

SING FOR YOUR SUPPER COMPETITOR

The motives would be so much clearer for a stranger: an insane fan, a deadly rival who she beat on *Sing for Your Supper*. And stalkers don't even need a proper motive. They latch onto people without any reason at all.

Perhaps if I was the police, I might have settled for Tim as the least improbable option, too.

Her death – and Tim's – make about as much sense as my essay question.

I hear the doorbell ring. For a while after Meggie died, no one bothered us. The charity collectors, religious converts, brush salesmen seemed to know to keep away, as though a dark cloud hung directly over our house. But now they're back. Another sign we're returning to 'normal'.

'ALICE? You've got visitors,' Dad calls from the hallway.

I'm not expecting anyone, unless ...

'Is it Lewis?' I call back, surprised at how needy I sound. He does seem to have this knack of being there when it counts. Maybe he's had a breakthrough with Burning Truths.

I hear Dad's footsteps on the stairs, then he pushes open the door. 'No. It's not Lewis. Um, it's ... Maybe you'd prefer to meet them downstairs?'

'*Them?*'

I go onto the landing and look down.

Suspects number 1 and 3.

Instinctively, I dart back, out of sight.

Dad sees my face. 'I could send them away,' he whispers, 'but ...'

But they've come all the way from Greenwich for a reason, I think. 'No. I'll be down in a minute.'

'Sure. I'll sort them out a tea or something ...' he tails off.

I go into the bathroom, comb my messy hair, splash my face with cold water and when I look up, my eyes are wide. They're not my friends. So why have they come here?

As I dry my hands, they're trembling. Whenever Sahara is near me, so is that *fear*. Is this how my sister felt? Perhaps it's why she started pushing Sahara away.

Deep breaths ...

'Hey, you guys,' I say, forcing a smile onto my face as I head downstairs. 'What are you doing here?'

They're in the hall, jackets still on, carrying his 'n' hers crash helmets.

'We were on our way to see friends,' says Ade, 'in the area. But we wanted to see how you were. After ...'

'Oh, God, Alice,' Sahara cries, opening her puffa-padded arms. Her thin hair has been flattened by the crash helmet, and it's hard to tell where her skull ends and her hair begins. 'How are you coping?'

I submit to the hug for a few moments, before twisting my body out of her grasp. 'I'm all right. But what about you, Ade? It must have been so shocking.'

He shrugs. In his biker's leathers, he looks tougher, though he's still deathly pale. His hair's swept back like a fighter pilot's and I wonder yet again why he's with Sahara. He's so much better looking.

Dad appears holding a couple of cups of coffee. 'Sorry about the delay. Make yourselves comfortable down here. I'm going to get some jobs done in the garage.' He offloads the coffees and rushes out.

In the dining room, they unpeel their layers, put their helmets on the table, and sit down. It still makes no sense that they're here. I didn't even know that they knew where I lived.

'Ade has been more deeply affected than he's letting on,' Sahara says. 'It's been a very difficult time. We've been terrified that the media would make the connection between him and me and that they'd come after me too.'

My sister's dead. Tim's dead. Ade must be traumatised by finding his best mate dead. Yet Sahara still manages to make it all about *her*.

'How had Tim seemed?' I ask Ade. 'Before . . .'

Ade scratches at a patch of imaginary dirt on the visor of his helmet. 'Low. Paranoid. Well, you spoke to him last year, he was pretty bad then but with the anniversary coming up—'

'You spoke to him, Alice?' Sahara interrupts him. 'I didn't think you'd had any contact with him since he killed Meggie. What an odd thing to do.'

She thinks she's in a position to tell *me* what odd is?

'I was desperate to know if he killed my sister.'

'Well, I think we all know now, don't we? How desperate you must have been, Alice. I understand why you did it, but . . .'

81

she turns back to Ade, 'I can't believe *you* helped her. *So* irresponsible.'

He looks like a man who's used to being in the doghouse. 'Sahara, you know I thought he could be innocent. Until I found him ... well, dead.'

We stay silent for a moment or two because, guilty or innocent, no one wanted Tim to die the way he did.

I make eye contact with Ade. 'So now you *do* think he did it?'

He shrugs.

I feel so ashamed making him go back over it, but this has to be done, for Meggie's sake. 'How was he acting before that? Was he scared of something?'

Ade shakes his head. 'There was nothing, Alice. I promise.'

'Was he drunk? The police said there were bottles.'

'When I saw him there ...' Ade closes his eyes, 'I panicked. Ripped the bag open, tore at the scarf, in case he was still with us. You know the rest.'

'The scarf?'

He blinks. 'That was what he used, a red silk scarf. To tie the bag in place. The police think it was probably Meggie's though they said they're trying to keep it out of the press. He might have kept it as a trophy. They said it's what killers do. Perhaps *that* was his way of admitting he was responsible.' Ade shakes his head.

I stare at him. The scarf could implicate Tim. Or it could be the real killer mocking the police, proving they can get away with murder for a second time.

But then again, Meggie never really wore scarves. They're what older women wear.

None of it makes sense.

Sahara frowns. 'Alice, this might not be what you want to hear, but what other explanation could there be? Someone broke into the flat, got Tim drunk against his will, faked his suicide and then got out?' Ade was only gone a couple of hours.' Her voice is gentle; maybe I've misjudged her. She might genuinely want to look after me. Or perhaps I simply remind her of my sister.

'He sat in the dark.'

Sahara and I both look at Ade.

'He wouldn't have the light on. The last few weeks. He seemed to be getting more depressed.'

Because your sister was everything to me, Alice. She lit up my world. She was like the brightest flame, and now the world feels so dark without her.

I can't get that last conversation with Tim out of my mind. Even though it was a conversation Sahara thinks I should never have had.

Then I think of something else. 'Was there anything on the web that could have upset him, sent him over the edge? You know how bitchy people get.'

Sahara's face doesn't change, neither does Ade's. He shakes his head. 'Not that I know of.'

The hall clock ticks. The coffee's gone cold.

'We ought to head off,' Ade says. 'To see our friends.'

'Except there aren't any friends round the corner, are there?' I ask. 'I mean, I understand you wanted to see me. You don't have to pretend.'

Silence. 'We're going . . . to lay flowers on her grave,' Sahara says eventually. 'I know there's no point. She can't see them. Other people can, though, when they pass her headstone. It shows she was loved.'

I feel tears pricking at the back of my eyes. I haven't been back to her grave once, because I can see her every night. But Meggie left a huge hole in Sahara's life, I see that now.

'She knew that,' I say.

83

Ade shuffles in his seat. 'We don't want to lose touch. Just because . . .'

'We were a part of her life too, Alice. We won't forget her. Or you. In time I was hoping you might come to see the two of us as . . . good friends of yours, too. Maybe we can even help you, as a brother and sister would.'

It's hard to know how to respond. I had a sister. I don't need a substitute.

Sahara's still talking. 'We can't replace Meggie, but we are that bit older than you, so if there are things you can't discuss with your parents, we're just a call or a bike ride away.'

I can't imagine asking her for advice, yet I can tell she's being sincere.

'Come on, Saz.' Ade pats her hand, as though she's a small girl. 'Let's leave Alice to enjoy the rest of her Saturday now.'

'I do need to go back to my homework,' I say, feebly.

Sahara stands up. It always surprises me how tall she is. She wants to hug me again and I let her. 'And don't forget Ade's birthday get-together. There'll be people there who loved your sister. It could be . . . nice.'

Ade doesn't hug me, but he smiles sympathetically.

I wave them off at the door and watch them walking back along the close. Sahara forces her helmet over her head, and climbs onto the front of the motorbike. Ade climbs on behind her, his arms tight around her waist, before Sahara starts up the engine, takes a long last look back at me, then speeds off.

Perhaps I should scrub their names off that stupid suspects list upstairs. Accept it's doing me no good at all to question everything, and everyone.

And then it occurs to me. *Flowers.* They were going to lay flowers on Meggie's grave. Yet they weren't carrying anything, and there's nowhere to put them on that bike without them getting crushed.

It's probably nothing. Maybe they are going to buy some at a garage now.

But even so … Maybe I won't tear my list up just yet.

19

'Brother and *sister*? Is that seriously what Sahara said to you?'

I'm beginning to regret telling Cara about my weekend visitors. She's taking a slightly unhealthy interest.

'She meant it, Cara. OK, so she's intense. But she was very sincere.'

'Sincerely *freaky*, more like. What about *Adrian*?'

Something in the way she says his name makes me look up from my sandwich. 'How do you know Ade?'

Her cheeks colour. 'Um. From the funeral.'

'Bloody hell, Cara.'

The other girls in the common room look at me. I don't care.

'Sorry, Alice. Was that, like, completely inappropriate?'

'No, no. I suppose I'm just *surprised*. I didn't even know you'd met him.'

She pulls a face. 'It was the last thing on my mind that day, obviously. But sometimes even if you're not *looking*, you can't help but feel a connection with someone. You can't explain it, it just happens.'

Like with Danny. I wasn't exactly on the pull the first time I saw Meggie's friends on the Beach, but I felt a connection with Danny all the same. Not that I can share that moment with my best friend.

Instead I say, 'At least you didn't ask me for his phone number at the church.'

'No, well, obviously even I know that'd be wrong.' She waits a few seconds. 'I did *friend* him, though. And guess what? He's invited me to a party!'

'A party?' I stare at her. What the hell would he be having a party for? Then I remember. 'Oh. His birthday thing. Sahara mentioned it too. But it's not really a party, is it? Just a quiet get-together. I mean, his best friend isn't even buried yet.'

'Ah. Sorry. I just assumed it was a party … On account of it being in this really loud tapas bar in town, and the length of the guest list on Facebook.' She goes quiet.

I feel stung on Tim's behalf. But perhaps they'd planned it as a party before Tim died and couldn't cancel. I try not to think about it. 'You're serious about *fancying* Ade?'

'Why not? He's cute. That pale, intense look appeals. Especially as I found out this weekend that my darling Sergei has buggered off back to the Ukraine without telling me. I am never eating chicken Kiev again!'

I never even knew there was a Sergei, but her new crush unsettles me. 'Ade does have a girlfriend, remember?'

'Well, Sahara's no threat, is she? I reckon he's only seeing her because he's scared she might beat him up if she's dumped. But I'm not scared of her.'

Maybe you should be. 'I don't like this, Cara.'

She shrugs. 'I totally understand if you don't fancy coming along. But then again, you are meant to be exploring your wilder side, aren't you? And don't you owe it to your best mate to cheer her up after the sad loss of Sergei?'

Sometimes I can't tell when she's serious and when she's kidding. The bell goes before I get a chance to work it out.

As I walk to Media Studies, I think about it, and realise I'd *like* to go out with Cara anyway. Plus, Mum will think I'm getting back to 'normal' which means I might get my laptop back sooner.

And, most important of all, there's a chance Ade or Sahara

87

might let their hair down after a few drinks and reveal something useful. I can't afford *not* to go.

I try to remember the last time I went to a party for fun. It seems like a whole lifetime ago.

On the way home, the sky is dark grey, like the slate rocks that enclose the Beach. I crave sunshine, and Danny.

The wait till four a.m. seems endless. When the time finally arrives, I leap out of bed and downstairs to the laptop.

He's there, in our place, beyond *our* rock. It's a ledge of black stone with room for two, just far enough from the rest of the shore to offer that most precious thing: a little privacy.

'Hello, beautiful.'

'Hold me,' I say. 'Warm me up.'

His arms around me feel like the only solid thing in my life. 'Is it so cold where you are?'

'They're forecasting snow again, even though it's spring.'

Danny grips me tighter. 'Remind me what it's like to be cold, Alice. How snow feels on your skin.'

I tell him in between kisses, and try to imagine him in the snow. Doing the goofy things couples do in romantic movies: building a snowman, throwing snowballs that are designed to miss, rubbing noses and feeling his icy skin against mine ...

It's hard to picture it at first, because the Danny I know exists only on the Beach, in shorts and t-shirts. I bet he skied, snowboarded. There is so much about him that I don't know yet, but we have time to discover everything about each other. At least, I hope we have time.

'What did you do in winter, Danny?'

'I skied in all the best resorts. Had the best instructors, best equipment. I was still pretty crap.'

'Danny! I'm sure you were great.'

'No, I really wasn't.' He scowls. 'I was a waster.'

I squeeze his arm. 'It doesn't matter what you were, what

88

money you had. I love the real you. Just plain Danny.'

He looks as though he wants to say something else, but then he smiles. 'Oh, Alice. I don't deserve you,' he says. 'But maybe I can be better. For your sake.'

'Don't be silly. You're good enough as you are. Don't look for problems where there are none. I don't have any shortage of those in the *real* world, so being here is all about making the most of you.'

And I focus on the warmth of his body against mine. I must concentrate on the good things. The Beach is a haven, not only for the Guests like Danny and Meggie and Javier, who have suffered so much, but also for me.

I won't let it be spoiled.

20

I'm so out of practice at parties that I have to make a list of what to do: straighten my hair, cover the spots on my chin, curl my eyelashes.

Of course, on the Beach, I am transformed into a beauty even when I've just dragged myself out of bed in the dead of night. In real life, it's harder.

Mum beams when she sees me. 'You look wonderful, darling.' Though she still stops to wipe an imaginary smudge off my cheek.

'I'm not five years old, Mum.'

'You'll always be my baby, Alice, though you get prettier every day. Tonight, you look just like . . .' She stops. 'Just like a young woman.'

Cara's much less impressed.

'Couldn't you be bothered with lipstick? Honestly. You're really not trying very hard at being badly behaved.'

On the train into town, she whips out her make-up bag and begins to make me over, one brushstroke at a time. By the time we pull into Waterloo, I almost don't recognise myself in her pocket mirror. My eyes are bigger, my lips fuller, my hair puffed up.

'What do you think?'

'I feel like a new person,' I reply, and she links arms with me, grinning.

'I am the makeover queen.'

As we step down from the train I inspect myself a final time in the grimy window.

I stop. *Look again.*

'Come *on*, Alice.'

It can't be.

The third time I realise it's just my own reflection. But for a few moments, I was one hundred per cent certain I'd seen my sister smiling back at me.

We're outside a big tapas bar behind the station when my phone rings. Lewis. I haven't heard from him since he agreed to look into Burning Truths; I was beginning to think he'd met his match.

'Wait a second,' I mouth to Cara, but she's already pushing open the door to the bar. I hear Latin music and smell garlic before it swings shut again.

'Lewis. How's tricks?'

'Slow going. But my net's closing in on Burning Truths.'

'Really?' I try not to sound like it matters as much as it does. 'How soon might you crack it? Tonight?'

'What's the hurry?'

It doesn't seem like the right time to tell him I'm hoping I might be closing in on the person behind the site, or even the killer. He'd probably call the police. 'I'm just impatient, that's all.'

A group of girls on a hen night pass by, whooping and singing.

'You out on the town, Ali?'

'It is a Saturday night, Prof. I'm sure you've got a hot date for later, right?'

I hear him laugh. 'No, but I do have a number of very hot leads in the domain registration world.' Behind the joke, he sounds lonely.

'Thank you. For doing this for me.'

'Hey. It's how I relax. Some people get pissed or do paintball. I like to crack cyber mysteries.'

Cara sticks her head round the door, waving a bottle at me.

'Well, thank goodness someone does or I'd be stuck, Lewis. I am super impressed. Shall I call you a bit later? Find out how you're doing?'

He says nothing for a minute. 'Sometimes I wonder if I'm doing you any favours here.'

'You are, Prof. And one day, I hope I'll be able to explain why.'

He sighs. 'OK. Back to work, then. Have a lovely evening. Take notes. Then you can remind me what it's like, back in the real world.'

I shiver. I'm not sure I'm ready to face the real world myself.

Ade has more friends than I realised. His birthday party begins with a meal in the dark back room of the tapas bar, and the table is set for twelve.

Twelve. So much for a quiet get-together. But I shouldn't judge him. Everyone deals with grief in different ways.

Unless he's not grieving at all . . .

Sahara is wedged into the corner, her handbag, hat and phone arranged in front of her like a castle's defences. She's the reason I thought Ade wouldn't have many friends. I thought she'd scare a lot of them off.

'Hi, Sahara,' I call out to her across the crowded room.

She smiles at me, and scowls at Cara. Perhaps she's sensed the threat. It must be awful to live like that, to fear being dumped because your boyfriend's better looking than you are.

Ade's different tonight. He doesn't have a glass in his hand, but he seems drunk on the company. Perhaps he's relieved to be out. Having a murder suspect for a flatmate can't do much for your social life.

'So great you could both come! It's going to be a great night!'

He kisses Cara on both cheeks, to be friendly, nothing more, but she gives me the thumbs up behind him. I wish she wouldn't.

When he goes, I turn to her. 'You're not going to try it on now, are you? With Sahara here?'

'No way,' she says. 'Half the fun is in the chase. I'll wait for the mini-break.'

'Mini-break?'

Before she can explain, Ade's coming towards us again, flanked by two guys in rugby shirts. The one on the left can't take his eyes off Cara's cleavage, but the other one is smiling at me. For a moment I wonder if I can face this pretence, when the only boy I want to be with is Danny. But then I remind myself yet again that I'm here for Meggie's sake: the more time I spend around Ade or Sahara, the more likely I am to hear something that might help me work out what really happened.

'Cara and Alice, let me introduce Matt and Craig. They might look like rugger buggers, but these two have got a few brain cells left.'

I wait for him to explain how he knows me, and for the looks of sympathy when they realise why my face is familiar. But instead Ade winks and turns away, and then Craig is asking me why I don't have a drink in my hand.

Normal can be quite good fun. I'd forgotten.

The boys are sweet and funny and I might have wanted to see Craig again, if I didn't already have a dead boyfriend.

Cara's getting wasted. She refused to touch the tapas because they were too fatty, and now the food's been cleared away and the table pushed into the corner to make a dance floor. Playing at normal will have to end soon, before Craig

93

asks me to slow dance. I almost wish I could have kept up the pretence a little longer.

'I'm so pleased you came. I didn't think you would.'

Sahara is standing next to me. It's the first time she's moved out of her corner.

'Ade's been good to me. You both have.'

She beams and I feel like crap for all the times I've been cool towards her.

'I wish you'd left your friend behind, though.'

Even for Sahara, that seems blunt. 'How come?'

'She's a bit *tarty*.'

I stare at her. Has she guessed what Cara's up to? Or is she just being a bitch? 'Please don't say that, Sahara. She's my oldest friend.'

Sahara wrinkles her nose, like she's just smelled something awful. 'Sorry. I can't help speaking my mind sometimes. Still, once you get to uni, you'll make *real* friends. Like Meggie and me.'

'Right.'

'Anyway, I'm so pleased you came tonight,' she repeats. 'Hopefully you'll be joining us in Spain, too.'

'Spain?'

'We're going away for a weekend, to Barcelona. Cheap as chips. Or should that be cheap as *patatas bravas*? That's why Ade decided to have his party here. Get us in the mood for flamenco.'

'Barcelona, right.' *Where Javier comes from . . .*

'There's some big festival that weekend, for midsummer. Fireworks. All night parties. And it's *after* the anniversary of Meggie's death, of course. We made sure of that.'

I nod. 'That's something, I suppose.'

'Plus, while we're there, we can make sure Zoe's all right. Poor thing.'

'Zoe?'

94

'Mmm. She's teaching English over there. Still devastated by what happened, you know. When I had to tell her Tim had died, well, I was so upset for her. I still can't quite believe she came tonight. She's been avoiding people ever since.'

'Tonight?'

'Sure. Oh. I forgot. You never met her, did you?'

'No.'

But I saw her in the papers. I remember one headline in particular – *Haunted: The Girl Who Found The Songbird*. And below it there was a shot of a red-haired student with such dark shadows under her eyes that it looked like she hadn't slept for years.

'Let's put that right, then. Zoe? ZOE!' Sahara calls out and waves, before I have the chance to stop her. 'I'm sure you have plenty to talk about.'

21

I see her before she sees me. She's sitting on her own, clasping a half pint of lager in her hands. I notice her fingernails are bitten, the skin around them raw.

Zoe's not exactly dressed for a party in loose black jeans and a grey hooded fleece zipped to the chin. Her eyes dart about, not settling on anything or anyone, until Sahara calls her name again. She jumps, like someone's sneaked up behind her. When she notices me, she looks away.

'She's funny with strangers. Better if I introduce you,' Sahara says, and grabs my hand.

'Hi, sweetheart.' Sahara gives Zoe a quick kiss. 'Are you enjoying yourself?'

Zoe gawps at her. Her eyes are huge and grey, the same colour as the shadows underneath them.

'Alice really wanted to meet you,' Sahara lies, 'and I thought it might be good for both of you.'

She pulls out a chair for me to sit down. But now what?

Sahara smiles nervously. 'Shall I get you both a top up?' she says, and scuttles away without waiting for a reply. If Zoe was anyone else, I'd walk away too, but perhaps Sahara *has* done me a favour. Zoe found my sister's body. It's the one part of the story I've never heard direct.

Zoe says nothing and my mind's completely blank. Eventually I say, 'So Sahara tells me you're working in Spain?'

She nods.

'You speak Spanish?'

A shrug. 'I can do hello, goodbye and thank you.' Her voice is lower pitched than I expected.

'That'll be quite a short conversation, then.'

She gives me a sharp look. 'I hate chit-chat. I went to Barcelona with my parents, once, realised it was a place where I could lose myself. This time, when I went over to find a flat, no one asked me anything about me. Or, more to the point, about your sister. No one knows who I am there. It's what I wanted.'

I stare at her.

'Sorry,' she says. 'That sounded really harsh. I didn't mean it to. Like I say, I don't do chit-chat anymore. But none of this is *your* fault.'

'Or Meggie's.'

Zoe frowns. 'No.'

'But it's OK, Zoe. I know what it's like to feel like everyone's looking at you because of her.'

She nods. 'I guess you would. You look like her.'

'No, I don't. But my picture was in the paper. And so was yours.'

I see a half-smile, a look of recognition. She clinks her empty glass against mine. 'The last thing I wanted was to be famous. Not like your sister, eh?'

It's all I can do not to slap her. Sahara puts two drinks down and hurries away.

Zoe picks up her beer and downs half of it in one go. She looks up at me. 'Yeah, I know, I shouldn't drink so fast. But life's marginally less horrible when I'm drunk than when I'm sober.'

Perhaps I've been too quick to judge her. 'Are you OK, Zoe? Not now but ... generally?'

She seems to be having trouble focusing. 'I'm a no-hoper college drop-out. I've come face to face with one dead body, and one of my best mates is six feet under now too. Apart from that, I'm ... *fine*, thanks.'

Best mates? 'You were friends with Tim?'

She downs the other half-pint and then stares into her glass, as though she doesn't know where her beer's gone. 'Not a good enough friend. Poor bastard. I was in Spain. I wasn't even *there* for him. If I had been, maybe ...'

'You think he killed himself?'

This time when she looks at me, she's not cross-eyed. 'Why? Don't you?'

'I know it's what the police think, but I can't quite believe it.'

'Denial. It's part of the grief process, apparently,' her voice is softer now. 'My parents made me go to counselling after ... Well, you know.'

'It's more than denial. I liked Tim. A lot. I can't see him giving up on life. Plus, he never left a note.'

I see the hurt in her face. If they were that close, perhaps she'd have expected a last message from him herself. 'He was a deep thinker, Alice. Serious-minded. No offence, but I never quite understood why he and your sister were together.'

I wince at her bluntness. Though I suppose she has a point. 'You didn't like Meggie much, then.'

'I didn't know her very well. We shared the same fridge. That was as far as it went.'

'But the way you talk about her—'

'Look, she used to nick my bread. I knew it was her. Sahara has a wheat allergy.'

I think it's meant to be a joke, but she doesn't smile.

Could Zoe have killed my sister? The police ruled her out ... but then maybe the police were so convinced Tim did it that they didn't look any further.

'Why are you staring at me, Alice?'

I look away, but she's shaking her head. 'You don't think *I* did it, do you? *Come on.* You don't murder people because they steal your bread. Indifference doesn't turn people into killers. But love just might. It's the people who adored her you should be frightened of.'

I think I believe her. But is she hinting that she knows who it could have been?

'Oh, Alice. I'm sorry. I've brought it all back for you, haven't I?'

'No. I live with it every day. There isn't a minute that goes by when I *don't* think about what happened to Meggie.'

She looks stricken. 'Of course. I'm an idiot. And I know it won't help but it's the same for me. I see her, Alice. When I close my eyes. When I open them.'

My head throbs. 'Is there anything else you saw? Anything you didn't tell the police, Zoe?'

She sighs. 'I wish there was something I could tell you, but I can't.'

Her wording is odd. Too precise, as though she's talking to a lawyer. 'Zoe, if you have any suspicions, please tell me . . .' I lean in closer but she recoils, and her hood drops to her shoulders.

'Oh, my God, Zoe!'

Zoe's red hair isn't red anymore. She's completely bald. Her skull glows harsh white, just skin and bone.

She cringes, then closes her eyes. Children do that when they want to be invisible. 'It . . . happened after I found your sister. Within a fortnight. Less, even.'

'Zoe, please. Keeping this to yourself is making you ill. You can trust me. I promise.'

She shakes her head. 'A trouble shared is a trouble halved? No. You're wrong, Alice. You don't want to end up like me. Accept that your sister's gone. Move on. While that's still an option.' And she pulls the hood up over her head again, stands up, and almost knocks over her empty glass as she pushes past the table.

I try to follow her, but there's a hand on my arm.

'Alice, my best friend in all the world. Are you having a good time?' Cara's drunk.

'I'm not feeling very good.'

'You want to go *already*?'

'You don't have to come with me, don't worry. I just need some time to think.'

'Oh, Alice, you've spent the last ten months thinking about what happened. What is there left to think about?'

I could give her a long list: murders and mirages, dead people who live forever, living people obsessed with the dead.

The party guests are swaying and singing. This isn't the right place for me to be now. My head's full of unformed theories and fears that I can't share with anyone, and it makes me feel so lonely.

'I'll get a cab. Mum gave me the money.'

Cara tries to smile. 'No. No, don't worry. Let's split. I've seen what I came to see!' And she glances over at Ade.

'What about Matt? You've been flirting with him for hours.'

She turns and smiles at him. He mimes holding a glass, offering her another drink. 'He's cute. But Ade is so much more interesting. Next stop, Barcelona!'

'Barcelona? You can't go with them, Cara.'

'Who says? Mum won't mind. I'll tell her I'm thinking of doing Spanish at uni.'

Someone turns the music up. Ade is on the dance floor, doing salsa moves. I wouldn't have expected that of him. I thought he was sensitive, introverted, like Tim, or Lewis.

Lewis.

He's the one person I trust to listen without pushing me further than I want to go.

'Cara ... If I wanted to leave but not actually go home yet ...' I leave the question unasked.

She smiles at me. 'Alice Forster, what *are* you plotting?'

I shrug. 'I was thinking of dropping in on Lewis.'

For a moment, she doesn't respond. Then she laughs. 'Oh! I knew you two were perfect for each other. No wonder you weren't interested in those boys tonight.'

'No, it's not like *that* ...'

But she's not listening. 'Remember. I told you that you'd find someone who'd convince you there was more to life than moping around. Lewis could be that someone.'

It's simpler to agree with her, even though I hate lying. 'You never know. I'll text him and then is it OK if I call Mum, and tell her I'm staying over with you?'

'Sure. You've been *my* alibi often enough. Just promise me one thing ...'

'Mmm?'

'Don't do anything I wouldn't do.' And then Cara starts to cackle like an old lady, because *that* doesn't rule anything out at all.

22

Lewis doesn't sound remotely surprised when I call and ask if I can come over. Maybe he's always getting midnight calls from damsels in cyber-distress.

'Sorry about the mess,' he says, as he opens the door. 'I wasn't expecting company.'

But the flat isn't messy. All the candles are lit, and there are spotlights under the plants, which makes them look fairy-tale green. Though some things don't change: there's the usual collection of Diet Coke cans in the bin under his long desk, plus a row of empty coffee cups.

'Burning the midnight oil?'

'Not on Burning Truths. But only because there's nothing going on there tonight.'

Because whoever's behind it was at the party, I think, but I don't say so, because it might sound paranoid.

'So what are you having, Alice? Wine? Beer?'

'I think I've had too much already. Cara's been trying to lead me astray.

He raises his eyebrows. 'Hmm. Not sure I approve of that. You're not even seventeen, yet, right? Not till . . .' and he stops. No one can think of my birthday without also thinking of Meggie's last hours.

'Thanks for the advice, Granddad,' I say, to cut through the tension. 'Could you spare a Diet Coke? That is, if there's any left.'

'Pretty much all there is in my fridge.' He goes into the kitchen area and opens the fridge door. 'Other millionaires have shelf after shelf of champagne. I have low-calorie caffeinated drinks.' He hands me a can.

'A millionaire. Is that what you are?'

He blushes. 'It's just what I tell girls to impress them.'

I blush back. 'The party was crap, anyway. Ade and Sahara invited me. And now they want me to go to Spain with them, too. To Barcelona, for some midsummer firework fiesta. It'll be not long after the anniver— After my birthday.'

'It'll be nice weather, I bet. It'll probably still be snowing here.'

'I don't know if I'll go, to be honest. They're a bit full on. Hey, unless you fancy coming along, too?'

I don't know why I just said that. I sound embarrassingly needy, as though I'm scared to do anything without him at my side.

Lewis doesn't say anything else, but goes to the microwave and puts something inside. Within a few seconds, explosive pops fill the silence. 'You'll join me in some supper? Corn counts as one of my five a day.'

'According to who?'

'Me.'

I laugh. 'And I guess when you drink Cherry Coke, that counts as a fruit, right?'

'I like your logic, Ali. So you didn't fancy going home yet. What shall we do instead?'

I want to go onto Burning Truths myself, and the Beach, to see if I can make more sense of what happened at the party. But it'd be seriously rude to come over here only to ask Lewis to go to bed while I go online. 'Tell me what you've been working on, Lewis.'

'Why, have you got insomnia?'

'No. I'm simply interested in what you get up to when you're not cracking international mysteries.'

He's weighing up whether I'm joking. 'Well, OK, if you

really want to know.' He goes to the desk, pulls up a second chair.

'This is the day job.' Lewis points to the first screen, which shows a constantly changing set of figures. 'Routine maintenance. Virus diagnosis. Yawn. But it pays the rent on this place and finances this ...' he points to the middle screen, which has five or six different windows showing news pages and live chat, 'which is the fun stuff. Experiments. Hacker baiting. One day I'll design a trap that won't just stop the bastards getting into your computer, it'll root them out, too.'

'Aren't hackers ... kind of cool?'

'The ones you see on the news. The ones hacking into the Pentagon to point out security flaws, they can be cool. But most of the others are criminals. They exploit people. I hate the idea that the web ends up dangerous. It shouldn't. It's about democracy.'

'You sound really passionate about it.'

He nods. 'Sure am. And not just because if I crack this, I'll end up richer than Zuckerberg. It's why I like puzzles like your Burning Truths site. The answers aren't always about fancy code. They're about psychology, about ... Alice?'

I lean in closer to the screen.

'I know you think I'm a geek, but it's a bit off to ignore your host while they're telling you about their life's mission, don't you think?'

I sigh. 'Sorry. I just got distracted by something.'

'My handsome face, obviously.'

'No! Not that it isn't handsome, but ...' I point at the screen. In the top right-hand corner, there's a page headlined *Breaking News from the Hackosphere*, with news items scrolling underneath.

He turns, too. '*New North Korean Crackdown on Civil Rights Challenged by Uni Hacker?*' he reads aloud. 'Yes, he's a good guy. They're doing great work out there.'

'Not that story. *That* one.' And I point to the headline that caught my attention:

Kidnappers of Tragic Teen Gretchen Found Guilty in Berlin: Sentenced to Life

He scowls. 'Oh. That. Hmm. Very depressing case. Her dad was some high-up in the German government, Erik Fischer. Poacher turned gamekeeper, used to try to guess what the hackers would do next. But he got too good at it.'

Gretchen Fischer. It is her. Javier's new best friend.

'What do you mean?'

'It was meant to be classified, but geeks are terrible gossips. Fischer built a program that can get into pretty much anything. Starts off as multiple clumsy hacking attempts, like a million houseflies, but while the anti-virus systems are swatting them off, Phase Two kicks in. It's a classic Trojan Horse, but so elegant. They call it Fischer's Ghostnet.'

'But what did that have to do with *Gretchen*?'

'She was kidnapped for the program, not money. Ghostnet would have been the prize that kept on giving. It's intelligent, you see. Learns from its mistakes. With something like that you could blackmail governments: pay up, or we mess with your hospitals, your defences, your nuclear power stations.'

He clicks on the link.

The first thing to load is a school picture of Gretchen; on the giant screen, it's larger than life size. I feel a shock of recognition, even though the Gretchen I know doesn't look quite like this one. On the Beach, her hair is more blonde than red and her eyes bluer, her features more delicate, her skin less freckled. But there's an innocence in the real Gretchen's wide smile. She doesn't know what's coming. How could she?

'Poor kid. The police found her alive, in the derelict recording studio where they'd been holding her. But they'd ... cut her. First her hair, to prove to her father that they had her. Then worse. She died in hospital. Blood poisoning.'

Below Gretchen's photo, there are defiant mug shots of three men with harsh faces.

Lewis scans the story. 'One Russian, one German, one Czech. The German claims he was coerced, that he tried to persuade the others to release her. His evidence meant the trial was over in a day. It didn't help him, though. They all got life.' Lewis shakes his head. 'I don't believe in capital punishment but what they did to her ... An eye for an eye begins to make sense.'

There's a last image at the bottom of the page, of an older man with freckles in a butterfly pattern across his cheeks, like Gretchen's. He has hippie-length salt-and-pepper hair, and wears a collarless suit jacket. But what I notice most is the sadness in his hooded grey eyes.

'Her dad?'

'Yes.' Lewis touches the screen, and the photo comes to life.

'This is no happy ending,' Gretchen's father says, in perfect English. 'Nothing can bring her back. She suffered terribly. But even in hospital, she fought. My daughter was special, worth a thousand, a *million*, of those cowards, those killers.

'But at least now we know what happened. They failed to break her and they failed to get what they wanted. Their conviction is not enough, but at least it is a kind of justice.'

'Justice.' I whisper the word as Mr Fischer's image freezes again.

If Gretchen has justice, then tonight she may also find her freedom. But what will that mean for Javier? I don't know if he can cope with losing another friend.

I *have* to be there for him.

23

Lewis must be immune to caffeine because pretty soon his eyelids start to droop. He offers me his bed, says he'll take the sofa.

'No. You don't have to be a gentleman. I'd prefer to sleep in here, so long as I can go online, too. I'm still getting serious withdrawal symptoms because of the bloody internet ban.'

He knows better than to argue. I wait till he's closed the door to his bedroom before I log on.

My email loads super-fast, and as I click on the link to the Beach, the huge screen fills with colour. On the horizon, the sky glows apricot, shot through with deep pink stripes, like memories of sun rays. In the last week, I've got used to arriving later than this, once the place is in darkness and the only light is from Chinese lanterns and the beach bar. But this time I've made it just in time for sunset.

I spot them almost immediately. Gretchen is sitting on the sand with Javier. She's got a pen and is drawing patterns on his hand, the way junior school kids do. Suns, moons, stars. His skin is dark next to hers.

'Hi, guys,' I say, sitting down.

I half expect them to scowl at the interruption, but instead Gretchen leans over to kiss me on both cheeks, her lips skimming my face. Her skin feels feverish. 'How is Planet Earth, Alice?'

'Complicated,' I say.

'You should never leave Soul Beach,' Javier says. 'Things are always *so* simple here.' Whereas when you are living, well, whatever you do, there are always consequences.

Gretchen smiles at me. 'Ignore Mr Sharp. You seem weary, Alice. But now you're here, you have nothing to worry about. I insist you relax with us. Watch the sun go down.'

There's something odd about her voice. Can she sense what's going to happen?

'The view of the sunset is best from the chiringuito bar, of course,' Javier says, 'and even better with a drink.'

We scramble up from the sand, which is gritty between my toes. How come it feels so much more real than the stripped floorboards that are actually under my feet? Gretchen and Javier pull me up, taking one hand each, and again, I notice that she seems to be burning up. Is this what it's like when a Guest is about to leave?

No sign of Meggie or Danny tonight. But that's OK. I must focus on Gretchen.

The bar is quiet, though the handful of Guests still nudge each other when they see me, perhaps hoping I might be able to help them. Weird. Since Triti went, I've almost come to believe my own publicity – that I'm all-powerful. Yet if Gretchen goes tonight, it will have been nothing to do with me.

We sit at the table nearest the sea. Within seconds, Sam has brought a tray over with three deep-orange tequila sunrises. 'I know you can't drink it,' she says putting one in front of me, 'but you can enjoy the view, and I'm sure they'll finish it for you.'

I wonder, does *she* know that soon she might have one less customer to serve? Maybe everyone knows, and the joke's on me.

'To sunset,' says Gretchen, holding up her cocktail glass for a toast.

'Except it's a tequila sun*rise*,' Javier points out.

She laughs. 'OK, then. To ... endless horizons.'

When we do clink glasses, it triggers a sunrise, as blood-red grenadine at the bottom of the cocktail spreads upwards, like scarlet mist.

Gretchen takes the first sip. 'It tastes of sunshine.'

Javier sips his. 'But not of alcohol. Sam is giving short measures again.'

'You're just used to Barcelona measures, Javier,' Gretchen says.

He smiles. 'Maybe. I had connections, it's true. I always got the best service, the catch of the day, the cutest waiters . . .'

I gaze out at the shore. The apricot glow has gone from the sky now. It's cherry red, deeper than any sky I've seen in real life. But then again, I've never been further than Greece. Perhaps in Thailand or India or the South Pacific, sunsets are this fiery.

Is the Beach modelled on a real place? Perhaps each wave and each grain of sand has a twin on earth.

'Alice?'

'Sorry, Gretchen, I was miles away.'

'I was saying that on nights like tonight, the thought of being here for eternity seems less frightening,' Gretchen says. 'Hearing my little song thrushes preparing for bed. Watching something so magnificent, with my friends.'

'Lately Gretchen has been hearing things,' Javier says, laughing.

'What things?' I ask. Any change on the Beach interests me.

'It sounds ridiculous, maybe, but yesterday I heard something familiar that I had never heard *here* before: birdsong.'

Javier shakes his head. 'Catch up, Gretchen. We've had birds here ever since Alice helped Triti get away. It was one of her *extra special gifts* to us.'

'Not those screeching gulls, Javier. Beautiful melodies. The birds who sing best are drab little things. I used to go to the park, on my way home from school. It was where they took me – the kidnappers. But that sound kept me going. It was the last lovely thing I ever heard.'

'I can't hear anything,' Javier says.

'Because you don't listen,' Gretchen tells him, but not unkindly.

Javier raises his eyebrows at me, but I look away. The way they tease each other, it's like they're brother and sister. Perhaps she reminds him of his little sisters in Spain.

'Maybe I *am* imagining the birds,' Gretchen says. 'But here I am grateful for the littlest things. They might help me understand what my death is supposed to mean.'

Javier groans. 'As though any of our deaths actually *mean* anything.'

I look at him. Should I warn them somehow, so they have the chance to say goodbye, to tell each other how they feel? After Triti escaped, Javier was almost destroyed by the know-ledge that he'd never had the chance to tell her how much she meant to him.

I'm trying to find the words to warn them, when Sam reappears with a platter of tropical fruits. Pale pink water-melon polka-dotted with black seeds, thin slices of pineapple leaking juice onto the plate, perfect strawberries sliced in two so that each half resembles a love heart.

As she puts them down on the plate, she says, 'Compliments of the management, because we don't often get a night this gorgeous, do we?' and then whispers directly into my ear, 'Don't even think about it, Alice. She might try to fight it. Let her go.'

'You OK, Alice?' Gretchen says. 'Only you look like you've seen a . . .' she doesn't finish the sentence.

'She's annoyed she can't have any of our fruit,' Javier says. 'Hey, Alice, maybe if you set another Guest free, you'll progress to the next level and be able to drink and eat with us too.'

I could repeat what he said to me: *there are always consequences.* But I just smile back. 'Actually, I *am* thirsty, guys. Need to get myself a real drink in, you know, in real life.'

'You'll miss the last minutes of the sunset,' Gretchen says.

'Don't go anywhere. I'll be back in two seconds.'

I tiptoe to the fridge. Here in London it's one in the morning, and through Lewis's kitchen window the pitch black sky is already full of stars.

This is going to break Javier's heart. And even though I'm not responsible, even though I would never have dreamed of helping Gretchen without talking to him first, I feel this all started with me. If I hadn't helped Triti, had never meddled in things I don't understand, then Javier would be just fine.

But what can I do now? Except see the end of what I started. Try to support Javier if Gretchen *does* go. Or even . . . help him escape too?

At first, the idea shocks me. Javier is so much a part of the Beach that the idea of this place without him seems as crazy as no sea, no sand, no sky.

I've always believed him when he says he loves his afterlife, but what if that's not true anymore?

Perhaps it's almost time to offer him the choice. But not quite. For now I must be normal – and I must be there for him.

I take a Diet Coke from the shelf, and return to the computer.

'OK, you guys. What have I missed?'

24

My mouth is gritty, as though I've fallen face first into the sand.

I can hear weeping. *What's going on?*

Now I remember. I'm staying up with Gretchen, so I can be with Javier if she leaves. But a stark blue light hits my face. I look up.

I'm still at Lewis's flat, and the light is coming from the outside world. I fell asleep. How *could* I?

Though maybe I'm OK. Maybe dawn hasn't broken on the Beach yet.

I blink hard. My neck is stiff because my head has been hanging down over the desk. I can taste the metallic tang of Coke. I blink again. Soul Beach is still on the screen in front of me. The palest pink sky is reflected in a silk-smooth sea.

There's a louder cry, like an animal caught in a trap. I see a man crouched on the sand with his back to me.

'Javier?'

'Go away.'

'What is it?'

'Leave me alone. You *knew*, didn't you, Alice? You *knew*.'

I stare at the screen. At some point during the night – I don't remember when – we must all have moved onto a blanket right by the water's edge. I am on one side, he's on the other, facing away from me, his legs hugged to his chest. In the middle there's an indentation in the sand, covered in crimson fabric.

I know, then, for sure: Gretchen has gone.

I touch his shoulder, but he rolls away onto the sand.

'Don't you dare deny it. You knew she was leaving, didn't you, Alice?'

'Yes.'

'*Bitch.*'

I reel backwards. It stings more than a slap. 'Javier. It's what she wanted.'

'How was she supposed to know what she wanted? Guests get so obsessed with escaping the Beach that they never consider that what comes after could be *worse*. Loyalty means nothing, *friendship* means nothing.'

His shoulders tremble.

'Gretchen deserved justice.'

He sits up. His face is twisted in what looks like hate. 'You helped her.'

'No.'

'You did. You think you're some saint. Some *God.*'

'I had nothing to do with it. I promise. My priority is Meggie.'

'Stop lying, Alice.'

'I swear. I know how much Gretchen means to you. I would never have made changes without the consent of both of you.'

He shakes his head. 'What is it about me? I get close to someone, they leave the Beach. Cursed in real life, now cursed here too. I must have done bad things, huh?'

'Javier, I'm certain Gretchen didn't want to leave you. But perhaps there was no alternative. You know ... what she suffered. The people who did that had to pay, didn't they? '

And that's when his face crumples. I reach out to him but he still backs off, the tears soaking his t-shirt.

'Will you be OK?' I ask.

He squeezes his eyes shut. 'I have no choice. Do I?'

The few wispy clouds in the sky are disappearing, promising another beautiful day. Sometimes I think the powers-that-be should arrange the odd grey, drizzly day, just to remind Guests why sunshine is so special.

'You *could* have a choice.'

He says nothing.

'I could try to help you.' I don't look at him, because he might hate me even for suggesting it. 'Of course, you could stay here. The Beach is a good place. But the option is there, for me to . . . look into what happened to you.'

Our eyes meet. His are defiant. 'I know exactly what happened to me, Alice. There is no mystery, no detective work to be done.'

I nod. 'But if you know . . .' I stop, but the question *then why are you here?* seems to hang in the air.

Eventually, Javier says quietly, 'Maybe I am curious about why I came here when my death was so . . . simple. Perhaps I'm curious about what happened to those I left behind.'

Then I remember last night. *Barcelona*. Sahara and Ade are going to Barcelona, where Javier came from. 'I could help, Javier. You only have to say the word. I owe you that.'

This time I *do* look into his eyes. They're red, from crying, but I'm sure I see hope there, momentarily. Then he frowns.

'There are many others here more deserving of the help you gave Gretchen.' He nods towards the huts. Guests are emerging from them, shading their eyes as they take in another bright morning.

How long before they notice that Gretchen has gone, and start jumping to the wrong conclusions too?

'It honestly wasn't me who set her free.'

'So you say. Yet forces like these are unpredictable, surely? Nothing comes without *consequences*,' he says. That word again.

'I would help you first, Javier. But you have to tell me what you want.'

He laughs. 'I am a human, Alice. Or at least I was. So what I want, inevitably, is what I cannot have.'

In the distance, I see my sister leaving a bamboo hut and blinking in the morning light.

'You don't have to be lonely, Javier. Meggie's still here. And Danny.'

'I am merely a way of passing the time when they can't be with the ones they love. Danny prefers you. And now Tim is here, Meggie has no need of others. She can be happy twenty-four seven.'

I look again. Tim has emerged from the hut, too. It's the first time I've seen him smiling on the Beach. His face is transformed. 'Maybe love isn't a bad way to pass the time, Javier.'

Javier smiles. 'I was in love, before, thank you. Second time round would be second rate.'

A seagull scythes through the sky, towards the horizon, before it disappears.

'Javier, did you see Gretchen go?'

He shakes his head. 'If I had known what was about to happen, I would have tried to stay awake. You could have told me.'

'Maybe,' I say, though I know I wouldn't have dared risk the wrath of Sam and the Management. 'But it's a Guest's decision. A Guest's fate. Not mine.'

Again, I see the implications of what I've said sinking in. He sighs. 'Gretchen's escape has left me ... what is the right word?' He holds out his hands. 'Empty. Perhaps it may be best for me to seek a way out, but I cannot rush my decision. It's a once-in-a-death-time opportunity, after all.'

I smile. Sarcasm from Javier is a good sign. I sense that he's on the point of saying yes to my help. 'You must know what you want, deep down?'

'I know I do not want to feel like *this* forever.'

'Is that a yes?'

He frowns. 'What of you, little Alice? What becomes of you when you've spent a lifetime helping the lost souls here? Because they'll keep on coming, won't they? As many tragedies as there are grains of sand on this beach.'

I shiver. It hasn't occurred to me before that *their* eternity could be *my* eternity, too. As long as Meggie's on the Beach, I will be too. But if I never find her killer, is this forever for both of us?

'Meggie comes first,' I say, trying to make it sound simple. 'Only after she has justice can I think about what happens next.'

25

Javier blows me a kiss – I think it's his way of apologising for calling me a bitch – then drifts away to the far end of the Beach, where he can be *almost* alone with his thoughts.

I'm on my own, too. I should log off now, in case Lewis catches me. Though there are no sounds of movement in the flat. Nothing but the whirr of computer fans.

The world goes black.

I struggle as unseen hands cover my face.

'No!'

'Guess who?'

'Danny!' I stop struggling, but my heart is pounding. 'You scared me.'

His grip relaxes, and he turns me gently. 'I'm sorry. Let me make it better.'

Our Hollywood kiss goes on for ages. He stops now and then, whispering my name above the gentle shushing sound of the waves.

When our lips are so numb that we have to break apart, Danny frowns. 'You're not getting tired of me, Alice? I know you came last night, but you never even looked for me. And you're not here as often as you were.'

'Just, you know, life getting in the way.'

He flinches, and I hate myself for using the L word. The other L word – Love – is easy to say and easy to get on the Beach. But Life is out of his reach.

'I'm sorry, Alice. I don't want to make you feel bad. What matters is that you're here now.' He takes my hand. We walk towards a new hammock that's been strung up between two palms so slender they don't look like they'll hold my weight.

'I'm not getting up *there*. I'll break the rope. Or the trunks.'

Danny laughs. 'I wonder what you look like in the real world, because I promise you that right here on the Beach, your figure is adorable, and represents zero threat to the health of the trees. Come on. It's super-cosy.'

His hands grip my waist, and he lifts me up as though I really do weigh no more than a skinny supermodel. I allow myself to fall against the warm cotton of the hammock. It smells of coconuts and the sea.

'Hang on, now,' he says as he vaults up and into the hammock: strong as an athlete, graceful as a ballet dancer.

Mine. How can *he* be mine?

After a few more seconds, the movement turns mellow, like being rocked in a cradle. It's delicious to feel the sun on my face, his skin next to mine. He leans towards me . . .

Ah, kisses like this should go on forever.

Except I sense someone watching us. I open my eyes and I see Guests watching. They've realised Gretchen's gone, and now they're waiting. Hoping they'll be the next one to get away.

'What's up, Alice?'

I realise Danny hasn't noticed yet that Gretchen's left the Beach. I should take it as a compliment. He only notices me. Yet I would have expected him to be more sensitive, somehow.

'It's Gretchen, she—'

A text rumbles in my pocket. I take out my phone: **Morning, dirty stop-out. Time to go home. Yr mum's just rung. I told her u r in shower. Call me later, I want details of night with Lewis the sexy geek. Love from yr alibi, Cara**

'What?' Danny asks.

'I have to go. Sorry.'

'You only just showed up.'

I kiss him one last time. 'Parting is such sweet sorrow,' and I can see from his face that he's never read *Romeo and Juliet*.

I click off the Beach. Do I have time to check Burning Truths again? Otherwise it'll be the early hours of tomorrow before I can sneak online again at home. Yes. It'll only take seconds, and then I can wake Lewis and go home.

The site looks less disturbing to me this morning. Am I used to it – or is it because I feel, at some deeper level, that the person behind it might be on the same side as me?

> FURTHER NEWS UPDATE, 2 MAY:
>
> THE INQUEST INTO TIM'S DEATH WAS ADJOURNED WHILE POLICE INQUIRIES CONTINUE. BUT THERE'S NO SIGN THAT THOSE POLICE INQUIRIES ARE VERY EXTENSIVE. THEY SEEM TO HAVE MADE THEIR MINDS UP.
>
> BURNING TRUTHS WILL KEEP GOING, WHATEVER HAPPENS. THERE IS MORE TO COME. MUCH MORE. BUT TIMING IS ALL. WATCH THIS SPACE IF YOU CARE ABOUT JUSTICE TOO.

'You've not been online all night, have you, Ali?'

Lewis! I click away from the site.

'Just checking my horoscope,' I say.

'You don't seriously believe in all that superstitious crap?' He sounds disappointed in me.

'Only the ones that say I'm going to have a brilliant day.'

Lewis smiles. 'Well, you're not going to have a brilliant day unless I get you home, are you?' He shakes his head. 'Come on. You've had all night. Your parents must be wondering where you are. *And* what you've been up to.'

He's blushing, as though we *have* actually been fooling around or something. The idea makes me blush too.

Lewis can't get me out of the flat fast enough, driving like a Grand Prix champ, but stopping on the main road so no one sees me getting out of his car.

'You look hung-over, Alice,' Mum says, when I let myself in. She tries to sound stern, but she's smiling. Perhaps a sleepover with Cara is a Sign of Normality. 'I'll make you a coffee, shall I?'

I clutch my head, like the worst ham actor in the world. I'm not hung-over, though I do feel wrecked.

'So how was the party?'

'Fun, I mean ...'

I don't tell *actual* lies about last night. I don't have to; Mum laps up the stories about me and Cara and Matt and Craig. She wants to know what they look like, what they're studying, which one I fancied. It seems like months ago somehow – I have to invent extra details and I feel guilty when I see the hope in her eyes.

'It's such fun when your best friend is going out with your boyfriend's best friend. You know it's how I met your father,' she tells me.

Finally I fake a few yawns, and she sends me upstairs to 'sleep it off'. She promises me a full Sunday roast later. 'Just like we used to have.'

I am knackered, but when I get into bed I'm wide awake. My head's full of unsettling pictures: Gretchen floating away to the sound of birdsong, Javier fighting back tears ... and here in real life, someone, somewhere, hunched over a laptop, trying to choose the right moment to tell the world how Meggie met her death.

Oh, Alice, really. For a bright girl, you are exceptionally slow to learn.

You are too young to let bad things concern you. Life should be all about cupcakes and parties and sunshine. But let the wrong people in, and you open the door to cruelty and passion and sadness.

Was what happened to your sister not enough of a lesson? An ego out of control, a desire for fame that made her reject those who loved her in favour of those who could make her name?

Meggie should be a cautionary tale. Yet instead of seeing that, you seem determined to pursue danger at whatever cost.

Unwise, Alice. Please, focus on your own future and let your sister rest in peace – before you pass the point of no return.

26

For a week or two after Ade's party, we act like an ad family. Mum and Dad are all loved up: she laughs when he does something daffy, he brings home flowers. We eat together, home-cooked food with real gravy. I work hard on my revision.

Except a couple of things don't quite fit the cheesy image. One, I sneak downstairs every night to read about conspiracy theories and meet my 'imaginary' friends. Two, my forthcoming birthday will also be the anniversary of my sister's death.

Normality is stretched thin. It has to break sometime.

This morning, when I come down to the kitchen, Mum is talking on her mobile. She sees me and walks out into the garden, even though it's freezing.

Dad shrugs his shoulders and butters his toast. I get some cereal and watch the breakfast telly.

She comes back after a couple of minutes.

'It's over,' she says.

Dad flinches. I freeze. Time compresses. Mum's leaving Dad? Who for? Her therapist?

But then she says, 'That was Fran from family liaison. She wanted to catch us before we saw the *Mail*. They're running an exclusive about Meggie's murder team being disbanded because the case is closed.'

'And is it true?' Dad asks.

Mum nods. 'There was a meeting yesterday. They were meant to come and tell us in person today but someone leaked it to the press. They're waiting for the inquest into Tim's death but Fran said they're certain they got their man.'

I feel calm, which surprises me. Maybe now the real murderer will relax, thinking it's all over. And when they relax, they might start making mistakes.

It's cold for May. Too cold. Every time Dad sprays washer fluid onto the windscreen, it freezes like frosted glass.

We sit side by side in the car, waiting for the heater to melt the ice. I thought Dad had offered me a lift so we could talk about the news, but he's saying nothing.

I fiddle with my nails, my gloves, my hair. But then I catch Dad staring at me and shaking his head.

'It's only mascara,' I say. Since Ade's birthday party, I've started wearing the odd bit of make-up again. It keeps Cara off my case if she thinks I'm making an effort. And, OK, it makes what I see in the mirror a bit less scary.

'What?' Dad frowns. 'Oh, no, Alice. It's not the make-up. You know me, I wouldn't notice if you were wearing black lipstick and a safety pin through your nose. No, it was ...'

I see it in *his* face. 'I look like Meggie, don't I?'

He nods. 'I only noticed it just now. Of course, you're still *Alice*, but you're growing into a young woman and so the resemblance is bound to become more ...' His eyes dart across my face, and I know he's seeing what I saw in the train window. 'More *obvious*.'

I glance at him and realise he's squeezing his eyelids together, trying to stop the tears, but they're still spilling out through the tiny lines at the edges of his eyes.

'It's OK, Dad.'

'*Stupid*,' he mumbles.

The heater is working, now. As the ice melts, the windscreen clears, revealing the world to us, and us to the world. In a few seconds, the neighbours will be able to see my father in tears.

'Everyone says it should get easier.'

He tries to smile. '*Everyone* hasn't lost a daughter. Or a sister.'

That shocks me. Till now, Dad's repeated the same glib phrases as everyone else: that the hurt will fade like a scar, that we'll always feel my sister's absence, but that there will be times when we'll forget it – only for seconds or minutes at first, but then for hours, perhaps even for a whole day.

Has he *ever* believed that or was he lying for my sake?

'Forgive me, Alice. I'm worn out, middle-aged. My hope reserves have run dry, but it's different for you. It has to be. Otherwise the killer won't just have murdered Meggie, he'll have killed both my lovely girls.'

I know what's coming next: the usual about how I must live my life for my sister as well as me. Trite instructions to squeeze in twice as much fun and love and success. When people say that, they forget I was always destined to be the shadow sister, the one in the background. I didn't mind. Life's easier when people don't expect you to be a star.

'I don't think I can live up to everyone's expectations.'

He stares at the steering wheel for ages. 'You know, Meggie wasn't better than you. You were just different.'

Yeah, right, I think.

Dad smiles. 'She'd had slightly longer on earth to work out where she was headed, that's all. Plus, her love of singing meant she never had to work out what she was going to do with her life, the way the rest of us have to.'

Cara would be raising her eyebrows now; parents trying to get down with the kids is her number two hated thing in the entire world. After Lady Gaga.

But I know he's trying so hard, and it makes me feel special. In return, I wish I could hug him and tell him Meggie is OK.

'Because I see you every day, I hadn't noticed what a lovely young woman you've turned into. But you're not Meggie.

You're beautiful in your *own* way.' He sighs, and looks away. He starts the engine and we reverse out of the drive and I pull down the shade against the winter sun, and there it is again, in the mirror.

My sister's face.

Sure, if we were standing next to each other, I'd look dowdier. My eyes are greyer and my hair mousier. But without the golden girl at my side, I am a decent enough imitation.

It's only as Dad is pulling over, outside school, that I realise what this might mean. Whatever I do, wherever I go, people will look at my face and see Meggie, and think of loss and tragedy. I will go through life having strangers feeling sorry for me.

Unless I take action. If I can find the killer, perhaps they will see me as Alice – a person in her own right. Strong, determined. Someone who never gave up fighting for justice for her sister.

27

Mum and Dad are out tonight: the first dinner party they've been to in almost a year. I half expect them to take the laptop with them to make sure I can't use it, but they're giddy, like kids, and forget all about the ban.

I wave them off into the dark night. Outside, red-grey clouds are coming down like an old army blanket, smothering the stars.

But on the Beach, a ripe peach sunset is filling the sky.

Danny is waiting for me by our rock, even though I'm visiting so much earlier with my parents out of the way. Perhaps he has a sixth sense, or maybe he spends most of his time here, waiting for me.

We say nothing, just hold each other. Our kisses get better and better. Danny isn't the first boy I've kissed, but this is the real thing. A century could pass, or a hurricane could lift us up and fling us back down to earth, and I'm pretty sure we wouldn't notice a thing. And despite the passion, it never feels rushed. Danny, at least, has all the time in the world.

'You save me from going crazy when you're here with me,' he whispers.

'And the thought of you saves me from going crazy when I'm not,' I whisper back.

'I never thought I'd meet a girl like you,' says Danny. He's stroking my arm, raising the tiny hairs with his fingers and then smoothing them down again. Every single nerve in my skin tingles, and I feel safe. *Cherished.*

'Especially on the internet.'

He stares at me. 'Yeah. Beauties like you don't hang out on internet dating sites.'

I'm not a beauty, but I can't expect Danny to know what that's like.

On the Beach, everyone has their old imperfections airbrushed away, but I've seen the pictures of Danny when he was alive and he didn't need any upgrading. His square jaw makes him the perfect movie leading man. And he has thick blond hair that cries out to be rumpled, and *those* green eyes. They were the first thing I noticed about him, and they're the last thing I think of at night. They're full of so much intelligence and sadness – though less sadness, since we found each other.

Danny breaks away suddenly. 'I need to show you something.'

He reaches into his pocket and pulls out a bundle of paper. There must be twenty different pages, each one yellow and brittle-looking, like an ancient manuscript or a message in a bottle after it's bobbed across an ocean or two.

'What are those?'

'They're for you. I didn't want to give them to you, but I . . . promised.'

I hesitate, just for a second. They stink of damp and despair. *Too late now.*

The handwriting on the first one is scratchy, as though the person who wrote it had never held a pen before.

'*Please Alice,*' I read aloud. '*You are only hope to get message to my family about water. The water kill me. My family must know or the same will happen. Thank you. From Li.*

Danny takes the page and then points through the gap in the rocks to an athletic looking Chinese girl who is pretending not to notice me as she plays chess with a friend. 'Li has never written in English before. It took her hours. She thinks she was poisoned by the chemical works upstream from her village.'

I take the second of the sheets. The letters are fancy, with looped js and ys and little circles over every i. This time I don't read it out loud.

Alice, the war in my country must stop before it destroys the new generation who could build a different future. The Beach is torture, knowing my people suffer. If they know I was a pawn, it could be stopped. And maybe I will escape too.

'That's from Olivier,' Danny says. 'He was one of the ruling elite in his home country in North Africa. He was killed to stoke civil war. Thousands die each week, he says. Don't tell him I said this, but I think it's hopeless. The UN have been there for twenty years and it's made no difference.'

Suddenly the letter feels red hot, burning my fingers. 'They're all like this?'

Danny sighs. 'After Triti disappeared, people thought it might have been a one-off. But since Gretchen left the Beach ...'

'I told you, that wasn't down to me!'

He raises his eyebrows. '*I* know that. But they don't believe it.'

I look away. 'Can't they see I've had no new gifts? Nothing's changed on the Beach, either.'

Danny looks back at the Guests. 'Maybe nothing physical. But they're more hopeful now. They believe in you, Alice.'

I shake my head. 'I'm no miracle worker. Nothing special.'

'I can't agree with that. You *are* special. And you also have what we don't. Freedom. *Life.*'

Perhaps I *should* work harder for them. Forget stupid exams and stupid parties. Dad talked about finding a purpose: maybe this is what I'm alive to do. But I already have my sister's death to resolve. And Javier's. And surely Danny must be a victim of some kind of injustice, too. It's overwhelming.

'Where would I start, Danny? How would I choose between them?'

He takes the letters, then puts his arm round me, stroking my neck. 'I'm sorry. This is my fault. The first girl to give me a letter promised she'd keep it a secret and I couldn't bring myself to say no. But nothing stays secret on the Beach and, next thing, I'm like your personal mailman.'

The pile of letters sits on the rock. The last one is written in old-fashioned writing – what's it called? Copperplate. The shapes are beautiful but the words are ugly: *death, war, poison.*

'Once they started, I couldn't accept one and refuse another. Who am I to say who deserves your help? It'd be like playing God.'

A pair of bright green parakeets skitter through the sky, resting on a palm tree. Who is playing God here? I've spent so many hours on the Beach since September that it's become normal, but every now and then I wonder: is this a hoax? Or, worse, am I imagining it all?

Dozens of Guests are watching. Waiting. Each hoping that they'll be the one whose story moves me enough to make me take action in the real world.

'I'll do my best,' I whisper, and they seem to hear me, because they drift away.

'Try to forget them now.' Danny turns my face back towards his. 'No more nasty surprises. Just you and me . . .'

I'm in bed by the time my parents get back. I hear the car door slam, then raised voices.

'. . . it won't help her. Or Alice.'

'It's the right thing to do, Glen. She'd have wanted us to *do* something, to stop other girls suffering like she did.'

There's a metallic scrabbling as a key keeps missing the lock in the front door.

'Come here, Bea, I'll do it.'

Once they're inside, they try to argue more quietly, but I still hear fragments. 'Meggie can be a force for good . . . make a difference . . . Olav says that . . .'

'. . . not a conversation to have when you're too drunk to . . . I can't reason with you—'

'It's not about reason! It's about emotion! Though I can't expect you to understand that! Well, you won't stop me, Glen. I'm going to follow my heart.'

Another slammed door, then my mother's unsteady feet on the stairs, then silence. The truce between my parents has lasted less than three weeks.

How quickly a year goes by.

I miss you so much, Meggie. Your luminous skin, your delicate hands, your fragile grip on life. I wish things could have been different. Though often I do feel you are still with me.

In a way, because of Alice, you are.

Seventeen is such a special age. What advice would you give your baby sister? To make the most of every minute, perhaps. To be careful what you wish for. To cherish those closest to you.

Happy anniversary, Megan London Forster. Forgive me if I haven't given you as much thought as I should have, lately.

Distractions, you know. But tonight is full of precious memories. Sweet dreams.

28

On the morning of my seventeenth birthday, I wake up *way* before four a.m.

Exactly a year ago, someone crept into Meggie's room and stole her from us. I sneak downstairs to the laptop. I should check in on Burning Truths. It's gone quiet on there since the inquest – no comments, no new posts – but surely there'll be something new on there today. The date is bound to mean something to whoever is running the site.

Yet I can't quite face that yet. It is my birthday, after all. So I head to the Beach first of all.

There's a football game happening on the shore, lit by a full moon. Meggie's playing, along with Danny and a few Guests I recognise but have never spoken to. Tim is watching her from the sidelines.

When my sister sees me, she waves, but keeps on playing. So she must be oblivious to the date, and its significance to her and to me. Even though I knew that would probably be true, it hurts me more than I expected.

'Strange time to be playing, right?'

Javier's at my side. 'What do you mean?'

He shrugs. 'It is very late at night for a match.'

I say nothing.

'What is it, Alice?'

I shake my head. The rules silence me, yet again.

'I get it. You have to be careful. But I can guess, right? It's your sister?'

I nod.

'It is one year ago, am I right?'

I stare at him, but his face gives nothing away in the low light from the paper lanterns.

'How did you know?' I ask.

'I think I am the only person here who keeps count of each day.'

'But Sam told me no one does. That it drives Guests mad.'

'Sam does not know everything, even if she thinks she does. It's good to have secrets, especially from nosy bar girls. Makes me feel I have a little ... control. When, of course, I have none.'

'Right.' Javier has always claimed to be happy here, yet why would a happy person bother to tick off the days in paradise, like a prisoner counting down his sentence?

'You know, Alice, it is better for Meggie that she does not remember.'

'I know,' I say. 'Except ...'

He looks at me. 'What?'

'It's my birthday, too.'

'Ah! And I suppose if you tell her that ...'

'Then she might remember her own anniversary and I don't want to make her feel bad.'

Javier nods. 'You are a good person, Alice.' He leans over and kisses me on both cheeks, which is closer than he usually gets to me: I smell alcohol. Is he drunk? *'Felicitaciones!'*

'Thank you.' I give his body a squeeze. 'Have you ... have you thought anymore? About my offer?'

'I haven't *stopped* thinking about it. It comforts me, when the perfection of this place makes me want to scream. But let us be realistic. You are an English schoolgirl. My story begins and ends in another country, in a language you do not speak.'

'I can't promise anything, Javier, except that if you give me permission, I will try. And there are means. Ways that even a schoolgirl can make a difference. The internet, for example—'

He laughs. 'My father didn't even know what the internet *was*.'

It's the first time he's mentioned his father. 'Whatever you can tell me could help. About your father, too—'

'ALICE!' Danny calls out, abandoning the football game, and then striding towards me. 'You're early. What a fantastic surprise!' He kisses me, and over his shoulder, I see Javier slinking away. Did he ask me for help? I don't think I got an answer.

My sister follows, as the game breaks up.

'Hey, little sister. What a treat!' She puts her arm round me, and for a moment I really want to tell her what day it is. But it's not fair on her.

'Who won the game?' I ask.

Meggie laughs. 'It's not the winning, it's the taking part. Didn't Miss Gregory always tell you that in your hockey class?'

'Yeah.' Miss Gregory retired last term. For some reason I don't want to tell her that either. Even the littlest things must make her realise the world is changing without her.

'You look very serious,' she says.

'I'm worried about Javier. How does he seem to you?'

Danny answers. 'Still cut up over Gretchen. That's normal, right?'

'Do you think he wants out?'

My sister frowns. 'Come on, Alice. Stop worrying about other people and make the most of your time here, eh? It's paradise!'

Tim's behind her now and she shrugs apologetically. 'I'll leave you two in peace, OK.'

When she's gone, Danny looks worried. 'It's my fault, isn't it, Alice? Passing on those letters put ideas in your head. But you don't owe any of us anything. Just enjoy being with us. With me.'

He kisses me again. For a few seconds, I pretend we are normal, that he knows what day it is, has presents for me hidden in a bamboo hut, a reservation in my favourite restaurant . . . I long for even a few moments of ordinariness with the boy I love.

'Alice? Is that you?'

My eyes spring open.

Dad.

I slam the laptop lid without shutting down the Beach, and as I stand up and spin round, he's coming into the living room.

I grab my water glass and stand up. 'Dad! You gave me a fright.'

'So did you.' He rubs his eyes. 'What are you doing up so early?'

'Couldn't sleep. Got up to fetch a drink of water.' I look down at my glass, and see the fluorescent blue light in my mouse is glowing in the half-light. I edge in front of it, hoping he hasn't seen it too.

'I couldn't sleep either. I've been doing better, lately, but what with the date . . .' and then he realises, and comes towards me and gives me the biggest of bear hugs. 'Happy birthday, Alice. A new year. Let's make it your best, eh?'

29

My parents take me to lunch at my favourite pizza place. The weather seems to have changed overnight, so it's warm sitting by the open window. We drink a glass of champagne each, and Mum hesitates before toasting 'my two girls'. Dad checks my reaction, and I smile, because it feels like the right thing to do, as though Meggie is here celebrating, too.

The waiter appears with a small Victoria sponge loaded with fizzing sparklers, and when the other customers look at our table, it doesn't feel like they're staring because they recognise us from the news.

At home, I feel woozy from the champagne, and tired from my early morning Beach walk, so I snooze through the afternoon. Then Cara comes round to get me ready for later.

There's no party. My sixteenth was cancelled after the police came to tell us the news and to make plans for a party this year felt too much like tempting fate. Instead, we're having a few drinks at a new bar she wants to try near the river, with Lewis and with James, Cara's latest arm candy.

'What did you get, then?' Cara is brushing my hair so hard it makes my eyes water.

'Driving lessons. A new phone. Plus a cheque.'

'Enough to pay for an end-of-exams trip to Spain?'

'Maybe.'

She turns me round. 'You might go, after all? Oh, Alice, it'll be brilliant!'

'I haven't decided for sure,' I say. 'But maybe someone needs to keep an eye on you.'

'Why?'

'Where do I start, Cara? You're going to a foreign country with people you hardly know, to try to get off with a guy who is already dating this really intense, slightly scary woman with muscles like a bouncer's. Oh, and "the guy" happens to be way too old for you.'

'Ha! I've been out with loads of older men. Plus, little miss perfect Alice, Lewis is older than Ade, and his age isn't stopping *you*.'

'Lewis is a mate.'

She laughs at me. 'Just a mate? Does *he* know that?'

'Of course.'

But when the taxi drives straight past the new bar, and stops outside Lewis's flat, and when he opens the door and I can hear music and see dozens of flickering candles, I wonder if he *does* know that.

'Surprise!' he says, and Cara winks at me as we go inside. James – a catalogue model who is ninety-four millimetres too short to do catwalk – is already there. I've never seen the French doors open, didn't even realise there was anything beyond the wall of adopted plants, but a line of fairy lights leads out onto a square patio, where a table is set for four.

'Lewis, have you been *cooking*?' Cara says, as though cooking is some kind of perverted hobby.

He blushes. 'I raided the chiller cabinet in the supermarket. I know how much you drink, Cara, so I thought I'd provide something to line your stomach, or you'd start singing and the neighbours would call the police.'

But the food doesn't taste mass-produced. Maybe it's because we're sitting outside, but the tomatoes taste of summer, and the bread is warm from the oven. The crockery doesn't match, and neither do the glasses, but it feels less formal that way and it's absolutely perfect. Exactly what I wanted, even though I didn't know it till now.

James says nothing but looks very pretty, Cara helps herself to wine, and I drink loads of water because the champagne at lunch has left my mouth dry. Lewis keeps getting up to change the music, top up our drinks, add more candles.

'Relax, Lewis,' Cara tells him, when he gets up for the fifteenth time. 'This isn't a royal banquet.'

But then he relaxes, and his dry humour makes Cara laugh, and she keeps giving me the thumbs up under the table.

Finally, when James starts asking Lewis if he can order him some extra-strong growth hormone off the net, Cara gets restless and drags her mini-model off to a club where his lack of conversation won't matter. I stay behind to help Lewis clear up.

'No, no. It's your birthday!'

But when I sneak back in behind him, I spot the bin's full of dark blue packaging from the posh deli in town. Even my mum thinks that place is too expensive.

I don't know what I do to deserve Lewis. He always does the right thing. I guess I just have to hope that one day I get a chance to repay his kindness.

Now we're inside, the bank of screens makes me think of the latest favour he's been doing for me.

'I meant to check Burning Truths today, but I haven't had time. Do you think I could . . .'

Then I see the look on his face. What a self-centred cow I am. But I can't take it back.

'I'd hoped I'd have something to tell you by now, but . . .' he sighs. 'I could have another go, now, if you like.'

'No. Not tonight. Not after you've gone to so much trouble.'

'Don't pretend you're here for the pleasure of my company, Ali.'

'Oh, God. Sorry. That came out wrong. I . . . I don't know what I'd do without you, Lewis, honestly. Today could have been so difficult but you made it OK.' I'm blushing now, but even though it's embarrassing, I *want* him to know how important he is to me. 'It was *so* sweet of you to do all this.'

'Sweet. Hmm.' He grabs two cans of Coke from the fridge and throws me one. I only just catch it, and he smiles.

He sits down. 'Let's take a look. It's been quiet on the site for a bit, but I'm sure the significance of today won't have escaped them. There was a sarcastic comment after the inquiry team was disbanded, but nothing interesting since.'

He navigates half a dozen different security screens.

'What are you doing?'

'I visit via a VPN so the host never knows who I am.'

'VPN? Is that like a Visible Panty Line?'

Lewis laughs, and I feel *almost* as though all is forgiven. 'Virtual Private Network. Makes me look like I'm in Slovenia one minute, Singapore the next. Same technology the designer uses.'

The header loads, as nasty as ever.

Underneath there's a single word, in huge font:

ANGRY!!!!!!!!!!!!!!

'Aye, aye. That wasn't there when I checked earlier,' Lewis says.

We both lean in to the screen.

> AS IF IT'S NOT BAD ENOUGH THAT TIM ASHLEY WAS EFFECTIVELY CONVICTED BY INNUENDO WHEN THE POLICE STOPPED THEIR INQUIRY INTO MEGGIE FORSTER'S MURDER, NOW MRS FORSTER HAS DECIDED TO PUT THE BOOT IN!

'What's Mum done?' I read as fast as I can.

> THIS STUPID INTERVIEW COMES OUT IN THE DAILY MAIL TOMORROW BUT IS ALREADY UP ON THEIR

WEBSITE. IN IT, MRS FORSTER POINTS THE FINGER
AT TIM BY SAYING SHE'S SETTING UP A TRUST IN
HER DAUGHTER'S NAME 'TO HELP YOUNG WOMEN
FACING DOMESTIC VIOLENCE IN THEIR
RELATIONSHIPS'.

APPARENTLY, SHE'S SO CONVINCED THAT HER
CONFIDENT, REALITY TV STAR DAUGHTER WAS
ACTUALLY A VICTIM OF DOMESTIC VIOLENCE,
THAT SHE'S GOING TO CAMPAIGN 'FOR YOUNGER
GIRLS, WHO OFTEN ASSUME THEY'RE ALONE, OR
THAT ABUSE IS ONLY FACED BY OLDER, MARRIED
WOMEN.'

WELL, FOR MRS FORSTER'S INFORMATION,
PLENTY OF PEOPLE HAD REASONS TO HATE MEGGIE
FORSTER, AND – FOR REASONS BEST KNOWN TO
HIMSELF – TIM ASHLEY WASN'T ONE OF THEM.
EVERYONE COULD SEE THAT. SO WHY ISN'T MRS
FORSTER CAMPAIGNING AGAINST REALITY TV
SHOWS LIKE THE ONE THAT PORTRAYED HER
DAUGHTER AS AN EGOMANIAC? OR AGAINST THE
NEWSPAPERS THAT HOUNDED HER FAMILY – AS
WELL AS TIM – AFTER THE MURDER?

NO. THAT'D BE TOO EASY FOR BEATRICE
FORSTER. AND FOR THE PAPERS. BUT SOMEONE
OUT THERE KNOWS EVERYONE IS GETTING IT
WRONG. AND ONE OF THESE DAYS, THEY'LL GET
A KNOCK ON THE DOOR . . .

'Bloody hell, someone wasn't joking about being angry,'
Lewis says.

But who? I try to imagine Ade saying those things out loud;
he seems too calm for those bitter words. And then I think of
Sahara saying them. That seems more likely. Sometimes
when she talks, she goes too far.

'Can I look at the news story?' I ask, and Lewis brings it up.

It's headlined *Exclusive: My Meggie Did Not Die in Vain*, and features one of the photos of Meggie on TV, plus a creepy picture where it looks like Tim is grabbing her by the arm (in fact, he was stopping her from tripping on her long dress). And there's a third photo, of Mum, walking by the Thames looking wistful.

I bet Dad doesn't know about *this*.

Mum only mentions the idea of a trust in passing, as something she's considering. It must have been what she and Dad were rowing about after the dinner party last week. Why did she even mention it? She must know how angry it'll make him . . .

The rest of the article is harmless, full of memories of my sister. I half expect Mum to go through the whole piece without mentioning me, but right at the end, the interviewer comments on how the rest of the family is coping.

'My husband and my daughter are more private than I am. It's how they cope. But without them, I'd be lost. Seeing Alice grow up and become independent is all that's keeping me going, some days. She's the best thing in my life.'

The screen blurs. I blink hard. Of course, I know Mum loves me, but sometimes, in the last year, I've wondered whether she'd have missed me as much as she misses Meggie, if *I'd* been the daughter who died.

Without speaking, Lewis clicks back to Burning Truths. 'I think the person behind the site might be online. The front page is changing.'

I look up again. There are fewer lines of text, and when Lewis refreshes the page again, the headline ANGRY!!! has disappeared. 'They're taking it down?'

'Yeah. But that means . . .'

Lewis moves across to the other keyboard, begins to type

incredibly fast, bringing up several different windows of text, images, maps. As I watch the screen nearest me, it goes black for a moment, then a large blank square appears.

'Something's being uploaded,' I say.

'Come on, come *on*,' Lewis mumbles, but he's not talking to me. He's still typing furiously, without looking at his fingers. My mum – who still boasts about her hundred-and-ten-words-a-minute in secretarial school – would be impressed.

The screen in front of me changes agonisingly slowly, like in the dark ages at home before we got broadband. It's definitely an image. A photo.

The background is white. Then pink shapes begin to appear.

Lewis looks up, but doesn't stop typing. 'Too bloody fast.'

He's right, the download has speeded up. Then the whole photo is there.

It's a *hand*. The semi-circles are fingernails, painted with glittery pink polish. Those nails are perfect almonds, at the end of slender fingers.

'Damn.' Lewis is hitting the return key over and over. 'Offline again. I was so nearly there, unless ...' And he's off again.

A right hand. On the index finger, there's a ring with a huge purple stone. Too big to be real.

I gave her that ring.

'Lewis. Lewis, it's her hand. Meggie's hand.'

He stops typing, and studies the picture more closely. 'There's something odd about that picture.'

'What, other than the fact that it's been taken by some kind of *nail* fetishist?'

'You're certain it's your sister's hand?'

'Yes. Of course. But why would someone take a photo of *just* her hand? It's too weird.' Something awful occurs to me.

142

'Lewis, do you think ... could this have been taken by the killer?'

He runs a hand through his hair. 'It's possible, Ali. But ... well, isn't it more likely that it's one Tim took? We know there's a connection between him and the person behind this site.'

'But I can't see why he'd do that. He could hold her hand anytime he liked.'

Lewis leans forward. 'There's something else. The colours are all wrong. The skin, it's too pale and the nails are too pink.'

'No, that's her favourite colour, but the skin ...' And that's when I realise. 'Oh, God, Lewis. This is Meggie. But whoever took this photo took it ... I think they took it *after* they killed her.'

30

Lewis reaches out to grab my hand.

'You don't know that,' he says, but he doesn't sound very confident.

'Look at it, Lewis. It's ... lifeless. The colour you noticed, it's because ...'

And then I can't speak anymore because my eyes are full of tears.

'Oh, Alice.'

Lewis holds me, now, as I sob into his t-shirt. It's not sadness that's making me cry, though, it's shock and *anger* that anyone could be so heartless. Who could do that? Murder my sister, then hang around long enough to photograph her.

'What else did they do, Lewis? *What other pictures did they take?*'

He doesn't say anything, but just lets me cry, holding me tightly. At first, it doesn't help, but then gradually I feel the tears beginning to slow, and, as they do, the shock wears off and the anger grows.

'The bastard. This is the sickest thing. The *sickest* thing.'

'I know. I know, Ali. But what you have to remember is that she would have known nothing about it. Nothing can hurt her anymore.'

I pull away from him. There's a huge damp circle where I was leaning against his chest. 'Sorry.'

Lewis smiles. 'Come on. Do you think I care about a wet shirt? It's not as if I'm Mr Immaculate.'

I smile back. The embarrassment's gone. I'm a little bit surprised at him, how he held me instinctively, not like an awkward geek at all, but like a best friend who *cares*.

'It's bad enough that someone took it. But what's that photo doing on the site, Lewis?'

We turn back to the screen and I flinch. Lewis scrolls up, so I don't have to see the image of my dead sister's hand, though I don't think I'll ever forget it. But there's nothing under the picture, no caption, no note. And the rant about my mother's disappeared.

'You know, I was *that* close to finding their real location. But it's still possible that some of the diagnostic stuff could crunch a result, of sorts. It might take a while, but I'll try, shall I?'

'Please.'

He types some lines of code at the middle keyboard, then sighs. 'It's going to be hours. I think after the shock you've had, perhaps I should run you home.'

I don't have the strength to argue. And actually, he's right. It's the only place I want to be.

I get back just after one in the morning. Mum and Dad are already in bed, but when I sneak into the dining room, my laptop's gone.

What the hell? The first thing I think of is that Meggie's killer has been here – is *still* here.

I run upstairs, not caring if I wake my parents, and the panic lasts till I get to my room and find the computer back in its old place on my desk, ready for action. There's a note next to it, in Mum's writing:

A final little birthday present. We've always trusted you, darling, we only wanted to help.

When I get my breath back, I realise it means I can carry on my own investigations into how Meggie died, right now.

Or venture back onto the Beach to feel my sister's warm hand in mine, to try to replace that horrible image of death with one of life.

But my eyes smart from my tears and from staring at a screen for so long, and the thought of Soul Beach is exhausting. Maybe Mum *was* only trying to protect me. God knows there are some things on the internet that shouldn't be there, that *no one* should have to see.

Yet even though I feel sick at the thought of it, I'm glad I did go to Burning Truths tonight. For months, I've been trying Lewis's patience with suspicions and theories that must have tested his belief in me.

Now he's seen it, he must also see what it is we're up against. Whoever took those photographs didn't see my sister as human, but as some kind of ... specimen, or trophy.

I know Lewis isn't as convinced of Tim's innocence as I am. But when we said good night, I saw it in his eyes: he wants to know the truth, too. He's not going to give up on me or Meggie now.

Somehow I fall asleep almost instantly. When I wake up at nine on Saturday, it takes me a few seconds to remember I don't need to set a four a.m. Beach alarm anymore.

It's a few seconds more before I remember what Lewis and I found on Burning Truths last night. It makes me shiver, but I have to focus on the investigation. We will find the person behind the site, I know we will, and then we'll find out where they got the photo.

It might even happen today.

Downstairs in the kitchen, the *Mail* lies open on the breakfast bar. I've interrupted a row, I'm sure of it.

'Morning, Alice,' Mum says, too brightly. 'You look very well this morning, considering!'

'I wasn't that late.'

146

'Ten past one is late enough for a sixteen— sorry, a seventeen-year-old,' she says, then smiles. 'I know I'm fussing but I couldn't sleep till I knew you were back safe.'

Dad's smile is forced. 'You had a good night?'

'Brilliant! And now I'm meeting Cara for breakfast so she can help me spend my birthday money.'

'I could run you in,' Mum offers, in a fairly desperate bid to get out of facing the music with Dad.

'No, thanks. The walk will clear my head.'

We meet in the Marks and Spencer coffee shop. Cara's nicked her mother's free breakfast vouchers and is already breaking the world Danish-pastry-eating speed record.

'How's your head?' I ask her.

'Thundering. How's yours?'

Full of horrible images and a roll call of names: Sahara, Ade, Tim, Zoe. It's my updated suspect list. I worked it out on the walk over here.

'Wake up, Alice! I asked you how you're feeling.'

'Not too bad, considering.'

'So what did you and your *just good friend* Lewis get up to after we left?'

'Surfed the web, obviously, because that's what geeks do.'

'You're not a geek, Alice.'

'Well, I am compared to you and your pin-up guy. So what happened at the club?'

'Unbelievably they asked *him* for ID, but I managed to talk the bouncers round . . .'

And off she goes. I let the details wash over me, but it makes me feel normal to be here with my best friend, hearing about her crazy night. Helps me block out all the details of my sister's hand, her sparkling nails and her—

'Your phone's going, Alice.'

I stare at Cara, then realise what she's saying. I dig around in my bag.

'Lewis,' I say, answering it. Cara grins and gives me the thumbs up.

I get up from the table and walk towards the fruit and veg.

'Ali, I think I've worked one thing out. Don't get too excited, but unless it's some quadruple bluff, then whoever's behind Burning Truths isn't local,' Lewis tells me.

'Meaning what? They're not from West London?'

A woman tuts at me because I'm getting in the way as she squeezes the apples.

'Meaning I'm pretty sure that they're based in another time zone. At least they were last night. Central European Time, to be exact.'

'You said they had that private network thing, though, Lewis. That could make it look like they were anywhere in the world.'

'Hmm. But I got *past* that last night. I didn't want to say anything till I'd run that program, but the data was conclusive. I got past the mask. It could be Paris, Berlin, Amsterdam. Did your sister spend time in Europe? Or have a uni friend from outside the UK?'

I move away from the fridges, because the hum is stopping me from thinking straight. 'Well, according to the press, she had plenty of fans all over Europe, all over the world, but ...'

And then I think of someone who couldn't *ever* be described as a fan. 'This time zone. Would it include Barcelona?'

But I know the answer even before he confirms it. 'Yes. Why?'

'Oh. Nothing. It's just been on my mind because ... it doesn't matter. Look, I'm with Cara at the moment. Let me have a think and call you back?'

'Sure, Ali. Are you OK, by the way? After last night?'

'Fine. Thanks. Not just for asking but for this, for not giving up.'

There's a pause. Then he says, 'I'm a stubborn sod, you know. I'll get to the bottom of it if it kills me.' He stops himself. 'Sorry, that probably wasn't the right thing to say, was it?'

'The day you start censoring yourself around me, Prof, is the day we're not friends anymore.'

I end the call, knowing what I have to do. I walk back to where Cara's sitting.

'So how is lover boy?' she asks. 'It must be all of ten hours since he last spoke to you.'

'Ha ha, Cara. You should be on the stage.' I take a sip of my hot chocolate. The sugar's making me sharper now. 'Hey, you know Barcelona?'

'Spanish city with a beach and a wonky cathedral?'

'That's the place. I've decided I'm definitely going.'

'*Seriously?*' She leans over the table and gives me a big slobbery, boozy kiss.

'God, Cara, how much did you drink at the club?'

'Shush. I don't want a lecture. I want to celebrate. Mum'll book our flights right now if I call her.'

'I thought you'd booked to go already?'

'I was going to, but then . . . It wouldn't be the same without you, hon.'

'One thing. Promise me you won't go after Ade?'

She laughs. 'All's fair in love and war, Alice.'

The pastry sits on my plate. I'm not hungry anymore. 'No, it's not.'

'Hey, you're not my mum. Remember what I keep telling you about being a teenager? Part of that involves, you know, having fun, flirting with boys.'

I sigh. How do I explain that she could flirt with any other boy in the world and I wouldn't care. But not this one, because there's a chance that either Ade or Sahara might be a killer.

I try making a joke of it. 'Sure. But this is all a bit close for comfort, somehow. Sahara's unpredictable, you know. Fiery. Get on the wrong side of her, and you might come back from Barcelona in a box!'

'Alice!'

'What?'

'People don't joke about stuff like that. Especially not you.'

I sigh. 'If anyone's allowed to joke about death, it's me. But I'm serious.'

'I can handle her.'

'You don't know what she's capable of.'

Cara frowns. 'Is there something you're not telling me? You're not saying you think *she* killed Meggie?'

For a moment, I wonder if I should tell her about my suspicions. Even if she thinks I'm crazy, it might be enough to make her more cautious. Here, everything feels under control, just about. In Spain, who knows? But going there is the best chance I've got of working this out.

'I'm just saying . . . We know what jealousy can do. It drives people mad. Don't risk it. I couldn't bear it if something happened to you.'

'Oh, honey. Nothing's going to happen to me.' She reaches out to touch my hand and I squeeze it back. 'Right. I'll phone my ma, shall I? Just think, we'll be soaking up the sun and sangria in less than a month.'

'Better wait to book till I've asked my parents for permission.'

'Your mum will be over the moon. She seems to think you're turning into a weirdo loner recluse who spends her life on the internet. Can't *imagine* how she got that idea.'

'I'm not *that* bad. I went out last night.'

'Oh, yes. Hey, Lewis could come to Spain, too!'

'So you can go off with Ade?'

She laughs. 'You know me too well, Alice Forster.'

I laugh too, though it doesn't seem that funny, because Cara doesn't know the real me anymore. How could she? Wherever I go – even the bloody Marks and Spencer café – my baggage comes with me: the letters from Guests on the Beach, the mystery behind Burning Truths, my list of murder suspects, Javier's story.

These days, I am ten per cent Alice Forster. And ninety per cent secrets.

31

I can't find Danny.

I'm not panicking, not yet. Though the Beach is too small to lose people. Javier is trying to hide from everyone as he grieves for Gretchen, yet everyone knows exactly where *he* is: in the same spot where Triti went when she was suffering. With luck, I may be able to help end his torment, too.

But where the hell is Danny?

I tried the rock first, of course. That was where I'd imagined we'd spend the whole afternoon today. The exams are finished, Mum's out, Cara's off on a uni Open Day with her mother, and I have nothing to do except lie next to Danny and talk nonsense between kisses.

When I've found him ...

The last week or two have been weirdly settled. It can't last. Spain is bound to change everything; that's the whole point of going. But right now, my time feels like my own for the first time in forever. I've passed my driving theory test, and taken my first practical lessons. I've gone for long lazy lunches with Cara after our exams, flirting with boys on the riverbank.

Once or twice, I've even forgotten to go online after a night out, and Danny's told me off. So this afternoon I am planning to put that right, by spending time with him, alone.

The sun is high in the sky, and dazzling. I can't even look at the white hot sand without screwing up my eyes. I guess it's midday on the Beach; in the real world, only mad dogs and Englishmen would risk the heat. But here, where Guests' skin is pre-bronzed like a Christmas turkey, no one burns, so they're lined up on the shore as usual.

Like sausages under the grill.

Where did *that* come from? Not an observation the glamorous Guests would appreciate. I spot my sister and Tim sitting in the beach bar, feeding each other scoops of ice cream. Her hand holding the spoon reminds me of *that* photograph. Nothing new has appeared on Burning Truths since then, not even a comment, but every time I check the site, it makes me nauseous.

Meggie spots me, then leans in to say something to Tim. She leaves their table and comes over to give me a huge hug.

'It's my baby sister!'

She sits down on one of the rough wooden steps down from the bar, and pats the space next to her. Since Tim arrived, they've been in this bubble and it's been hard to get any time alone with her.

'So, what news?' she asks. And I manage to make her laugh with the tale of next door's dog being chased by a cat, plus a whole bunch of other stuff that doesn't matter. I've never even mentioned my birthday, and she hasn't brought it up. Perhaps she feels awkward too.

'And how's everything going with Tim?' I ask.

Her smile says it all. 'When you arrived, I was ecstatic. Now he's here too, the Beach feels different. It's more like contentment. Boring word, right? But it's the right one.'

I hug her again, then see Tim over her shoulder.

'He's looking at me again, isn't he?' my sister asks.

'Like a baby chick who's lost his mother.'

She giggles. 'There are worse things in the world than being adored. As you should know, because Danny's pretty adoring himself.'

I sigh. 'Yeah. That's why I'm here right now. Things have been so busy, lately. I wanted to spend time with him.'

Meggie kisses me again. 'Off you go, then. Come back later if you like. Tim's getting more used to things. And I want you two to be as close as you were ... before.'

She skips back up the steps and I carry on towards the set of beach huts lined up just beyond the bar. I tend not to come near these, because it's where Guests go to make out or argue, but I want to find Danny, and there's nowhere else he could be.

'... but if it's that important, why not ask her?' It's a girl's voice, coming from one of the huts.

'Because I'm scared of her answer.'

A man's voice. *Danny's voice?*

The huts are on skinny stilts. I take a couple of steps closer, then wait. And listen. It probably wasn't Danny at all. Of course, he gets on with everyone – he's that kind of guy – but he doesn't have any close female friends apart from Meggie and me.

You're enough for me, Alice. And when you can't be here, your sister reminds me of you, of how you're worth waiting for.

'What's the worst thing she could say?' The girl's voice again. I think it's coming from the end hut, the sound leaking through the struts of the bamboo wall.

'That I can't give her what she wants.'

I stop breathing. It couldn't be anyone else. I wriggle into the gap between the huts and the scrub-covered rock. I don't want them to catch me spying. I can't believe I'm doing this, but I can't drag myself away either.

'Yeah, right. Even though you're, like, every girl's dream? The very charming, very handsome Danny Cross, heir to the throne of one of America's most *major* corporations?'

When Danny laughs, he sounds so sad. 'An heir has to be alive, right? That's what I can't give Alice.'

'But you always knew that, Danny. A relationship between a Visitor and a Guest could never have had a future.'

I imagine a future without Danny and it hurts like a punch with a clawed knuckleduster.

'DON'T SAY THAT!' Danny calls out. I hear movement from the hut, and I move backwards, hitting the prickly bracken that grows on the rocks. I suddenly feel so ashamed for eavesdropping, yet I can't stop now.

'Sit down, Danny. Listen. I don't know Alice, but she seems like a nice kid.'

Kid? How old is this girl, with her idiotic Minnie Mouse voice?

'She's not a kid. She's wonderful.'

'But she's also a Visitor, Danny. They come here for one reason. To help the person who called them here.'

'You don't *know* that. No one knows jack about what this place is really about, Roberta.'

Roberta. An irrational jealousy begins to burn inside me.

'Well, I know things are different since she helped Triti get away. It changed stuff, right, Danny? And it's been worse since the German girl disappeared. People are restless.'

'It wasn't Alice's fault. She had nothing to do with Gretchen going.'

'Whatever.' Roberta sighs really loudly. 'If you're not interested in what I think, why ask for my opinion?'

Yes, why confide in her and not me, Danny?

'Because I'm so scared of losing her. I wanted to talk to someone neutral.'

'None of us are neutral here. Your friends . . . we're worried about you. What happens when she goes? Because she will, you know that, right? Either she'll fix what happened with her sister, or she'll get bored and get a life in *her* world.'

I won't.

'I'll . . . accept it. What other choice will I have? But I'd rather have loved her than not.'

Even though he sounds so sad, I feel warm inside.

'It's already happening, Danny. Even we've noticed she's not here so much.'

'Alice has exams. She's busy.'

'I give up. You're beyond help.' The hut creaks as she gets up.

He laughs, softly. 'Maybe. But I'm happy, while it lasts.'

'I hope for your sake it lasts forever. But whatever happens we'll still be here, Danny. We'll pick up the pieces afterwards.'

I squirm backwards as she steps down from the hut. Roberta is a perfect Beach blonde, in a bikini so small it must have shrunk in the wash. Would he be happier with a girl like her, instead of me?

After a minute or so, Danny climbs out of the hut too. He has to crouch to fit his powerful body through the doorway. I think he's heading for our rock.

I give him a head start, then squirm out of my hiding place. As I walk towards the edge of the Beach, I wonder whether it's better to tell him what I heard, or to pretend everything's good. When I reach him, he smiles up at me, as though he already knows I was there.

'Hey, Danny.'

'Hey, beautiful.'

I blush. I always blush when he says that, because it isn't true. 'I'm sorry I haven't been around much. It's been a strange time.'

He says nothing, but keeps looking into my eyes. I look away first.

'I've been busy in my world. It's just a phase, though. It doesn't mean I love you any less, Danny.'

'No?' He looks up at the sky. 'Are you having doubts? About us?'

'Not about you. Sometimes I worry about what happens next. If Meggie . . . goes, will I go too?'

Danny shrugs. 'I hate the idea, but I understand if you

want to end this now, Alice. You have a life to live. Maybe I am stopping you from doing that.'

I look at those hands, that neck, those lips, and I know that I can't turn my back on him.

'I love you, though, Danny.'

'And I love you too, Alice. *So* much. But the longer we spend together, the worse it will be if we're separated forever. Logic says I should let you go.'

'Logic?'

'And fairness.'

'You could *do* that? End it? For my sake?'

'I . . .'

When I look into his eyes, they're guarded. But the idea of never looking into them again . . .

'Logic and fairness and common sense. They're words, Danny. They can't compete with how it feels to be here, with you. I don't want to end this. I can't.'

He doesn't look up straight away but I can see he's scowling. I freeze. Maybe an end to this is what he wants, after all. But then he stands up, and leans in to kiss me, and I see his eyes are wet.

'I was kidding myself too. I couldn't have borne it if . . . No, I can't even say it aloud. Just come here. Now.'

We fall into each other's arms, a little unsteady. The sharp edge of the rock scrapes against my leg but I hardly feel it. We're together again. This is how things are meant to be.

32

'Bar-ce-LONA, la, la, la, la, la. BAR-cel-ona, la, la, la, la, LA, LA, LAAAAA!'

I think Cara might be quite excited.

She's staying over before Dad drives us to Gatwick tomorrow, but at this rate, neither of us will get any sleep.

'I definitely think Ade's noticed me already, don't you, Alice?'

'Probably.'

'No, it's not probably, it's definitely.'

'Then why ask me?'

'Spoilsport!'

I'm beginning to wish she hadn't come to stay.

'You will be careful, though, won't you?' I say. 'Just because you *could* have Ade, doesn't mean you have to go through with it. You don't always have to be the kid in the sweetshop.'

'Why else would I be going?'

I try not to snap back, but it's hard. 'Um, because you want to explore one of Europe's most exciting capitals? To learn Spanish? To spend some quality time with your best friend?'

I'm not in any position to lecture her; my own motives are hardly straightforward.

Cara goes silent and I wonder if she's sulking. But after a couple of minutes her breathing changes, and I realise she's finally fallen asleep.

It's two fifteen a.m. We have to get up in two hours, but before that, there's something I need to do. I could try going online under the duvet, but Cara's a light sleeper. She always says it's so she knows if a guy is trying to sneak off in the night. Sometimes I wonder why my best friend acts so strangely and whether it might be because I've not been there for her enough.

After Spain, it'll be different. It has to be.

I carry my laptop downstairs. Since I've been allowed back online in my own room, visiting the Beach has felt less exciting. Being here in the dining room, where I could be found out, brings some of the edginess back.

It's darker on the Beach than it is outside. In my world, this weekend is the summer solstice, so it never seems to get completely dark. But there's no moon on the Beach tonight, and someone has laid out more of those Chinese lanterns across the sand, glowing pink and purple. In the distance, I hear singing: strange melodies, from unfamiliar instruments. It could be mermaid music, the kind that brings sailors crashing onto the rocks.

I walk along the water's edge, trying to pick out the shape of my sister or Danny from the strange silhouettes, but not daring to go closer to the Guests. Apparently they're growing restless because I haven't responded to their notes and appeals. I *want* to, but events in real life seem more urgent right now.

It feels like a clock is ticking ...

Then I spot the person I really need to speak to, on the pier.

'Javier!'

He waves me over.

'*Hola*, Alice. If you're looking for Meggie, she's in one of the huts with Tim.'

'Actually, I'd like to talk to you.' I sit down next to him. 'You've been avoiding me. I'm worried.'

Javier kicks gently at the water. 'Perhaps I enjoy being melancholy. It's a Catalan thing.'

'Catalan?'

'Where I come from, we have our dark side.'

'Ah. Is everyone in Barcelona like that then?'

'The stories I could tell you, Alice. It is a place of high emotion.'

'I'll find out for myself, soon. Very soon. Tomorrow. Well, later today, really.'

He turns round to look at me. 'That's not a very funny joke.'

'It's not a joke. I'm going to Barcelona. That's why I'm here now. I wanted to make sure I'm doing the right thing.'

Javier stares at the water. 'Ha! The right thing? How would I know?'

I say nothing.

'You are doing this for me, Alice?'

'Mainly. I mean, my friends were going anyway. But I hadn't decided, until Gretchen left and I saw how sad it made you. It's a coincidence, but a good one.'

'Coincidence? Or perhaps everything is connected, but we're too blind to see. But Barcelona ...' He whistles. 'It's a beautiful city, Alice. I miss her. The beach ... well, it's not like Soul Beach. Not Paradise. More raw, but more real. Well, it could hardly be *less* real than here, right?'

'Tell me what I should do, Javier. Where I should go.'

There's a long pause; all I can hear is fluttering like paper wings, as the breeze blows through the Chinese lanterns. 'There is someone ...'

I wait, but then he shakes his head. 'Except, maybe it is better not to haunt the living.'

Perhaps I got it completely wrong, and he doesn't want to leave the Beach at all. But the force field of sadness that surrounds him is *so* powerful.

'It is up to you, Javier. I'm not pushing. It's just that you've seemed so lonely and so hopeless, but perhaps things are better now.'

'Better?' He laughs. 'I wish it were so. I fear making things worse, that's all. I have no idea of what I left behind at home. Maybe it will pain me more to know.'

'It's your choice.'

A lime green parakeet flies past us, screeching; in the lantern light, its feathers shimmer. 'You know, sometimes I think *that* might be Gretchen,' Javier murmurs. 'Or more likely Triti. She loved bling and bright colours. But then I think I am stupid because surely after this there is *nothingness*. It would be even more of a punishment to be here as a bird than to be here as a Guest, right?'

He's not expecting an answer. He follows the bird with his eyes, then looks back at me. 'And then sometimes I am afraid of nothingness and sometimes I think it would be the best thing ever. So I am trapped in my indecision. If I had a coin to flip, I could choose.'

'I have a coin,' I say, reaching behind me to the box where my father dumps his change every night after work. 'Would you prefer to leave it to chance?'

A twisted smile appears on Javier's face. 'I think I do like that idea. *Que será, será.* It's appropriate for a world where nothing is under our control.'

'Heads or tails?'

'In Spain, we say *cara o cruz*. Face or cross. So let me see. Face, you do nothing. Cross, you do what I ask.'

It occurs to me that I could lie. Make it cross anyway, because I believe it's the right thing for Javier.

I throw.

The coin lands on the table.

'It's tails . . . cross.'

Javier throws his head back and laughs. 'Ah. There it is. And now I realise it *is* the right thing for me, Alice. Because if it had not been the cross, the tails, I would have asked you to throw again until it was.'

I don't have much time left before I have to leave this Beach for the one in Barcelona. 'So what now?'

He smiles at me. 'Let me see. I cannot send you to my city without some ... traveller tips, right? The Sagrada Familia is better from the outside than the inside, so do not bother to queue. The Ciutadella Park is very nice all year round. Very pretty. Oh. And do you like chocolate brownies?'

I feel impatient. There are guidebooks for this. I need to know how I can *help* him. 'Yes, of course, but—'

'Go to the Dulce café, on Carrer de Balboa. They have the best brownies in town, served warm, with ice cream on the side. Best waiters in town, too. Tell the cute one you know me. But, beware, he might drop your plate.'

'And that's all?'

'You're a smart girl, Alice. I trust you will understand what is required once you are there.'

And then he reaches out to hug me, something he never does. I let him hold me, and I feel his heart beating against my chest. He wants this. I will do my best.

After Javier leaves me, I walk towards the huts that lie beyond the beach bar, taking careful steps in the dark. All I can hear is slow breathing; no one is awake. The intensity of the blackness here is making my own eyelids heavy.

I peep through the door of the first hut. A single candle burns in a fisherman's lantern, illuminating my sister's face, and Tim's next to her. Strange how two people who died such awful deaths can look so peaceful. They're holding hands in their sleep.

For a moment, I consider waking them up. This weekend could bring the breakthrough we all need, and if I manage to corner her killer, then it might possibly mean the end of her time on the Beach. And my own.

My breathing quickens. *That would be too soon.*

But she looks too sweet to wake, and anyway, what could I tell her without being banned? Plus, I can't believe the journey will end in Spain. Surely it would be right for justice to be done in London, where she died.

Or perhaps that's just me trying to convince myself that I have any control over what happens to her or me or any of us.

'Sweet dreams, Meggie. I will be back soon. Promise,' I whisper. She smiles in her sleep and I think she might have heard me.

33

In the departure lounge Cara is still singing the Barcelona song.

I'm drinking Diet Coke, Sahara's got a soya protein shake, and Ade is eating a breakfast panini. And we're all wishing Cara would change the record. I was already on edge at the thought that I'm going to be in Spain with three murder suspects *and* this huge responsibility towards Javier.

The tune is making me even edgier.

'Does she have to announce where we're going to the entire bar?' Sahara mutters. Though she doesn't seem to have the guts to tackle Cara directly. Perhaps she's not really scary at all.

The singing stops.

'*Adrian?*' says Cara, twisting a strand of newly dyed white hair round her finger. 'Alice and I would love a tiny drink. Just to, you know, help us get in the holiday mood.'

Sahara frowns. 'We promised your parents we'd take care of you. And anyway, it's not even half past nine yet.'

'Mum always lets me have wine with dinner. She says it's the reason why French children don't turn into binge drinkers,' Cara replies. Sure, her mum *does* let her have a small glass in the evening, but that doesn't stop Cara necking more in the pub afterwards.

'I suppose they *are* on holiday,' Ade says to Sahara. 'And I quite fancy a beer myself.'

Sahara holds up her hands, and those long pointy fingers

seem to have grown since I last saw her. 'So what I think doesn't matter to you?'

'It's not that, I just—'

'Can I get anyone a drink?'

The voice is the last one I was expecting to hear. I turn round.

'Lewis?'

He smiles at me. His face is red behind his designer specs, as though he's been running. 'What a coincidence, bumping into you guys!'

'What are you doing here, Lewis?' I'm surprised – he didn't exactly jump at the idea of coming with me when I joked about it at his flat.

'There's a conference in Barcelona this weekend. Lots of potential contacts are going.'

'You never said.'

'Only confirmed my place at the last minute. Thought you'd be pleased. I'll be busy during the day, but I was hoping to hang out with you guys at the fiesta!'

'Great!' I say. And it is great – he's probably the only person here I really trust. It's just a bit weird that he's showed up like this without mentioning it before.

Lewis parks his black leather trolley case under our table, then takes a step forward. 'You must be Sahara?' he surprises her with a quick, confident embrace, and then holds out his hand to shake Ade's hand, 'and Adrian. Delighted to meet you. Alice has told me all about you. What you've done for her.'

'Oh. Right. Well, we've tried our best,' mumbles Sahara.

'Don't you recognise me, Bill Gates?' Cara demands.

Lewis grins and gives her a hug. 'How could I forget you, Cara? Now, where was I? Drinks, right? What can I get everyone?'

'White wine and soda,' says Cara.

'I'm sticking with Coke,' I say, pointedly, even though this situation is getting so odd that maybe it'll only seem normal after an alcoholic drink.

When Lewis goes to the bar, Cara leans in close to me. 'Romantic, or what? It's like a Hugh Grant movie.'

'Rubbish! He's working.'

'Looks good in a suit, too. Who'd have thought it?'

'I didn't notice.' I was so surprised to see him that I hadn't thought about what he was wearing till now. But his linen suit fits him so well it must be tailor-made.

'Nice arse,' she says, then giggles. 'Don't worry, I only have eyes for Ade. But you should have ordered wine. Soft drinks make you look like more of a kid in his eyes. Not a woman.'

'I don't *want* him to see me as a woman,' I hiss back. But then, I don't want him to see me as a little kid, either.

'How are we doing for time?' Ade asks Sahara.

Sahara looks up from her phone, checks her watch, then leaps up from her chair. 'Shit. We're late. We might be denied boarding, you know these budget airlines.' And she throws her khaki-rucksack onto her back and starts to run.

We struggle to keep up. She could be a soldier on exercise. Cara ends up slugging her white wine on the way to the gate, while Ade tries to keep up with Sahara, and Lewis and I do a fast walk on the travelator together, trailing behind.

'Why do I get the feeling this is going to be one of those trips, Ali?' he says.

'I still can't get over you being here.'

'The conference will be worth it. Plus ... well, I'd like to get a measure of this Zoe girl. You know how I love a puzzle. Not to mention a bloody great bonfire.'

'I think the fireworks might kick off *before* we get to Barcelona,' I say.

'Hmm. Sahara seems very intense.'

'I'd forgotten you'd never met her before. It just seems like you've been part of our lives forever and ever. Sahara is odd, though. It never made any sense that she was my sister's closest friend at college.'

Lewis shakes his head. 'No, I can't see the two of them sharing much of a world view.'

I really wish he wouldn't say stuff like that. Stuff that suggests he actually *knew* my sister, when he's always insisted he didn't. 'Perhaps she was a different person once she got to uni.'

'People are bloody unpredictable, Ali. That's why the objects of my desire generally have lightning-fast chips and a serious oversupply of RAM.'

And he grins in that self-conscious way that always makes me relax.

When we get to the gate, Sahara is hyperventilating because the queue's so long. I look out of the triple-height window and I see the plane and I freeze.

Flying's never bothered me before, so why do my legs feel as though someone has sliced through all the muscles? Then I understand: this is about Danny. Danny died when his plane fell out of the sky and smashed onto the desert below. Until I met him, crashes happened to strangers, in strange lands. Now they're terrifyingly possible.

'You OK, Alice?' Cara says, and I realise I'm blocking the tunnel that leads onto the plane.

'Sorry,' I mumble at the tutting passengers behind me. We're at the plane door and Cara pushes me inside with a no-messing shove on the small of my back. I fall into the cabin, and the steward has to catch me.

'Wow, you're keen to get there, aren't you, sweetheart?' he says.

I'm trying not to freak out as I breathe the stale-air smell. There are too many seats packed into too little space.

'Over there,' Cara says, steering me into the fifth row. 'The

167

nearer we are to the front, the sooner we get off the plane.'

And the closer we are to the emergency exits.

Meggie would laugh at me. She loved flying. She told me she knew it was only a matter of time before she turned left into first class instead of right into economy. She was going to spend her flights sipping champagne or wrapped up in cashmere, before the inevitable paparazzi reception committee at the runway. But she never made it to first class.

Sahara and Ade and Lewis file on board behind us; in Barcelona, Zoe will be waiting. My suspects are all lined up. I am never going to stand a better chance of discovering who killed Meggie.

My breathing slows a little. This flight isn't where the danger is. But when we touch down in Barcelona, that's when I'll be playing with fire.

34

Even in the sea of faces in Arrivals, Zoe stands out.

It's not just her pale skin, or the skullcap she's wearing even though it must be twenty-five degrees Celsius. It's an aura of unhappiness so powerful it seems to repel people. All around her, families push and pull and call out, but there's open space around Zoe. No one gets near.

Get a grip, Alice, you're starting to sound as weird as Sahara.

We head towards Zoe, and she holds up her hand in a half-wave that also keeps us at arm's length.

'You're late,' she mutters to Sahara, then starts marching off without bothering to check that we're all here. Zoe walks *at* people, and they seem to get out of her way. 'Bloody tourists everywhere, thanks to the bloody fire fiesta.'

The way she says it leaves me in no doubt that we're a nuisance. Any euphoria we felt on landing safely and seeing the *real* sun for the first time in months is extinguished.

'Little ray of sunshine, she is,' Lewis says behind me.

'Do you see why I think it could be her?'

'Burning Truths?' he whispers. 'Or . . .'

'Don't.'

I'm hot and sweaty by the time we get to the train station. Zoe hands out tickets like we're ten years old. But when she gets to Lewis, she stops. Her face contorts.

Is that *fear*? Or just irritation? 'What's going on?' she asks Sahara, as though Lewis isn't even there.

'Sorry, Zoe. Last minute addition. Lewis is a friend of Alice's. He's here mainly for some conference.' Sahara frowns. 'You're not planning to join us in the hostel, are you, Lewis? Only I'm not sure there's room.'

Lewis shakes his head when she mentions the hostel. 'Don't worry. I've made my own arrangements.'

Zoe still won't look at him. 'So long as he doesn't expect me to take him where he wants to go. I'm busy enough as it is.'

Lewis raises his eyebrows at me. It's not much of a welcome.

'Watch your bags, passports, everything,' Zoe says, in the weary voice she must use with her language school students. 'Barcelona is more famous for pickpockets than Picasso now. They're on bikes, skateboards, on foot and especially on the Metro. Better not to take anything valuable out with you. But I wouldn't leave stuff in your hostel, either; it's one of the dodgiest in the city.'

'Welcome to beautiful Barcelona,' Cara calls back, and everyone laughs.

Everyone except Zoe.

The hostel isn't *that* bad.

OK, the communal bathroom is grim. And our shared room is a sectioned off area of corridor, with bunks stacked four high. And I'm sure I spot two different kinds of cockroach. But the bathrooms and bunks aren't the point. The point is that we are *thirty-six* steps from the beach.

I kept seeing glimpses of it through gaps between buildings as we struggled through narrow streets with our trolley bags. Zoe seemed to be leading us on a crazy route, but then finally we turned a corner and she watched our faces, as though she'd handed us the best present ever, wrapped in a giant bow.

The sea, dreamboat blue, with nothing on the horizon except a few windsurfers and a shimmering building in the shape of a boat sail.

I glanced at Zoe and she looked ... proud, as though the view belonged to her. It was the first time she'd acted like a human being since we arrived. But then she scowled and told us we were making her late for her intermediate conversational English class.

Sahara and Ade stand by the window and coo at the shimmering sea and the purring waves.

Cara calls down to Lewis, who is waiting in the sun while we check in. 'You can keep your posh hotels, mate. We've got the best view ever from up here!'

This was Javier's beach, of course. His secrets are buried here. But not for much longer. I reach into my pocket and feel the slip of paper with the address of the café on it. I'll find it today. I promised.

'Hey, daydreamer, let's get down there,' says Cara, abandoning her stuff.

'Wait for me,' Ade shouts out, then sees Sahara's glowering face. He corrects himself, 'Wait for *us*!'

They leave the room. Zoe and I are alone.

'How are you finding it here?' I ask. 'Better than home?'

She shrugs. 'Honestly?'

'You don't have to lie to me, Zoe. I know what it's like to lose someone.'

'Then you'll know it doesn't seem to make that much difference where you are. Though at least the sun shines more here than it did in London.'

I study her colourless face. I bet she never sunbathes.

'What about you, Alice? Did you take my advice to move on?'

'I'm here, aren't I? My first holiday since it happened.'

Zoe seems to see right through me. 'Holiday? Is that what this is?'

The odds are that this is the person behind Burning Truths. I could ask her right now if she is, and where she got *that* photo and who she believes killed my sister.

Unless *she* killed Meggie herself.

No. If she did kill her, surely she'd have been happy to let Tim take the blame. I'll only have one chance to catch her off guard. I don't feel ready now.

'You coming to join us on the beach?' I ask, gesturing towards the door.

'No. Apart from having to earn a living, I think beach bums are the dullest people in the universe.'

'Funny place to live if you hate beach bums.'

She shrugs. 'Funny choice of boyfriend, for a girl like you.'

'Lewis? He's not my boyfriend,' I snap back, before realising something. 'Do you know him?'

Zoe stares at me. 'How would I? But I know his type. Be careful, Alice. Not everyone is on your side.'

'What do you mean? What aren't you telling me, Zoe?'

'Leave it, Alice.'

'I can help you. You don't have to live with this alone. If there's anything you know, you should share it. It might ... keep you safer.' It's the nearest I can come to hinting that I know about Burning Truths.

She shakes her head. 'You're very young, aren't you, Alice? The world doesn't work like that. Not all stories have a happy ending.'

'Don't fob me off. At least *think* about it, Zoe. Promise you'll do that.'

She looks at her watch. 'I have to go, now. We'll meet later. I can tell you about the city. Oh, and prepare you for the *Correfoc* tomorrow.'

'The what?'

'The finale to the fiesta. *Correfoc* means fire run. It's not meant to start till tomorrow evening but they're letting off firecrackers already, so tell the others they should cover up tonight. People here have a thing about fire. After dark, nowhere's safe.'

35

Barcelona's beach looks all wrong to me. So many strange people: too old, too pale, too sunburned, too irregular.

I close my eyes, blink hard. Soul Beach has made me expect perfection but I'm not that shallow. When I open my eyes again, I make myself notice the laughing families and the old men playing board games, their eyelids hooded against the sun. I hear squeaky bikes and babies' cries and buskers' drums. I smell fried food and brine.

I feel a hand on mine.

'Everything all right?'

Lewis. I pull my hand away. 'Yeah, planes make me sleepy. I thought you'd gone to check into your hotel?'

'I did.' And he nods towards the sail-shaped building further along the shore.

'Wow. That looks amazing.'

'Yeah, and it costs amazing too. It's all there was left, because I left booking so late.'

'Good job you're a millionaire, then, eh? So what do you make of Barcelona?'

'Obviously the daylight's a bit of a shock to the system for someone who spends his life in front of a screen in a darkened room, but it seems fun – assuming we can avoid being robbed or pickpocketed or abducted by aliens.'

'She's quite something, Zoe, isn't she?' I say, watching his face.

He laughs. Or *most* of him does. Somehow the amusement doesn't reach his eyes. 'You think she's hiding something, Ali?'

'I don't know. I was so certain it was her after you found out the site was being updated abroad. But nothing's changed since that horrible picture appeared. Maybe whoever is behind Burning Truths has given up.'

Lewis shakes his head. 'No. There's some work going on behind the scenes, like the designer is getting ready for something. An update, maybe?'

'More pictures?' The idea is sickening, but I know I need more to go on.

'Your guess is as good as mine. Oh, and I've got their name, too.'

'*What?*'

'Not their real name. That'd be too easy. But I got as far as the admin page and found their avatar. It's *la Fée Verte*.'

'Spanish?'

'French. It means the Green Fairy.'

I try to make a connection between the name, and Tim or my sister. 'Means nothing to me.'

'Don't worry, Ali. We're getting closer. But try to enjoy being here, too. It's not all about playing detective, is it?'

Playing detective? I want to scream.

He points towards a bar in the distance. 'Let's grab something to eat with the others. A glass of sangria and a plate of Spanish sausage will set me up perfectly for an afternoon of geeky lectures and anti-social networking. Coming?'

No. It's not possible.

I stumble towards the bar, trying to make sense of what I'm seeing. Am I imagining it, because of tiredness, or stress . . . or total insanity?

Or is this beachfront bar in Barcelona *really* identical to the one on Soul Beach?

'Over here, guys!' Cara calls out. She, Sahara and Ade are sitting at a bamboo table which is laid with a glass jar of fresh lilies and a giant cocktail list. They're acting like everything is completely normal.

But it's not. This shouldn't *be* here. It's as out of place as a red double-decker bus on the Moon.

'Looks a bit kitsch, don't you think?' Lewis says to me as he helps me up onto the raised wooden platform.

I weave between the tables, trying not to stare, even though it's doing something very odd to my brain to see plump middle-aged tourists spilling out of the same chairs that usually hold the brightest of bright young things on Soul Beach.

As I sit down, Cara hands me a menu. On the front, there's a silhouette of a palm and the words *Bienvenido al Chiringuito Tropicano.*

'*Chiringuito?*'

'The waiter says it's a local word for beach bar,' Cara says, and then I remember Javier using that word.

Maybe this is where he used to come? I rack my brains for other connections between the Guests and their former lives. Didn't Gretchen talk about song thrushes, even though they're not tropical? And Triti's descent into madness was triggered by a firework display like the ones she remembered from home ...

But there's nothing on the Beach to remind Meggie of her old suburban life, or her star performance on *Sing for Your Supper.*

'We've ordered a pitcher of *sangria* and some *tapas*,' Cara pronounces the two Spanish words with the moody flourish of a flamenco dancer. A couple of young guys at the next table turn round and wave at her. She winks back and then whispers, 'I'm loving Barcelona so far, aren't you?'

I'm not really listening. Like Sam's bar, this one is open to the elements, but while this beach seems to go on forever,

Soul Beach is a bay that goes nowhere: prison disguised as paradise.

The water *here* is dark blue, and choppier than it looked from the hostel window, with dozens of surfers scudding across the horizon. Right in front of us, a large shaggy dog races into the sea, and straight back out again, joyously shaking seawater off his coat. It splashes onto my leg and makes me smile for the first time since I got to Barcelona.

'*Sangria, aceitunas, pan con tomate.*' A male voice, with an all too familiar accent. I turn slowly. If this waiter looks like Javier, then I am officially losing my grip on reality.

But this guy is short, with a bushy beard and beady eyes that are already sizing us up for tips as he puts down a glass jug.

'It's not red,' Cara cries out, not bothering to hide her disappointment. 'We didn't want orange juice, we wanted sangria.'

'Maybe the man thought *some* of us should lay off the alcohol,' Sahara mumbles.

'This is *sangria de cava*,' the man says. 'Orange juice and local champagne.'

As he pours the drink, it fizzes and bubbles, and splashes when the ice cubes and orange segments and sliced strawberries fall into the glasses.

When the waiter's gone, we hold up our drinks.

'Cheers,' says Ade.

'*Salud!*' Cara corrects him. 'It's the Spanish toast. Means good health. And I know a great weekend in the sun with my friends is going to do my health the *world* of good.'

Apart from a single glass on my birthday, I've never really drunk fizzy wine. But I could get used to it. There's a picture of Meggie the press always use, where she's holding up a glass of champagne at some premiere. No wonder she was smiling.

We've been here a couple of hours, and the sun is relentless, far crueller than on Soul Beach. I feel my skin burning already. Ade suggests a walk round the old city, and Cara agrees, which makes Sahara scowl as she was obviously hoping for some quality time alone with her boyfriend.

Without Zoe as our guide, we get lost in minutes.

'How can we not know where we are when I can *hear* the sea?' Cara says.

Lewis holds up his iPhone. 'We don't have to be lost.'

I don't know why he's still hanging round with us – his conference must have started by now.

'Don't cheat!' Sahara snaps. 'They say you only know a city once you've got lost in it.'

So we keep walking. The streets are long and straight, with canopies of washing hanging out from every balcony, and old women sitting in the road in plastic chairs, chatting to each other and to their dogs and their budgies, as though they're in their own front rooms.

And then we're in this big square, where kids are playing ping-pong on concrete tables. Sahara wants to go into the covered market, to 'soak up the local culture'. I'm thinking that apart from the sunshine and the budgies, the culture doesn't seem that different from home, but we follow her inside. There's a cheese seller at the entrance: it makes the market smell like sweaty feet.

Sahara goes from stall to stall, pulling impressed faces and giving the vegetables an occasional squeeze. I can't look at Cara or Lewis or I might burst out laughing, and even Ade seems to have a slightly fixed expression, as though he's trying to keep a straight face while his girlfriend gets her culture fix.

'It's all so *authentic*,' Sahara says.

'I'd rather get my hands on some authentic local wine,' Ade mumbles.

Sahara giggles. It sounds like a moth caught in a lamp-

shade. 'Sorry. Ade warned me not to be a bore. Let's go somewhere else.'

Cara gives me a look that says *what a loser*. The afternoon
sunlight has turned the yachts in the harbour pale orange,
and Cara keeps up a running commentary as we pass the
swishest boats. 'I'd like the white one. Oh, no, the pink one.
Lewis, you can probably afford a yacht already. Fancy sailing
off into the sunset with me?'

But she's reserving her biggest smiles for Ade. Sahara is
either not noticing Cara's flirtiness, or pretending it's not
happening.

'If we keep heading this way, we'll hit the *Ramblas*, which
is a freak show,' Lewis says. 'But we might as well take a look.
Hang onto your bags, like Zoe said.'

I catch him up as we cross the main road. 'You're an expert
on Barcelona. Sure you've never been here before?'

'Why would I bother when it's all on here?' he says, tapping
his phone. I'm about to tell him that it's sad to travel virtually,
then I think of how addicted I am to the Beach and realise I'm
no different.

Weirdly, though, I'm not missing Soul Beach right now.
Reality seems ... excitingly real and, as we're all together,
I feel safer. I can almost pretend I'm simply on holiday. Except
for having to observe *everyone's* behaviour, and look out for
Javier's café, of course.

We're on a pedestrian promenade that stretches endlessly
uphill. It's packed with ambling tourists and hurrying locals
and what must be the world's entire collection of living
statues.

'Welcome to the mad house,' says Lewis.

We have to use elbows to push through, tucking our
bags under our arms. Cara and Ade are grinning as they
launch themselves into the crowd. Maybe she's right about
them being a good match. Sahara looks like she'd rather be

anywhere else, as she clutches her rucksack to her chest like it's a bulletproof jacket.

'Come on. It's not *that* bad.' Lewis links arms with her.

I'm on my own again, being pushed past the stalls so fast I only catch glimpses of what they're selling. There are souvenirs celebrating landmarks I haven't seen yet: the spiky cathedral, a mosaic lizard, a statue of Columbus. Then pet supplies, plants, old clocks. Every few metres there's a café offering radioactively yellow paella.

I've lost sight of the others. I'm being jostled and pushed but that's not what's making my heart beat so fast. It's that feeling again – the feeling of being watched.

I turn round, but all I see are tourists. Sunburned ones, loved-up ones, nervy ones.

Maybe I'm only sensing the curious eyes of pickpockets checking me out. Except it feels more threatening than that.

The jam of people clears, and I see Lewis and Sahara ahead of me, looking at the living statues. There's a silver robot, a cowboy and a man sitting on a toilet.

Lewis reads from his phone, 'Toilet humour is an abiding theme in local culture. At Christmas one of the key figures at the nativity is a *caganer*, the so-called "shitting shepherd", who crouches behind the crib. He symbolises the cycle of returning goodness to the earth.'

Sahara pulls a face. Even though *she* was the one who was desperate to hear about local customs.

The statues get cleverer. A guy in the blue-and-red Barcelona football strip keeps a ball permanently in the air: heading, kicking, bouncing. Wrinkles divide his face into neat eighths. Maybe he's been standing in that same spot, heading that same ball for decades.

'We should catch up with the others,' Sahara says.

Lewis is the only one tall enough to see over people's heads. 'They're over there,' he says, pointing to the left-hand side.

Then he links arms with me too, and we move slowly but purposefully past the last of the statues, towards a large stone building. As we get closer, I see Ade and Cara, deep in conversation.

'Hey, you two. Are you trying to lose us or what?' Lewis calls out to them.

Ade and Cara spin round: he looks guilty, she looks pleased with herself. Sahara snarls at them both. Maybe I ought to tell Sahara that I've never known Cara fail to get a man she wanted. Keeping one, that's the bit she finds trickier.

'Thank goodness we've found you all again,' Cara says flatly. 'We must have been separated for at least, ooh, four minutes.'

'We thought we could get a coffee here,' Ade points at one of the busiest places, 'and watch the world go by for a bit. Then maybe do a bit of souvenir shopping.'

Sahara nods so enthusiastically that I worry she'll get whiplash.

'I ought to head off to the conference. Put in an appearance at least,' Lewis says.

I look at the other three. Perhaps I should stay with them. Keep an eye on them. But even Sahara wouldn't take Cara on in broad daylight, would she?

'I'll walk back with Lewis,' I say. 'That cava's gone to my head so I could do with a lie down before dinner.'

Though I might take a detour via the café serving the best chocolate brownies in Barcelona ...

36

Lewis doesn't talk on the way back to his hotel. We reach the corner where my hostel is, and there's an awkward moment when we say goodbye and don't know whether to hug. The Spanish people around us seem so physical and *kissy*.

We settle on a clumsy half-embrace, then I go inside. There are maps at reception, so I take one and look up the address of the café Javier suggested. On paper, it's easier to see that the streets round here are designed along grid lines, like New York.

After a couple of minutes, I go back outside and check Lewis is out of sight. It's strange to be alone, in a completely foreign place, and to be able to go anywhere I like. But it's not scary. The Beach has made me less afraid. I imagine Meggie watching me approvingly. *You're growing up, Florrie ...*

The route takes me back past the market, then along a narrow road lined with high buildings painted in terracotta and mustard colours. I turn a corner into Carrer de Balboa but realise I'm at the wrong end. It's quieter here. I pass a group of kids kicking a football around and I stare at their faces, looking for Javier's sisters, but they're all boys. One stares back at me, then pokes out his tongue. It makes me jump, then makes me laugh.

The blocks are so tall that even though it's still bright sunshine on the beach, only the narrowest sliver of light hits the road ahead of me. The plants on the balconies stretch out their leaves for a meagre ration of sun.

I'm hungry again. Obviously I want to help Javier, but the

thought of a chocolate brownie is a little bit tempting too. As I approach the end of the street, there's a burgundy-painted sandwich board outside a café.

Brownies, pasteles, cocteles, bocadillos.

The rest of the words are mysterious, but 'brownies' doesn't need translation. My mouth's watering.

I gaze through the window. There are rough brick walls and cosy sofas and a chiller cabinet full of cakes. It's almost empty and there's a red leather chair facing the street that's got *my* name on it.

Yet I'm hesitating.

There's only one waiter. He has his back to me, a black apron tied tight around his waist, and blond curls brushing against his shoulders. Is that the cute one Javier was talking about? And if it is, what the hell will I say to him?

BANG!

What the hell? The explosion behind me makes my eardrums sting. Yet the waiter hasn't flinched at all.

I turn round, but there's no car in flames and no assassin running away. I hear giggling. There's a smell like autumn, and then I realise: fireworks. I should have thought of it sooner, but it feels all wrong to be letting them off on a midsummer's afternoon in a Spanish street.

Two of the small boys who were playing football appear from the shadows. As they run away, they throw something. This time I hear the whine but before I can move, another firecracker explodes less than ten metres from me. Loud and so bright it seems to burn a hole in my vision.

In the café, the waiter turns round this time. Dirty blond hair frames a tanned face, and his eyes are denim blue. *Cute?* Yep. Despite the temporary damage to my sight, I'd say I've found Javier's waiter.

He beckons me inside. Everything seems to be moving too quickly. I want to turn round, buy myself time to work out what I should and should't say. But I can't back away now. I push the door open.

'Hi,' he says. 'What can I get you – late lunch, coffee?' His accent is Australian.

'Hi. How did you know . . .'

'. . . that you speak English? You haven't been in town long, have you, sweetheart?'

'No.'

'Don't get stressed about it. I could only tell because you're too pale to be a local. Get some sun while you're here, right? Sun makes you happy. As does cake. I believe that this seat is all yours.' And he points at the chair in the window and hands me a menu.

I shake my head. 'Already know what I'm having. Your famous chocolate brownie, with ice cream on the side, please.'

'Famous, eh? The chef *will* be pleased to hear that. Anything to drink?'

'Some tap water.'

He shakes his head. 'I wouldn't. Seriously. I promise it's not me trying to rip you off. The tap's unspeakable. Only bad thing about Barcelona. Well, that and the tourists.' He winks at me. 'I can do you a good deal on a bottle of still.'

'Fine.'

He takes my order to the kitchen. He's broad and big, a surfer dude, I guess. Unless that's just me thinking *all* Australians are surfer dudes. But was he also Javier's first love? His *only* love?

'So, what are you doing in beautiful Barca?' He pronounces the c as a soft hiss. 'Don't mind chatting, do you? It's quiet today. They're all out buying bloody firecrackers and balaclavas for tomorrow night.'

'Seriously? Is it really dangerous, the fire run?'

He sits down opposite me, on the arm of the other leather

chair. 'Depends on your definition. They *are* crazy about fire. Kids are given firecrackers almost before they can walk. A nation of pyromaniacs. Still, Australia and England are nations of alcoholics, right, and that is nowhere near as pretty as fireworks.'

'We're here for the weekend.'

'We?' He pretends to look around him. 'You and your invisible mates, right?'

'They're sightseeing. Shopping. I wasn't in the mood.'

'A girl who isn't always in the mood for shopping? Wow! If only I was interested in girls, we'd be perfect for each other.'

So he *is* gay. 'I'm Alice.'

He holds out his hand. 'Gabriel. Like the angel. But everyone calls me Gabe.' A bell rings. 'That'll be your brownie.'

By the time he brings it to me, butter-coloured ice cream is already melting into a pool around the warm cake.

'Enjoy,' says Gabe, putting my desert down in front of me. He goes off to clear a table, while I stare at the bowl. It smells amazing, but my appetite's gone.

I know I must say something before the moment is gone, but what? Gabe hands the bill to a Spanish mother and daughter who are the only other customers in the café. He's all smiles until they leave but then he scowls.

'You know what I said to you about the one bad thing in Barcelona? There's another one. The locals never bloody tip.' He stops. 'You OK? Don't tell me you don't like the brownie. Chef will commit *hara-kiri* with his truffle fork.'

'It's not that. Gabe . . . could I ask you something?'

'Sure.' He sits back down again. 'Though if you were expecting a *hash* brownie, I think you're a bit young.'

He might think I'm already on drugs when he hears what I've got to say. 'Listen, this might sound weird, but will you promise to hear me out?'

'Sure. Weird is good. I like weird. Especially on a quiet afternoon when I've got bugger all else to do.' He waves at the empty café.

'Did you know a guy called Javier?'

His eyes narrow. The smile's gone.

'Maybe.' He stares at me, giving absolutely nothing else away.

'The thing is, I know ... I knew him too. Not well, but well enough.'

'You said this was your first time in Barcelona.'

'It is.' I keep eye contact with him, though his face has hardened.

'J never left Spain in his life. What the hell *is* this? Who *are* you?'

'My name is Alice Forster. I live in London. I'm seventeen, and I'm doing A Levels in—'

'Don't dick me around. I don't want your school report. I want to know what you're playing at. Bringing up this crap. Did you read about J somewhere? Is *that* what it is?'

I gulp, angry with myself for not planning this better. But then I could have had till Christmas and I still wouldn't have been able to come up with something rational. He's either going to believe me, or he's not.

'Do you ... Do you believe in the afterlife, Gabe? I mean, in people having another existence after they're dead—'

'I know what the bloody afterlife is.'

'But do you think it's real?'

'Shit. I've heard it all now. Are you some trainee medium? Because if you're offering me a séance, I'm not interested.'

I've lost him. 'You promised you'd hear me out.'

'That was before I realised you were a flake, *Alice* – if that's even your real name. You'd better leave now, before I get really pissed off.'

'My big sister was murdered,' I say, hating myself for using her to win sympathy, but knowing it's the only way I might stop him interrupting me. 'She was Javier's age.' I pause, so it sinks in.

'Sorry,' he says. 'But I don't see what it's got to do with me.'

'I have this ... knowledge. I can't explain why. Anyway, it's made me certain that there is an afterlife, at least for those people who die before they should. People like my sister, and Javier.'

'But Javier jumped off a bloody roof! How does that constitute dying before he should, when he *chose* to take the easy way out? To leave the poor suckers who loved him behind ...' He stops.

I stare at him. 'Jumped?'

'Look, this is not crap I want to relive. I almost left the city because of it.'

'What makes you think he jumped?'

He holds his hands up to his ears. 'Enough. I don't want to talk about this ever again.'

I see the pain in his face, and it's like looking in a mirror. 'I'm sorry. I didn't mean to ... He told me ...' I tail off, knowing whatever I say, it won't be enough to heal the pain Gabe's suffering.

'He?'

I pull my purse out of my bag, put five euros down on the counter. Gabe puts his hand over mine.

'You're saying you really believe you've *talked* to him?'

I try to break free but his grip is too strong. 'I know it sounds mad, Gabe. But you said it yourself, how else would I know about him? And I don't believe he'd have jumped. He wouldn't have left his sisters, or his mum. Or you.'

Gabe lets go of my hand. When I look up, his face is even more distorted. 'I *did* leave me.'

'No. I think you're wrong. I'm going, I promise. But answer me one question: did Javier seem like a person who'd leave without saying goodbye?'

37

For a moment, I think I've convinced him, or at least bought myself more time.

But then he shakes his head and the haunted look is back on his face. 'Just go.'

I do as he says. I've screwed up. Let Javier down. Plus I have no right to inflict pain on someone I know has already had more than his share. I leave the café, making sure the door doesn't slam behind me. As if it matters . . .

Heading back to the hostel, I look up at the tops of the buildings. The thought of Javier falling so far makes me dizzy.

Falling? Or jumping?

How can I be so sure he didn't jump? He told me himself that his afterlife is a hell of a lot better than his real life ever was.

I walk faster, hoping Cara might find some way of cheering me up when I get back to the hostel. But the atmosphere in our room is oppressive. Sahara isn't talking to Ade, Cara isn't talking to Sahara, and I don't think I want to talk to any of them; their squabbles seem pathetic after what Gabe has suffered.

The space is so tiny that we end up sitting on our bunks. Sahara is snoring, Ade is playing a game on his phone, Cara's doing her make-up, and I'm still trying to make sense of what happened at the café. I can hear the people in the next room having a party. Outside, firecrackers explode every few seconds in random, bad-tempered bursts.

Zoe told us that no one in Barcelona goes out before nine at the earliest, so we're on our own till then. But Lewis has texted to say he's found a cool place to meet up.

'Is it safe to walk to this bar?' Sahara says, breaking the silence.

Cara grunts. 'Who do you think is going to come after us, Sahara? Banshees or werewolves?'

She's being sarcastic, but there's something about the joke that breaks the tension in the room.

Ade puts his arm around Sahara. 'I'll protect you, gorgeous. Banshees, vampires, zombies. Bring it on, forces of evil! We're British. We shall fight them on the beaches.'

Even Sahara can't help smiling at that. 'Maybe we should eat lots of garlic tonight. It fends off muggers *and* supernatural beings.'

We follow Lewis's super-detailed instructions, and find him in a place with stained glass windows, ancient leather sofas and a little terrace outside.

'Mojito for me,' Cara says, holding a five euro note out to Ade so he can buy it for her.

'Don't get *too* drunk,' I whisper. 'Sahara's already on the warpath.'

But Cara just laughs, enjoying the attention she's getting in her barely there skirt. Sahara sits down in a dark corner of the bar and beckons me over. As I approach her, the sounds of laughter in the bar seem to fade away.

'How *are* you coping, Alice?'

Where would I begin? 'It's strange, being here.'

Sahara nods. 'She should be here with us, shouldn't she? We were so close. It feels wrong to be enjoying myself when she should be here.'

'I understand.' But even though I know what she means, I can't forget what Meggie said about how they hadn't been speaking for a while before she died, and how clingy Sahara was. *Why* weren't they speaking? Could an argument have crossed over from frustration to violence?

'Sometimes, you know, I feel as though she is here. That probably sounds crazy, doesn't it, Alice?'

'No crazier than anything else that's happened.'

When Sahara says nothing, I look up at her and realise she's trying really hard not to cry. I reach out to touch her hand, feeling like a two-faced cow. But that's how mad my life is at the moment: one minute I am convinced she's a killer, the next I want to tell her everything's going to be OK.

'Sahara, it'll get easier.'

'Really?'

'Really.' I say it to make her feel better, not because I believe it. If I do somehow resolve Meggie's death, things could get an awful lot harder.

She smiles. 'I'll always be Meggie's friend. And now yours.'

I smile back. But why do Sahara's words sound more like a threat than a promise?

Zoe doesn't show till almost ten, and doesn't explain why. She moans that the bar is full of *gringos*, even though I can't hear any other English voices. When I get closer to her, at the bar, I smell alcohol on her breath.

'Have you been somewhere else first?'

She gives me an odd look. 'No. Just my flat.' And then she orders an absinthe. 'You should try one, Alice. It's special. It makes reality better. You and I could both do with that, couldn't we?'

'I'll stick to Diet Coke, thanks.'

The barman hands her a small glass with a yellow-green shot at the bottom.

'Not one for taking advice, are you?' Zoe says.

'What do you mean?'

'You didn't listen to me about Meggie, either. About the dangers of poking your nose in.'

Is she warning me off because she knows who the killer is and she's worried about me – or because she has blood on her own hands?

'Zoe, *please* would you tell me what you know? I only want the truth.'

'Whose truth do you mean?'

'Is everything OK, Alice?' Lewis has appeared behind us.

'Yeah. Long queue, that's all.'

He nods. 'We've found a table on the terrace, where it's cooler.'

Zoe pushes past Lewis without looking at him. The table is one of half a dozen outside on the square, where more local kids are practising their firecracker throwing. The dogs are so used to it that they don't even flinch when the bangers explode.

'So you were telling us about the conference?' Ade says to Lewis as we sit down.

'Yeah, yeah. Like I said, the lines are blurring. Cowboys and Indians, goodies and baddies. That's a bit last century. Now you don't know who the enemy is.'

Ade is nodding. 'So some of the delegates might be hackers?'

'Definitely. Or spies. Both at the same time, in some cases. There's more intrigue at the W Hotel tonight than in your average Bond movie.'

I've never heard Lewis talk quite like this before: he's out to impress his audience. And maybe one person in particular. Though Zoe is still not looking at him.

'But where do you stand *morally*?' Sahara asks.

Lewis smiles. 'They say the web is a morality-free zone. That's what I mean about the goodies and baddies. There's absolutely no black-and-white online. I definitely don't support the overthrow of democratic governments. Or cyber-terrorism. But look at something like Wikileaks. I'm a fan of openness.'

'Even though openness might lead to people getting killed? Some of the leaks revealed state secrets,' Zoe says. I'm pretty sure it's the first time she's addressed him directly.

He smiles at her. 'Information is neutral. It's what you do with it that counts. And it's not just the high profile ops that make a difference. One person acting alone can change stuff. There's a coder I really admire at the moment who is keeping everyone guessing about a miscarriage of justice case. It's a pretty obscure European thing ...' he looks at me, 'but this coder keeps drip-feeding information. She could really make a difference.'

'She?' Zoe's voice sounds strangled.

I try to catch Lewis's eye but he looks past me. Is this the right way to do it?

He laughs. 'Oh, there are plenty of geeky girls out there now – though it's only my hunch in this case, based on the many levels of the site. It's intricate, like ... embroidery.'

'You're a sexist, Lewis,' Cara says, teasing him.

Lewis grins back. 'Yeah, that's me. But it's definitely the site of a multi-tasker, and you know how crap we men are at that. Plus there's the username, too.'

Zoe takes a swig of her absinthe. 'What is it?'

Lewis looks at each of us in turn, and ends up staring at Zoe again. 'It's funny. I didn't know what it meant, at first. Then I Googled it. Perhaps she's French. Her name's *la Fée Verte*. It means the Green Fairy.'

I watch Zoe's face. Is that a tiny muscle twitching under her eye? I check the others: Sahara looks intrigued, Cara bored, Ade amused.

'Well, that's *got* to be a girl. Or a gay man who worries about the environment,' Ade says, pleased with his joke.

'Actually,' says Zoe, draining her glass, 'it's the old French nickname for absinthe. Because it's famous for being hallucinogenic, for making people see things *that aren't there at all*.'

She's staring back at Lewis. Is she playing along – or warning him off? Zoe is so unpredictable that I'm scared he's screwed everything up, like I did with Gabe.

I wait to see who blinks first.

A flash of light blinds me momentarily, followed by a bang. A firecracker has exploded right next to our table, and we hear laughter as a small girl in a flowery dress runs back to her friends.

Sahara shrieks, then laughs when she realises what it was.

'So where are we going to go after this?' Cara is asking. 'Have you got a "hottest-clubs-for-hot-Spanish-guys" app on your phone, Lewis?'

By the time I look back at Lewis and Zoe, they're no longer trying to outstare each other. But my instinct tells me that something has started, here, tonight – and I can't tell yet whether it'll help me find what I'm searching for, or close the door for good.

38

I'm falling.

The street below is brutally shiny with cobbles. No, not cobbles.

Flames. They glow blood-red, lapping hungrily at my clothes, my skin, my hair.

I wait for the impact, for the end. But the fire pit has no floor. The flames are coming from the centre of the earth and I'm falling, falling, FALLING ...

'... wake up, please, Alice! Stop screaming. You're here. You're safe. You're with me. With Cara.'

'Cara?'

She's so close I can smell her breath, and *that*'s what brings me back to reality: stale cocktails, cigarettes, garlic. *Last night, in a single, rancid breath.*

I move my head to the side. 'I need air.'

As I straighten up, I bash my head on a metal bar above me.

'Watch yourself, honey!' She helps me off my bunk. I'm dizzy, though *I* hardly drank any alcohol last night, while Cara's daisy fresh – except for the death-breath. There's no justice.

I realise the room is empty. 'Where are the others?'

She pulls a nasty face. 'Sahara dragged Ade out for a romantic walk on the beach. *Yuk.* So it's just you and me. Oh, and a mysterious guy called Danny, apparently.'

'Danny?'

'You've been calling out for him for the last five minutes.

I was trying to wake you up, but you were all "DANNY! DAN-EEEEEEE!"' She manages to sound just like a pathetically needy version of me. 'No wonder you haven't been playing tongue tennis with Lewis, if you're dreaming of another guy.'

'I don't know a Danny. I must have been shouting something else.'

She looks into my eyes, searching for the truth. 'What? Danone, maybe? I like yoghurt too, but not *that* much. Come on, spill the beans.'

I close my eyes. 'Leave the Spanish Inquisition, Cara. It was just a bad dream.'

She sighs, then goes to the window and holds her hand up to shield her eyes from the sun. 'You don't have to shut me out.'

'I'm not.' I hate myself for lying. Cara keeps trying, even though most people would have given up. I don't deserve her.

'Do you get them a lot, Al? The nightmares?'

I walk towards the window, standing close to her. 'Not as often as I used to.'

'Well, something's brought it all back. And I don't believe you about this *Danny*, but I can't force you to tell me.' She bumps my arm with her fist, to show I'm forgiven, despite my disloyalty. 'Let's get breakfast, yeah?'

'What time is it?'

'Past ten already, lazybones. And my stomach thinks my throat's been cut.'

'Better?'

I nod, because I'm still chewing the best chocolate croissant I've ever tasted. We're lying ten metres from the water, and the towel under us is damp from sea spray. I swallow. 'How did you know about that bakery?'

'Don't you remember that guy in the Mexican bar last night? The one who kept pestering me for my number?'

I don't remember *any* strangers, not because I was pissed, but because I was too busy watching everyone else for danger signs: how many times Cara found an excuse to stroke one of Ade's limbs, and how many times Sahara noticed. What Lewis said to Zoe, what Zoe said to Lewis, and all the pauses in between.

'I half expected to find him waiting for me outside the bakery,' Cara continues, sounding disappointed. 'You can't rely on men. Lucky you can rely on croissants.' She takes a huge bite and flakes of pastry stick to her lips. 'Bliss. So what's the plan for today, Miss Forster?'

I wish I could say, *Let's go shopping or take the cable car, or just hang out on the shore, watching the boys go by.*

But it's no good. No matter how beautiful Barcelona is, this isn't a holiday. When I'm not searching for Meggie's killer, I should be finding out why Javier is stuck on Soul Beach, so when I have the briefest moments of normality, like now, I feel guilty.

'Let's meet for lunch later,' I say.

I see the disappointment in Cara's face, and I hate myself. '*Lunch?*' she says.

'Sorry. It's just that …' I try to find a good reason to abandon my best friend, 'well, at home, I'm always being watched. By my folks, or teachers. Here, I guess I just fancied a little bit of time on my own.'

I hate how easily I lie now, especially to those I love.

It takes me almost an hour to find anywhere to go online. Eventually, in a backstreet, I find The Mobile Phone Shop That Time Forgot, which has a faded CAFE sign in the window, and two yellowing computers right at the back. Luckily the one that's working faces the wall, so no one will see what I'm doing.

The owner brings me a glass of coffee that looks like a tiny pint of Guinness – black beneath, with a head of milk. As he puts it down, I notice red scars all over his gnarled fingers.

I wait for him to return to the front of the shop, then I go straight onto Burning Truths. The connection is slow and stuttering and the computer's an antique, so while I wait for it to load, I wonder if Zoe's done anything to the site since last night. If it *is* Zoe . . .

But who else could it be? She necked four more absinthes, then disappeared without telling anyone she was leaving.

The page begins to load. There's a blank where a picture should be, and at first I think it's the horrible one of Meggie's hand. I scroll down and there's another photo-shaped gap. When the cursor hovers over the space, it tells me the photo is called *MeganForster_hand.jpg* – which must be the old picture. So what does the new one show?

I try refreshing the page, but nothing happens. The connection seems too slow. The only clue is the photo name: *MeganForster_lips.jpg*

Did the killer photograph her mouth, too? Perhaps even as she took her last breath? The idea makes me nauseous, but I have to fight the emotional stuff and concentrate on clues. I refresh a third time, but it's too much for this old computer. I take my phone out, try to call Lewis, but I get some message in Spanish and it refuses to connect. So I text him instead, telling him to look at the site, but he doesn't reply.

Now, time to try Soul Beach. I don't suppose I'll get very far on this rubbish PC. I follow my usual routine – plug in my Mp3 headphones, find the original email invitation from Meggie, and wait . . .

Nothing happens. I check my mobile. No text from Lewis.

This is never going to work. If the stupid computer won't even display a photo or two, it's hardly going to give me a dazzling beach with animation so real I think I'm actually there. I might as well give up – but I've paid for an hour's surfing and I've run out of other options to pursue.

The golf-ball sized webcam on top of the monitor lights up. I hold my breath. But the screen stays white and the light on the hard drive flickers desperately as the computer tries to keep up.

'Alice?' Javier's voice is clear through the headphones.

I lean in to the mic underneath the camera. 'You can see me? I can't see you.'

'You are . . . hazy. One moment you're there, the next you're more like a mirage, or a ghost. My ghostly *human* friend, Alice.' I hear him laugh.

'Hold on. It might just be loading.'

But nothing changes on the monitor. The white screen makes my eyes sting and I can't pick out any shapes. I *can* hear waves, though, and I know they're not Barcelona ones. Soul Beach waves sound different.

'You're not moving, Alice. And you have a really miserable look on your face.'

'I am feeling a bit down, Javier.' Or should it be *J*?

'Down, in Barcelona? Surely that's not possible.'

'It's a great city, but . . . the circumstances could be better.' I'm wary of volunteering anything until he asks directly.

'You've been to Dulce, haven't you, Alice?'

I nod, but still say nothing. Not just because I'm nervous about breaking the rules, but also because I don't know how to tell him I was thrown out.

'Was he there?'

'I met a waiter called Gabe.'

I hear a sharp intake of breath. '*Gabe*. How was he?'

'He was . . .' How am I supposed to describe him? '. . . low. Beautiful, but very low.'

'Because of me?' Javier's voice cracks.

'He thinks you deserted him, Javier. That you left him . . .' I struggle to find the words, '. . . on purpose.'

'On purpose? He thinks I *killed* myself? That I jumped?'

I nod. 'I tried to tell him that I couldn't believe you'd do that, but he wouldn't listen to me. Not that surprising, I guess. I turn up out of the blue with stories about a guy he was close to. He . . . seemed afraid.'

'Gabe? He's the most fearless guy I ever met.'

'He was afraid that I'd confirm his worst fears, I think. That you took the easy way out because life wasn't worth living.'

'No! I'd never have done that.'

'I said that. Told him you weren't the kind of person to leave without saying goodbye. Tried to tell him it was an accident. But he was angry.'

'You told him it was an *accident?*'

'*Wasn't* it?'

Silence. Have I broken the Beach rules by asking that question directly?

'There are no such things as accidents, Alice. That is what I have learned. But it is unbearable that he thinks I abandoned him. *Unbearable.*'

I'm almost glad I can't see his face, because the pain in his voice is bad enough. 'I could try again, Javier, but I don't think he'd listen to me a second time.'

'You could *make* him listen, Alice, with my help. You could tell him things only I know.' He pauses and for a moment I wonder whether the computer has finally broken the connection. But then I hear him again, speaking softly now, 'You could tell him how I died . . .'

39

'You're saying you *know* how you died, Javier? That you *remember*? I thought no one on the Beach could remember their last moments.'

'Most Guests don't. Perhaps it is a ... safeguard. To stop them torturing themselves with what could have been. But in my case, there is no mystery. I know exactly how I met my death, Alice, and who was to blame.'

I stare at the blank screen, willing it to show me Javier. 'But you wouldn't be on Soul Beach if it was straightforward. You'd be ...' I pause, ' ... at peace, I suppose. Or in heaven.'

'Heaven. Of course. Why did I not think of that?' He laughs bitterly. 'Tell me, Alice, where *exactly* are you right now?'

'Um ... in some ancient internet place not far from the sea. In the old fishing district.'

'In my *barrio*, then. My neighbourhood. It is very respectable, right? Very *neighbourly* and, where the tourists don't go, peaceful too. Appearances matter. So my father was the gentleman outside the house. And inside it, a pig. A bully. A *bastard*.'

I lean closer into the screen. I want to show Javier that I am listening to every word.

'From an early age, I understood this was not normal. And I saw something in my mother's face that was not there in the faces of my friends' mothers, who always seemed so smiling and bright. Later, I realised that what I was seeing in her face was fear.

'Papa was big on *respect*. If my youngest sister cried, that was lack of respect, never mind that Rosa was a baby, only a few months old. If my middle sister, Karina, wet the bed – and she did, very often – then that was an insult to him personally, an act of disobedience. So he lashed out – usually at my mother, to punish her for what *her* children did. We were *his* children, too, of course, but he forgot that when he was raging.'

'Oh, Javier.' I don't know what else to say.

'A little while after Rosa was born, I suddenly understood that *physical* pain hurt me less than it hurt my mother or my sisters. I don't know why. Maybe they turned the pain in on themselves, while I could pretend it wasn't happening and store it up for the day when I was big enough to fight back. So, I began to incite him. Find ways to redirect his anger. It was very easy. My father seemed to prefer to take his rages out on me. Perhaps it made him feel more *manly* to beat another male, even though I was only eight years old.'

I try not to think about the little boy in the photograph that illustrated the newspaper story of Javier's death.

'My mother coped by closing down. Karina talked mainly to her toy cat, even taking the scruffy animal to school with her. Ah, until she was six and Dad cut it into pieces to teach her to grow up. Rosa and I were the closest. She would save supper for me if I was sent to bed early, or sing to me if I was sore. Since Gretchen went, sometimes I think I can hear Rosa's voice, here. At night. When everyone is asleep.'

He sounds wistful. It reminds me of the way Gretchen talked of her song thrushes.

'Did no one know what was going on?' I ask.

'We made sure they didn't. My mother kept the lie going out of shame, and we children learned to do the same. We learned that it was better people did not realise we were wicked enough to deserve this. We lived on the top floor, so we were less likely to be heard. And I tried not to cry out. Dad helped in his own way; he knew where to strike me so it wouldn't show, and how far he could go so I wouldn't need a doctor. The funny thing was, I wasn't scared of him, Alice. I could always see in his eyes that part of him was under control.'

Somehow that's the most shocking of all the things he's said. 'He knew what he was doing?'

'Until that last night, yes. That night, as he shouted and screamed and pushed and goaded, he was an *animal*. I had decided to stand up to him, you see. To leave college. To take a job to support my mother and the girls. We would not need him anymore. And I told him so.'

'What happened?'

'It was a festival night. The *Merce*. The festival of Barcelona. There is always an energy in the air in that week – but also something wild.'

Like now.

'I could see he was getting angrier. I felt almost excited, but also a little afraid of the craziness in his eyes. I walked away, out onto the terrace, to give him time to calm down. It was a good night to argue. Parties would drown out our voices.

'Except he followed me out before he cooled off. Called me the usual names but with some hatred. You can guess. I never came out as gay to my mother or my father, but I think they knew. For him it was as though I was gay only to shame him.

'I argued back. For the first time ever, I pushed him away when he went to strike me.'

'And that's when you fell?'

He doesn't seem to have heard me. 'You should have seen his face, Alice. The idea that I might resist, it had never occurred to him. For a moment, I felt ecstatic. But then ... then he came back at me. I was taller than him. Broader. And, of course, alcohol had made him old for his age. But I wasn't expecting it ...'

'And?'

'And. Well, you can guess. But what maybe you can't guess is that as I toppled, I almost felt I had won. No pain. Just ... the knowledge that he couldn't ever harm me again. After I got to the Beach, I rationalised it – that it was better for Mama and the girls to believe it was an accident. Maybe my father would have learned his lesson by killing me. But now ... Alice, what if my sisters think the same as Gabe – that I left them on purpose?'

'Javier—'

Sweat forms on the back of my neck; someone is behind me. I turn slowly, half expecting to see Sahara or even Zoe.

But it's just the guy who runs the shop. 'Problem?'

We both look at the screen now. 'No. I'm just waiting for the page to load.'

The man gives me a strange look, then says, 'Now you pay one hour and half,' and goes back to the front of the store. He's soldering something, without gloves. That's where the scars must come from.

'Are you there, Alice?' Javier asks. 'I thought I heard something else.'

'It's nothing. Someone else in the internet place, that's all.'

'Ah. It sounded like ... fireworks.'

I can't hear anything in here except the hum of the computer and the monitors. 'Javier. I might have to go soon, but I want to say that I understand now – why you've always said you prefer the Beach to your old life.'

He sniffs. 'That was before I realised that being on the Beach did not mean I would be free of the pain of losing people.'

'You still want to leave, Javier? You still want me to help you?'

'What I want ... What I want most is to know if they are all right. My family. Whether I escape or not, now, seems irrelevant to me. Peace, or heaven, or whatever you want to call it. I want that for the living. We dead do not count.'

'That's not true, Javier, you deserve—'

He interrupts me. 'Alice. If you want to help *me*, help them.'

'Of course. But how?'

'It depends on whether he is still there. How long are you in the city?'

'Only till tomorrow evening.' I realise this means nothing to him. 'Another day and a half. Plus the night, of course. It's not long, but I'll do whatever I can.'

'I suppose it must start with finding out if they are happy. Although ... I am not sure I can bear it if they are not.'

'Maybe I should only tell you if it is good news,' I suggest. 'If not, then I will pretend they were not at home.' Even though it'll be another terrible secret I will end up having to keep forever.

'But if the news is bad there may still be a way for us to change things, Alice. Or for *you* to change things.'

Sometimes it's terrifying, the trust the Guests have in me. And why? Just because I'm alive doesn't mean I'm all powerful. Yet, what else can I do but say yes? 'You know this could mean ... things change for you, too?' I warn Javier gently.

Javier laughs softly. 'Life is change, Alice. So is death. Do you have a pen?'

I write down the address where he lived; he has to spell it for me. 'It means Happy Town Street, if you can believe that,' he says. 'If you are near the main beach, then you are also near my home. Rosa looks the most like me, you might see her playing in the street. I taught her football – how to kick, in case she had to. Maybe now she's different, though – into dresses and boys. Maybe now she's ... safe.'

'And if I see your father?'

He laughs but it sounds so hollow. 'Oh, Alice. I hope you

will not. Because if you do, I fear there is nothing left to be done.'

'Even though I know what he is? What he did?'

'I trust you to know when to leave things alone. Remember what happened when I tried to make things better. I will not have you endanger yourself, too, Alice. The last thing I want is another waste of a life.'

40

When I get outside again, the bright sunshine hurts my eyes and makes me dizzy.

No text from Lewis about Burning Truths, but Cara's messaged me: **MATE! Where we meeting for lunch? Come to the park. It's huge! There's beer! & sexy dangers! Besos – means kisses in Spanish. The guy told me lst nite. Guess how I found out, ha ha. Miss you, hon, xxx**

Sexy dangers? Perhaps she means dancers, though knowing Cara it could easily be either.

I smile. After the intensity of the conversation with Javier, a chilled-out lunch with my best friend is *exactly* what I need. I'm not a machine: an hour or two lying in the sun, chatting about nothing, will help clear my head.

Of course, I'm still going to keep my promise to Javier and go to see where he lived, but going straight away seems a bad idea. Look what happened when I rushed headlong into talking to Gabe. It's better to plan properly before I get my second – and probably my last – chance to help Javier find peace.

I follow the tourist map towards the park, though the crowds slow me down. On the main street, waiters try to ambush me with their seafood menus. Families tackle ice-cream cones heaped high with pastel scoops. It reminds me a bit of days out with Mum and Meggie in Brighton. One summer, when it had rained non-stop from May till July, she pulled us out of school the first time the sun shone. We tried to build castles with pebbles and we went on the rollercoaster and then ate so many chips we could hardly climb the hill for the train home.

Despite everything that's happened, Meggie and I were lucky, weren't we? Compared to Javier and *his* sisters, we had the perfect childhood.

It takes me half an hour to get to the park gates. Statues stand guard at the entrance: the male one has a body to rival the best on Soul Beach. But I realise it's not going to be easy to find Cara; the park is almost as busy as Barcelona beach. Everywhere I look, people are *doing* stuff: juggling, jogging, tightrope walking.

I set off anti-clockwise round the edge of the park, getting my bearings. Everywhere I look there's a fairy-tale building: a bright pink clock tower, a gothic castle with turrets, an enormous wooden greenhouse. There's a boating lake and a life-size sculpture of a mammoth with tourists posing for photographs underneath. There are dogs and babies and couples walking hand in hand.

Latin music is playing somewhere, so I follow the rhythm. In the distance I can see an ornate bandstand mounted on white marble. I catch glimpses of couples dancing.

Sexy dancers, I suppose. Which must mean Cara's around here somewhere.

The sun is shining through the fancy ironwork, which makes the dancers seem like silhouettes. The music and their movements seem to suit this city perfectly: passionate, energetic, but just a little bit edgy.

I wish I could dance like that. Meggie could, of course. One week she'd convince millions of viewers that she was the wildest Carmen ever, full of Latin passion. Then the next she'd be all in white, making even the most determined atheists believe in God with her *Amazing Grace*. She was almost as good an actress as she was a singer. But was she acting with us, too – pretending everything was OK when all the time she had a stalker or someone threatening her?

The music changes to something slower paced. I walk towards the bandstand, where spectators are clapping and calling out to the dancers. I've only ever seen dancing like this on *Strictly*. There's something different about watching it live. I guess some of these are real-life couples, so they're putting their love and passion into every movement.

Oh, God! No.

Cara and Ade. *Dancing.*

His arm is tightly wrapped around her waist, and hers is draped on his slim shoulder. I take a step back but I needn't have bothered. They're so busy trying to get the moves right that they don't notice anything except each other. They're giggling as they get it wrong, while the other couples on the bandstand weave around them.

As Cara and Ade keep repeating the same moves, I try to convince myself that they're just messing about, being tourists. Except they look so right together, far more right than Ade ever looks with Sahara.

The music builds to a crescendo and Cara leans back from her waist, her leg raised against his body, and her hair hanging down like a sheet of white silk.

The music stops. They stay like that. I look away, because it feels like I shouldn't be watching. Even when the other dancers stop for a drink, they're like statues in the middle of all that movement.

Finally Ade pulls her back upright and I wait for them to get the giggles.

They kiss.

Oh, no. Tell me this isn't happening. Not here . . .

They don't stop. Not for bloody ages. Finally, the music starts up again, and it breaks the spell. They stare at each other.

I'm pretty certain I've just witnessed their very first kiss.

What have they done? Anyone could have seen them.

I have to get out of here, before they see *me*. A line of tourists on orange bikes pass in front of me, and I use them as cover to get away. There's a multi-tiered fountain, topped by two gilded horse statues that blaze in the afternoon sunlight. I run past it, then round to the right, towards the boating lake.

'Sorry!' I say, as I barge into someone. '*Lo siento.*'

'Alice?'

The someone is Sahara. She's holding onto my arms. Her face is bright red, and her underarms are ringed with sweat.

'Are you O K, Sahara? You look really...' *Desperate!* I think, but I don't finish my sentence.

'I'm fine.'

'Are you sure?' Her pupils are huge, even though the sun is shining brightly. She could be on drugs. Might she have seen Ade and Cara, like I did?

'It's the heat. It doesn't agree with me. I've been walking and walking and now I'm dehydrated.'

'We could get some water, there's a kiosk...' Then I realise I can't take her to that kiosk as it's too close to the bandstand. 'Or maybe you should go back to the hostel.'

'That's what I'm trying to do,' she snaps. 'Have you seen the streets? The crowds are doing my head in, and they're putting up crash barriers already. There are ambulances parked all the way up the main road. It's worrying, Alice, don't you think?'

'I'm sure it's safe, Sahara. They wouldn't let it happen otherwise.'

She looks dubious. 'People are different here. Wilder. Unpredictable.'

'The Spanish?'

'Yes, but not just them. Us, too. Maybe we're all different when we're away from home. All at risk.'

I stare at her. 'Look. We'll be fine if we stick together. I mean, I know Zoe's been going on about keeping safe, but she's been before and she survived just fine.'

Sahara sighs. 'I suppose so.'

'Do you want me to come with you, back to the hostel?' At least that way I can make sure she doesn't go anywhere near the bandstand. Though I also need to stay focused on what I've promised to do for Javier.

She shakes her head. 'No. I'm not going to ruin your day, too.'

I try not to look too relieved. 'If you're sure ... I think the exit's the way you just came, Sahara.' I point away from the bandstand. 'Here, borrow my map.'

She takes it from me. 'Thanks, Alice. I probably do need it. I feel like I've been wandering around this park for hours without getting anywhere. '

Did she spot her boyfriend dancing with Cara while she was getting herself lost? I dismiss the idea. Sahara can't seem to keep anything to herself, so I'm sure she'd have told me if she had.

I sit on a bench for a few minutes till she's disappeared into the crowd. There's a guy on the bank opposite me, juggling with flaming torches. Every time he drops one, he smiles. A ring of scorched grass surrounds him.

Everyone wants to play with fire. Cara and Ade kissing in public, Lewis chasing hackers, even Zoe, if we're right and it *is* her who set up Burning Truths to try to get justice for Tim.

And I'm no different. Trying to solve Meggie's murder, offering to see Javier's family, even though I could make things worse, not better.

But the alternative is to feel nothing, do nothing. And my sister's death has made me realise what a waste that would be.

I text Cara: **Came looking for u. Found u! U seemed a bit**

busy for lunch so thought I'd leave u to it . . . also, just bumped into S!!! Sent her in opposite direction. C u at the hostel later, xxx

She texts back almost immediately with a smiley face and a long row of kisses.

Time to look for Javier's old address. I leave the park and head back towards the fishing district, trying to remember the way without my map. Sahara was right about one thing – the chatter and buzz on the streets is getting louder. Javier said his fight with his father was drowned out on fiesta night and I guess tonight will be the same. There are signs posted everywhere, on walls and lampposts, in Spanish or maybe Catalan. The only word I recognise is *Correfoc*. The fire run.

The sea's ahead of me now, in the distance, so I take a left into the dark streets of Javier's neighbourhood. There are fewer tourists now. The deeper I get into this maze, the quieter it gets. I guess if I can't find the address, then I can always get a new map from the hostel, but I think if I'm methodical about it, and work my way up and down the gridlines that make up the streets, I should be OK.

What I say when I get there is the hard part.

I take the first right: Sant Miquel. No, that's not right. I go to the end, take a left: Ginebra. No, that's wrong too. Right again. I'm trying to keep track, but I feel like I'm already losing my bearings and the heat makes my head feel woolly.

Carrer del Baluart.

I take another right. This feels familiar, now, although all the streets look similar.

And then I realise why it's familiar: I'm back on Carrer de Balboa.

I know it's just a coincidence. And yet, Javier is always telling me he does not believe in coincidences. So perhaps there is a reason I've ended up here. I *do* have unfinished business at Dulce. Last time I made things worse for Gabe.

Perhaps I should seize this chance to try to make things better again.

What was it Javier said? *You could make him listen, Alice. You could tell him how I died ...*

I walk fast, so I don't have time to change my mind. But the café's shutters are already down. I lean against them, listening for signs of life. Is the music coming from inside? I hit the metal with my fist. Sweat drips down my forehead. I've had nothing to drink today except coffee. The shady street is getting darker – or is it that I'm about to black out?

I lean against the shutters, my face touching the grille. The metal smells rusty. Like blood.

'Gabe?' I call out. 'Gabe? If you're in there, let me in.'

The shutter moves, suddenly. I only just get out of the way in time.

'You!' says Gabe. 'I should have known it was you. Play-acting being ill are you now? What a bloody attention seeker!'

He's about to close the shutter again.

'Wait! Gabe. Please listen. Um. Karina ... Karina's the middle sister. She had a toy that her father cut into pieces.' I try to remember more. 'And Rosa sings ... sang to Javier when he was hurt. She's the baby.'

Gabe stares at me. 'Is this another bloody trick?'

'No trick. Please give me a second to explain. I can't hurt you anymore than I have already, can I?'

He's thinking. Then, finally, he opens the door a little wider. I go inside, and he locks the door behind me and pulls the shutter halfway down. The café is almost dark, except for the tea lights still burning on the tables.

'I wasn't exactly in the mood for a big fiesta tonight,' Gabe says. 'Too many memories.'

'Because J died on the night of the fiesta, didn't he?'

'You think you're clever, don't you, Alice? But you could have found that out online.'

'You don't *have* to believe me,' I say. 'You just have to listen.'

'I don't know what the hell to believe. But you know about me and J – which is more than anyone else did in Barcelona.'

It takes me a few seconds to work out what he means. 'You kept it secret?'

Gabe nods. 'Not my choice, but with his father being the way he was, I understood why. It's less a big city, more a series of villages. Hell, I even call him *Jay* the Australian way because the Spanish don't pronounce their Js like that. To make certain no one local could ever make the connection between him and me.'

'So if no one knew you were together, then when he died . . .'

He nods. 'Right. When he died, no one told me. He didn't show up for the fiesta. I spent forty-eight hours getting angrier and angrier. He used to freak out, sometimes, about how his dad would react if he found out. I thought he was just having one of those moments.'

'Oh, Gabe . . .'

'Then I picked up the paper. He'd been dead all that time. That's why I'm not a believer in messages from the bloody afterlife. I should have *known*. If he was trying to get a message to anyone, it'd be me, not some little English kid.'

I say nothing.

'But here you are, eh, Alice?' The cynicism's gone. All I can hear is sadness.

We sit there in the dark as more bangers explode outside. 'Here I am.'

'His dad was old-school. They came here from the countryside down south, and his dad brought values that would make Hitler seem moderate. I thought that's why J ended it. He'd realised he couldn't ever be happy living this double life.'

'Couldn't the two of you have gone somewhere else?'

Gabe sighs. 'Don't you think I tried to persuade him? There was Australia for a start. Or anywhere in Europe. I didn't care. I just wanted . . .'

I think of Danny, and how torn *I* feel between the Beach and 'real' life. Yet the Beach always wins. 'To be with him?' I finish for Gabe.

'Anywhere would have been home with him there. But he wouldn't leave his sisters. I thought maybe he might go when they were older. And then . . .'

'He didn't kill himself.'

'No? How did he tell you that, Alice? One knock for yes, two for no?'

I ignore the sarcasm. 'He was fighting with his father. It went too far. Javier was pushed, and there was no barrier on the roof. Nothing to stop him falling.'

For a moment Gabe does nothing. Then he punches the flint wall so hard that a stone falls away, but he doesn't seem to feel any pain.

'The *bastard*.' He pulls out a chair, sits down, head in hands.

'Have you ever met his father?'

'No. I . . . I did see where it happened. The address was in the paper. There was nothing there, not even flowers. I went to the beach and collected a bunch of shells, and I scattered them where I thought he must have landed, on the street. Bet you think that's dumb. They'd have been smashed to pieces by a moped within minutes.'

'Nothing's dumb when you're grieving.'

He looks at me. 'I looked you up online, Alice. Your sister. So you know how it feels, don't you?'

I reach for his hand and he curls his fingers round mine the way a baby does, and won't let go.

'I'm going there now,' I say. 'To Javier's place. I want to see if his father's still there and if his sisters are all right.'

It's a risk, telling him. If Gabe didn't already think I was crazy, I bet he does now.

But his fingers stay tight around mine. 'And what will you do if they're not?'

I don't have an answer. Instead I say, 'I'd really like it if you could come with me. I think it's the right thing. For both of us.'

You're leading me on a merry dance, Alice.

It's too hot for this. Up and down the backstreets of this grubby, beautiful city, as though you're searching for something you'd lost. Or someone.

Who are you looking for? Me, perhaps?

All you have to do is look behind you.

41

It's lucky Gabe knows where he's going because I am totally lost now. Every street looks the same: the tall buildings, the washing lines, the kids playing in the road.

Except that the kids in this street might be Javier's sisters.

'I think Karina would be eleven, Rosa eight,' I say, and Gabe gives me an odd look but doesn't ask how I could know that.

There is a girl of about eight leaning against the building, watching kids in Barca football shirts kicking a ball around. She's facing the sea so I can only see the back of her head, silhouetted against the setting sun. She has long dark curls and for a moment I imagine she's holding a new cat toy, to replace the one Javier said his father had cut up out of spite. Except that was Karina's toy, wasn't it?

Then the 'toy' moves and I realise it's a young ginger cat.

'Could that be Rosa?' I ask Gabe. He doesn't answer, and when I turn back to repeat the question, I realise he's staring at the girl so hard that she must sense it too. She looks round, right at us.

She's striking rather than pretty. It's not her features that tell me I'm right, though. It's her gaze. Pure defiance.

'Jesus. She's the spit of him,' he says.

'Do we talk to her?'

Before we can decide, she puts the cat down and it trots behind her as she walks into the apartment building, out of sight.

'Did you see the way she walked?' Gabe whispers. There

was a self-assurance about her that reminds us both of her big brother.

I try not to get my hopes up.

'I was expecting her to be more ... more submissive, I suppose,' I say. 'After what Javier told me about their home life.'

'Me too.'

We want to wait, but there's only so long you can hang around a corner in this neighbourhood without attracting attention. We find a bench in a small square at the top of the street and watch from there.

The sky is still bright blue. Below it, the rooftops are flat, cluttered with aerials and old bikes. We count one, two, three, four rooftops along: the roof Javier fell from must be the one with the collection of bright plastic toys piled up against a low stonework wall.

Gabe lights a cigarette. Even in the open air, it stinks. 'So, have you found what you were looking for?'

I think it through. 'If it's definitely Rosa—'

'It's her. You know that as well as I do.'

'Then it might be good news. She didn't look miserable, did she? And the cat. Javier's father didn't sound like the kind of guy who'd put up with a pet. Perhaps he's left – out of guilt or something.'

Gabe takes a deep drag from the cigarette, shakes his head and then stands up. 'We could sit here guessing all day. I'm going to ask after his old man.'

I remember what Javier said about him. 'Be careful.'

Gabe smiles, and walks away. I watch as he approaches one woman with a baby in her arms, who shrugs and points to another, much older woman, sitting in a green plastic chair. She's pretending to knit, but I think she's too busy keeping a beady eye on everyone else to make much progress.

Something's nagging at me. If the little girl is as happy as she looks, then surely Javier's death is already resolved, so why would he still be on the Beach?

Gabe has offered the woman a cigarette, she's offered him a plastic chair, and now they're huddled together, talking. *Please* let it help him. I hate the idea that I'm making things worse.

My phone buzzes in my bag. It's Lewis: **Text me back ASAP about the pictures. Need to see you.**

Gabe's coming back towards me. His walk is carefully controlled, but as he links arms and drags me out of view of plastic-chair woman, I sense his excitement. Or is it anger?

'What?'

'He's back,' Gabe says. 'The bastard's back.'

'Back from where?'

'That old gossip knows everything about everything in the street, but even she's not sure. What she thinks happened is that he left – or was thrown out – soon after J died.'

'Maybe Javier's mother worked out it was no accident.'

Gabe nods. 'They all knew the father was a thug, of course. Not much slips past the neighbours when you're living so close together. Apparently, the daughters turned into different girls after he left. The older one was doing brilliantly at school. And you were right about the cat. J's mum bought it for them as soon as the father left.'

'But?'

He's grim-faced. 'A few weeks ago, they heard raised voices again. Well, *his* raised voice. That's how they knew he'd come back. The neighbour reckons he's wormed his way back in, somehow. When they saw him, he was thin. Perhaps he's been ill. Though she reckons it might just be the drink. *Shame it didn't finish him off,* she said. He's not exactly Mr Popular round here.'

'What story did you tell the neighbour?'

'Hinted at a few debts owed to me. Figured the old man

would be the type. Didn't take much to set her off. My Catalan is pretty good these days. Don't worry, I said nothing about knowing J. I know better than to blow his big secret out of the water.' There's a sadness in his voice.

My phone buzzes. I bet it's Lewis again. I wonder what he's found out.

'I'm sure he'd have told his mother and his sisters about you in the end,' I tell Gabe.

He lets go of my arm. 'I'll never know. I might as well never have existed.'

'If you didn't exist, why did J send me to see you?'

'Maybe you're a hallucination. Maybe I knew deep down J wouldn't have deserted me, so I've imagined you – to remind myself that he loved me.'

'No, no hallucinations. I'm pretty solid, Gabe.' I squeeze his hand to prove it. 'What now?'

His eyes narrow. 'I didn't have any plans for tonight. I'm going to wait for him.'

'*What?* What can you do?'

He shrugs. 'I'll rely on instinct for that one.'

'No. Gabe, this isn't what J would have wanted. His father's dangerous. I'm sure Javier just wanted this to be an end to things, not the beginning of a new vendetta.'

'With all due respect, Alice, it's not your decision.'

I hear the steeliness in his voice, but I can't let him do this. The consequences don't bear thinking about. And it's my fault. I brought him here. 'Please don't.'

Gabe sighs. 'I know you're being sensible. But you must see that I don't care about the danger. What I care about is putting things right. Justice, if you like.'

That word. It's one of the most dangerous there is.

'His father's crazy, Gabe. What if he kills you too?'

Gabe shakes his head. 'You know what? I don't think I care.'

Maybe Gabe and Javier will end up like Meggie and Tim,

on the Beach for all eternity. I don't want that to happen, but I also know I've started something I can't stop.

'All right, Gabe. But if you're going to do this, I want to be here.'

'You're a sweet kid, Alice, but I can take care of myself.'

'That's what J thought. I won't try to stop you, I promise. I want justice almost as much as you do.'

I can see him thinking it through and his face relaxes a little. Even if I am only a *kid*, I sense he's relieved that I want to see this through with him.

Gabe nods. 'OK. But you don't have to wait with me.'

'I want to.'

'Alice, don't be dumb. He could be hours yet.'

I look at my watch. It's just after four thirty. We're meeting Zoe at eight, to bag a prime position for the parade – though she laughed when Sahara called it that. *It's not clowns and Disney carnival floats. They take this seriously. So should you.*

'If I give you my number, will you promise to text me before you go anywhere near J's father?' I ask Gabe. 'Please? I'll be in this area, anyway. But I guess I should see my friends or they'll wonder what I've been up to.' *Friends?* Tonight has little to do with friendship. It's my last – and my best – chance to watch my suspects, and catch them unawares. And right now, I should be on my way to talk to Lewis about the Burning Truths photo.

Gabe nods. 'Thank you.'

'Don't thank me, Gabe. I know Javier wouldn't have wanted you to face this alone. And I *need* to see this through.'

42

Lewis's room is like something out of a Bond movie. His bathroom is twice the size of our shared hostel bedroom, and the view from the twelfth floor is like looking down from a giant ocean liner. If *I* was staying here, I don't think I'd bother going out at all.

Lewis doesn't notice what's beyond his window, or bother asking how my day's been. He's too busy frowning at his laptop screen.

'You need to see this, Alice.'

He's pulled up the Burning Truths site.

I look over his shoulder.

There's a close-up photograph of a crystal wine glass.

'What's that supposed to . . .'

Then I notice the lip print, in darkest crimson. A shade Meggie never wore; it was too garish for her golden colouring.

Yet that cupid's bow. I'm pretty sure it's hers. She went through a phase of signing off all her letters with lipstick prints and the perfect shape on the glass matches those exactly.

This is the image I couldn't see: *MeganForster_lips.jpg.*

'That's just weird.'

Lewis nods. 'This picture. And the other one,' he scrolls down to the first photo posted there, of Meggie's lifeless hand. 'I know it sounds odd but they almost remind me of collector's items – like you'd see in a museum.'

I think of another interpretation and it makes me shudder.

'Or the pictures they take on crime shows. At the post mortem.'

Lewis nods. 'If we can find out who took these, I think we will have found the killer.'

It's only what I was thinking, of course, but when he says that, the danger I'm in hits me harder than it ever has before. And it's not just me, but also Lewis. Or all of us. All of us, except the person responsible. And I can't help wondering . . . Was Sahara *following* me earlier on?

'Alice, there's another thing. I don't want to worry you, but I wonder if I should take this down. At the moment, hardly anyone has found the site. But if one person stumbles on these photos and realises what they are, it could go viral. And then . . . well, it might be a lot harder to get at the truth.'

'You can do that? Take the site down.'

'I could launch a denial of service attack right now. There's a ninety-nine per cent chance it'll work, at least until after the fiesta – until we've had a chance to talk to Zoe.'

'You still think it's her?'

'Alice, I *know* it's her. After the conversation we had last night about *la Fée Verte*, someone searched for information about me for hours and hours. And she wasn't quite as careful as she is when she's coding her site. I tracked the searches down to an area off the Ramblas called Raval. That's where Zoe lives. It's too much of a coincidence.'

I nod. I knew it already, really. 'But where would she have got the photos from?'

'Or who?' Lewis says as he sits down at the computer. The bin's full of Coke cans. This is a real home from home. I wonder if he's slept at all since he's been here, and how much time he's spent at the conference he's supposed to have come here for.

'Lewis, do you see now? Why I've got doubts about Tim being the one who killed Meggie?' I ask.

He doesn't look at me. 'It could still have been Tim who took those photos, couldn't it?'

'But he was going out with her. Why would he need to photograph her lips on a glass?'

'If he did murder her, Alice, then I don't suppose he'd have been worried about a bit of illicit photography.'

'Lewis, you don't really believe he killed her, do you?'

He smiles wearily. 'Look, I'm not saying your hunch about Tim is wrong. Zoe's reached the same conclusions, after all. She's trying to warn people. But she's afraid to come out with it openly. And with good reason, I guess, when you think that we're dealing with someone who might have killed two people, now.'

'She'll realise, if you take the site down. She'll know it's you.'

'I know. But I can time it for when we're at the fiesta. Give us a chance to talk to her. She might *want* to talk, you know, Alice.'

'I've tried, but—'

'Try again. You'll probably get further than me.'

'Why?'

He shrugs. 'I don't think she's keen on strangers, do you? But I'll tell you what I see when I look at that site, apart from the dodgy graphics. I see fear, but also a desperation to confide in someone. To share her suspicions.'

I nod, even though I can't help wondering why she can't just go and tell the police directly. I wonder if they're still watching the site – or if the detectives have already forgotten about my sister's case now that the murder team's been disbanded?

'Shall I see you later, then?' Lewis asks pointedly.

'You want me to go now?'

'I am *supposed* to be working. *Net*working. God knows this hotel room is costing me enough, so I should at least make an effort to do something productive other than stalk Zoe on Burning Truths.'

'Oh. Only I was wondering if I could use your laptop – just for a few minutes. There are a few emails I want to send.' *And another conversation to be had with a dead boy who lived just a few hundred metres from here.*

He frowns. 'Oh, Alice. For once I'm saying no. You're not running a FTSE 100 company. I'm sure they can wait. Why don't you go to the beach and eye up the boys or something, like a normal teenage girl?'

I look through the window, down to the shore, and then to the city beyond. Firecracker flashes light up streets and squares. I can't hear anything, but it's definitely getting wilder out there.

The line between normal and out of control seems to be at its narrowest in this city.

The hostel is a shock after the luxury of Lewis's hotel. Our room smells of Cara and Sahara's competing perfumes, and there's an oily layer of sand on the floor that sticks to my feet as I get changed.

I keep checking my phone, but Gabe hasn't been in touch. I hope he doesn't break his promise to wait till I'm there before he goes near Javier's father.

'I've had such a lovely afternoon,' says Sahara. 'The Picasso museum is incredible. I could spend a week there.'

Is she lying? I thought she was going to spend the afternoon back at the hostel, away from the crowds. 'You went on your own?' I ask her.

She nods. 'Adrian's the perfect boyfriend in almost every way, but he doesn't have much patience for art, do you?' And she reaches out to stroke his neck.

'I have tried,' he says, 'but I'm a cultural pleb.'

'Anyway, I'd rather have the chance to go at my own pace.

I literally studied some of the paintings for twenty minutes. People were staring at me,' Sahara laughs.

'Cara smiles. 'Well, we had a great afternoon at the beach, didn't we, Alice?'

I frown at her. I never agreed to be her alibi. Then again, I don't want to make Sahara suspicious.

'Time's gone so fast today,' I say vaguely.

'And we had a lovely late picnic lunch,' Cara adds.

Sahara frowns. 'A *liquid* lunch, was it?'

I look at Cara: she seems slightly cross-eyed, and her make-up's on the smudged side.

Cara pulls a face. 'We are on *holiday*, in case you've forgotten.'

'All the same, Cara,' I say, 'Zoe says this fire festival can get quite out of control. We should be careful. And she reckons we need to cover up a bit.'

Sahara holds up a balaclava and red scarf she bought earlier, and Ade is pulling on a thick blue cotton shirt with long cuffs that will cover his hands.

'Blimey, Alice, give it a rest. It's only a party. Seriously, mate, you never used to be such a worrier,' Cara says.

Sahara stares at her. 'Is it any wonder she worries about the people she cares about after what happened to Meggie? Honestly, Cara. You don't deserve her as a friend if you can't understand *that.*'

Cara blushes. 'Sorry,' she says to me. 'OK. You win. I'll cover up when it's time.'

'We're still going to have a great night,' I say. 'I know we will. But there's safety in numbers, eh? So long as we all stick together, we'll have the time of our lives.'

43

All the firecrackers in the world must have been shipped to Barcelona for tonight.

And now the sun's going down, they're being lit across the city. The flashes are almost constant, so it feels like day again.

The bars are full except for an Irish pub with a terrace where people are clustered round tall tables. Even though the evening's sultry, the locals are dressed in cold weather layers, while the tourists wear thin cotton shirts. Suddenly I see how Gabe could tell I was foreign; we stand out a mile among the smart Catalans.

Still no message from Gabe. I've been checking my phone every couple of minutes. I even texted to remind him, but I've heard nothing back.

'Zoe definitely knows we're here, does she?' Lewis asks.

It's ten past eight now. We were supposed to meet at eight, so we could find a spot with a good view *and* a fast escape route. *You don't want to get lost in the crowd*, she'd warned us.

Sahara reaches for her phone and texts Zoe again. 'She's normally punctual.'

Lewis and I exchange a look. He's arranged for the Denial of Service attack on Burning Truths to start at eight o'clock, because we thought she'd be safely away from her computer by then, but what if she's decided not to join us? Not only will we miss our best chance to talk to her, but she might panic, fight the Denial of Service, stay away.

The idea that all this might be for nothing, that I could go home knowing no more about Meggie's death than I do now, makes me dizzy. Lewis reaches out to touch my hand.

'We'll sort this, don't worry,' he whispers. 'Even if we have to go round to her flat and confront her there. The trip won't be in vain, I promise you.'

Cara has seen his hand on mine, and she raises her eyebrows at me, as though I'm up to no good – when, of course, it's her that's putting herself at risk. OK, so Sahara didn't see anything earlier, but that was pure luck. And if Cara and Ade were brazen enough to kiss in broad daylight, then I'm scared of what they might do under cover of darkness.

I take my hand away from Lewis's, and lean towards Cara. 'Let's forget about the boys tonight. I'd rather be with you than with anyone alive.'

At first I don't recognise the bandit who arrives at our table.

'Zoe?' Sahara says uncertainly, leaning forward to look into the bandit's eyes.

'Who the hell else would it be?' Only her voice gives her away. Her bald head is covered like it always is, but she has a second lime green scarf tied in an upside down triangle round her face and neck, plus a thick ski jacket, black leather gloves, old jeans and ankle boots. She must be boiling hot.

'We were about to give up on you,' Sahara scolds. 'It's almost time for the parade to begin.'

'I told you before, it's not a bloody parade!' she snaps. If anything, she's edgier tonight than she's ever been. Has she worked out what Lewis has done – or is something else freaking her out? 'I wouldn't dress like this for fun, would I?'

'Isn't that what tonight is about? Fun?' Cara says.

Zoe turns on her. 'You're not going into the flames looking like that, are you?'

'Ugh, not *that* again,' Cara says. 'You're worse than my mum.'

Zoe shakes her head. 'Things are different here. It's the culture. You look after yourself. You don't expect other people to do it for you.'

Cara is wearing the skimpiest of halter-neck dresses. 'Er, it is midsummer, in case you haven't noticed. But don't worry, Ade's already agreed to lend me his shirt.' There's the briefest glance between him and Cara that only I notice. Sahara is too busy trying out her balaclava and tying the scarf round her thin, slightly greasy hair.

'I'll be OK in this, will I?' Sahara asks.

'You could probably survive a nuclear bomb in that,' Zoe says. She turns to me. 'You're OK, Alice. Though watch out for your hair. Ideally you'd cover that too.'

'I'm a wimp anyway.' I tell her. 'I don't intend to get too close.'

I can't help thinking that Zoe's going over the top. How can the wide boulevard we walked down yesterday turn into some fiery vision of hell?

'Assuming I *don't* turn into a human firecracker, what happens?' Cara asks. 'We dance in the flames for a bit, and then what?'

'When I came with my parents the first time, they kept me safely on the sidelines and it seemed to last a couple of hours. But if you're in the thick of it, I think the time will go lightning-fast. Fear does that.'

Sahara's taken her balaclava off now, but her eyes are wide open, as though she's half expecting Satan himself to pop up out of the barrel our drinks are resting on.

I take my mobile out. No messages.

Cara winks. 'Not expecting a text from the mysterious *Danny*, are we?' she whispers.

If only she knew.

Dusk is falling fast and it's beginning to feel more like Halloween than midsummer. The bars and cafés are all candlelit, but a sea breeze has swept in so the flames keep blowing out.

It's still warm, but I'm shivering. Lewis catches my eye and then nods towards Zoe. I know what he's thinking – if the parade goes on for hours, maybe this is my best chance to talk to her. If he's right, and she wants to talk too, then perhaps all I need to do is break away from the group, let her come to me . . .

The others are chatting and laughing as I walk to the edge of the road, brushing past Zoe 'accidentally' on the way. I cross over, closer to the harbour and the city museum. There are lights on some of the yachts, but most of the people are headed to the right, into the city.

'You know, don't you?'

I turn round slowly. Zoe's dark clothing makes her look even smaller.

'I know what, Zoe?'

'That I am *la Fée Verte.*'

Even though I believed Lewis, it feels different to hear Zoe say it – like it's the first big step forward I've made in all the time since I found Meggie on the Beach and realised what I must do.

'We guessed.'

'You and your *boyfriend?*'

'He's not my—' I look at her and realise her eyes are wild with . . . what? Amusement? Or terror.

'That's what everyone else thinks, though, isn't it? But I'm more observant than that. I notice things, like the fact that you two seem to be on some kind of mission. So how did you guess?'

'I *thought la Fée Verte* might be you, but Lewis confirmed it.' I wonder if I should go further. 'I know what you're trying to do, Zoe, and I admire you for it.'

'Then why interfere?' She doesn't sound hostile, just curious.

'Because I think the same as you – that Tim didn't kill my sister – and that knowledge is risky. But so is all this secrecy. Shouldn't you go to the police?'

'Like Tim did, you mean?'

'What?'

A family with twin girls run into us, laughing, and the mother smiles in apology.

'Yes. Tim went to the police. They didn't believe him. They thought it was some attempt on his part to distract them from his own guilt. Next thing, he's "committed suicide".'

'You think the police were *involved*?'

'No. No. They're just too incompetent to look any deeper than following some kind of ABC children's manual of detective work that tells them to a) find an obvious suspect, b) tell the media even if you don't have the evidence, and c) hound him relentlessly.'

'Where *should* they be looking, Zoe?'

'I don't want to get you involved, Alice. You don't need to be tainted by this too.'

'I told you before. I want to help. I *need* to help.'

She stares at the ground. I wait.

Finally, she looks at me again. 'Well, If I were the police, I'd start with those photographs. The police said they were proof of nothing, but that's not how I see them.'

'Proof of ... nothing?' I think it through. 'But the killer took them, surely?'

'That's why I think Tim died. He found them.'

'And gave them to you?'

'No. Not exactly. You see, I'd set up the site before he died, because I was so angry. But it was never intended to feature *anything* like those pictures. They only arrived after he died. He'd told me that if anything happened to him, I should look

232

in this locker at college: a spare one. It belonged to a fresher who left. So I did, and I found memory sticks – a dozen of them.'

'With the photos on them?'

'Those. Plus *thousands* of others. Most of them mean nothing, as far as I know. It took me hours to realise the one of the wine glass was significant. I think Tim jumbled them up, so that if anyone but me found them, they'd think there was nothing to see. I've been going through them since he died, but I'm not even sure I know what I'm seeing – or looking for.'

'Or who took them?'

She closes her eyes. 'It has to be someone here, doesn't it, Alice? Someone here *with us*.' She's whispering now.

'You don't know?'

'Someone who was close to her, Alice. It has to be. If you saw the pictures ...'

'I could look at them, Zoe. I could come with you, now. There might be things I spot that you haven't. We can skip the fiesta. I can tell you don't care about it anymore than I do—'

'No! Don't you see? If we're not there, whoever it is will know. He'll know. Or she will.'

I stare at her. 'You think it has to be Sahara or Ade, don't you?'

'Alice, I—' Her eyes widen, as though she's seen a ghost.

'So this is where you're both hiding!'

It's Sahara. Ade, Cara and Lewis are right behind her. 'Honestly,' she says, 'those dark clothes of yours are *very* effective camouflage on a night like this.'

Zoe seems to back away, into the shadows. I reach for her hand, and stop her.

'We were just admiring the yachts,' I say. Weren't we, Zoe?' I squeeze her hand, then let go. 'After the fire run,' I whisper.

She nods, then marches ahead, forging a route through the crowd.

Lewis falls back with me. 'So?'

'So you were right. After the fiesta, I'm going back to her flat. There are more photographs, thousands of them. The answer's there, Lewis. I know it is.'

'But what do they show?' I'm about to answer when I feel my phone buzz. Gabe? I reach into my pocket and take the phone out: **He's here. Alone. You don't have to come, but I promised I would let you know.**

It's half past eight. It couldn't be worse timing, but I can't let Gabe confront Javier's father alone. I owe him – and Javier – more than that.

If I go now, I could still make it back for the fiesta – if I run.

'Alice? Are you coming?'

'Of course. Of course I am. But I just need a few minutes alone, to think. Tonight – well, it's pretty intense, Lewis.'

'Let me come with you.'

I smile. 'Alone, Professor. That means on my own, even without you. But I'll join you as soon as I'm done.'

'Don't get lost, Ali.' He squeezes my arm. 'I'll text you to tell you where we are. Apparently tonight is unmissable.'

44

Now, Javier's street is deserted. This is how it must have been the night he died.

No old women, no children.

No *Gabe*.

'Gabe? Are you here?'

But I feel like I'm the only person left in the middle of a warzone, where everyone else has fled. The coming fireworks could be an approaching army.

I go up to the front door that Rosa disappeared through earlier. There are no names, though, just a panel of silver buzzers with flat numbers next to them. The top one is *Atico*, which even I realise must mean *attic*.

Has Gabe gone in ahead of me?

I've got his number now on my phone, but, of course, when I try to call I get that Spanish message again and then a disconnection tone. So I text him instead: **I'm here. Come and find me before you do anything.**

But *will* he? I saw how angry he was when he found out that Javier's father was back. And anger makes people do crazy things, especially on a night like tonight when the city is alive with fire and explosions. Gabe may think he has nothing to lose.

In this street, the TVs and radios are silenced. All I can hear is a scaredy-cat dog, whining whenever a firework goes off in the distance.

'Gabe, where are you?' I shout louder this time.

Something smashes onto the pavement, just a couple of metres away. A firework?

I get closer. It's not a firework, it's a doll. At least, it *was*. Now it's a pile of pink plastic limbs, and a porcelain head with a fixed smile on a half-smashed face.

I look up and see two figures, close to one another, on the roof.

'Gabe?'

It's definitely Javier's building. I run backwards, dodging bins and uneven paving slabs. I still can't see the men clearly. But now I'm tuning out the sounds of the fireworks and trying to focus, because I think I can hear raised voices. A furious argument.

The bench where we sat just a few hours ago might give me a better view. I clamber onto it.

Two men are squaring up to each other, shadowy against the gunpowder-red night sky. Gabe is one of them, I'm certain. We recognised Javier's sister from her slightly arrogant walk, but Gabe gives himself away with his surfer-boy movements.

The other figure is shorter, stockier. The voices are getting louder but they're speaking Spanish, or Catalan. I can't understand the words, but the threatening tone is frighteningly clear.

'GABE!'

They start to fight. They're getting closer to the low stone wall that borders the roof. It's no higher than their knees.

I think of what happened to the doll. And of what happened to Javier.

I can't let it happen again. Yet there's no one around to help me. I cry out, 'Gabe, STOP!'

It's impossible to tell who is attacking who. But if Javier's father could murder his son without a second thought, then killing a stranger would surely be easier still. The sounds aren't words anymore, but screams and grunts and cries.

Is this history repeating itself?

No, it's even worse than that. Because if the worst happens, it will be *my* fault. I brought Gabe here. I am responsible.

'Gabe, he's not worth it!' I'm shouting so loud my throat hurts, but I'm nowhere near loud enough to be heard above the firecrackers exploding across the city.

And all the while, they're getting closer to the edge.

I jump off the bench, race back towards the front door. I should have done this sooner. I smash my fist against the wood, and press all the buzzers with my left hand in case *someone* is still in the building who could call for help.

And then the front door bursts open.

I fall into the hallway.

'Alice!'

It's Gabe.

I struggle to get up, my hands slipping on the tiled floor.

'Come on,' Gabe says, grabbing my arm. 'Let's get out of here.'

'What did you do to Javier's father? Did you hurt him?'

Gabe shakes his head, but his face is grim. 'No, though he bloody deserved it.'

'Where are we going?'

'Far enough away that I won't be tempted to smash his face in. But close enough for me to watch him leave.'

We're both shaking as we stumble back round to the bench. When I look up at the rooftop this time, all I can see is the silhouette of the wall against the sky. It's as if nothing happened.

Gabe's panting. 'Jesus, Alice ... I never knew evil had a *smell*. The guy looked normal from a distance, but when I got close to him it was stronger than body odour.

'How did you get in?'

'The mum went out with the girls, all dressed up for the

Correfoc. J's Mum looked upset, and Rosa was telling her that they'd have a good time, that Papa would have calmed down by the time they got back. He'd been there the whole time.'

'What did you do?'

'I sneaked in after some neighbours left. When I got up to J's old flat, right at the top, the old man was smoking on the terrace. He was too drunk to even look surprised that this stranger had appeared from nowhere. I told him my name but obviously it meant nothing to him.'

In the distance I hear drumming, but the fireworks have stopped – almost as if out of respect for Javier.

'The old guy was swearing, and then he turned to face me. Alice, it was like seeing this hideously warped version of J. And then I looked down. *Such* a long way down. I'd planned to be absolutely calm, but seeing the distance J fell, it made me angrier than I've ever felt in my life.'

'No one could blame you for feeling that way, Gabe.'

'I punched him, Alice. Hard. I mean, I never punch *anyone* but I did this time. There was a crunch. His nose going, I think. And then he started fighting back. For a drunk, he was doing pretty well. At that moment, I don't think I cared if I fell, so long as I made sure I took him with me.

'That's when I heard my name. You were calling me from down here. I think it's probably all that stopped me killing him.' He sounds ashamed of himself.

'No. You didn't kill him because you're a good person.'

He sighs. 'Maybe. But it brought me to my senses enough to do what I'd planned. I told him I knew how Javier died. He mumbled something back about not knowing a Javier. And when I said, "Your son, remember?" he shook his head. "I don't have a son," he kept saying, "I have daughters. And a slut of a wife, but no son".

'It was so hard to stay calm but I knew J would have wanted me to put his sisters and mum first. So I spelled it out, in

238

words a drunk can understand. Described J. How he looked. What he loved. His dreams.

'I saw the change in the guy's face. He *knew* I knew. And then I repeated the story J told you: about exactly how he died, and why.

'Finally, he got it. I told him that he had to pack. Tonight. Leave for good. Be gone before the family were back. That if he didn't, I'd be watching and waiting, and that if he was very lucky it would be the police that came after him. And if he wasn't, then it'd be me.'

'And he believed you?'

'Hell, Alice, *I* believed me. I reckon he realised that I was willing to die myself, to avenge J. And when you started banging on the door, I said that next time it would be the *Mossos*. The police. Told him he had ten minutes to get his things and go.'

'Ten minutes.' I check the time on my phone. Lewis has texted me, asking where I am. 'So J's father should be leaving about now.'

'You don't have to wait with me.'

'I think I do.'

A minute passes. Two. Will he go – or will Gabe have to carry out his threat?

Then the door to J's building opens. We both hold our breath.

'It's him,' Gabe whispers, and reaches for my hand.

The man is dressed in jeans and a hooded top. He has a black holdall on his shoulder, and carries a couple of large carrier bags in his other hand.

Maybe it's because I know what he's done, but there is something ugly about him, the way he scuttles out of the door like a cockroach.

He looks around him but doesn't notice us. With his head covered, I can't see any likeness to J. He pulls the door shut with a violent slam, and the noise seems to reverberate around the deserted neighbourhood, louder than any firecracker I've heard.

Finally the man looks up at the building, and the roof. I wonder if there's any regret about what he's done.

But then he lifts his head and I see the rage in his face before he spits against his own front door, and then swaggers down the street towards the city.

I realise I've been holding my breath the whole time. Gabe lets go of my hand.

'Do you think he'll come back?' he whispers, once the figure has disappeared.

'He's a coward, isn't he? And it doesn't sound like he was there because he loved them. More because it was an easy life. Hopefully you've scared him enough to make him realise staying away is his only option.'

Gabe nods. 'Thanks. For believing me. And for stopping me from doing something I would have regretted. I hate the fact I came so close.'

'The most important thing is that you didn't give in to that darkness. You were only trying to protect the people J loved, remember. But what will you do now?'

'Stay in town for a while, I guess. Check that he really has left for good. But after that, I think it's over for me and Barcelona. It's now my ex-favourite place in the world.' He looks up at the sky. 'Drop dead gorgeous, still, but time for me to go.'

I wonder if it's time for Javier to leave Soul Beach, too? This *must* be enough now. Justice has been done.

Even though the explosions have started up again, the street feels calm. As though J's father going has made everything lighter.

Of course, it means J will leave tonight. I feel a catch in my throat: the idea of the Beach without Javier's edgy humour and the vulnerability I know lies behind that, makes me want to cry. Whatever happens with Zoe at her apartment, I have to get online to say goodbye before the next Soul Beach sunset. Javier deserves that.

But before the sadness overwhelms me, I force myself to focus on the good that's been done here tonight. I was so convinced something was going to go wrong. That someone might lose their life . . .

And it didn't happen.

Suddenly, everything is brighter.

'I should go and find my friends,' I say, eventually.

Gabe squeezes my hand. 'I don't know what you're doing here, or how you found me, Alice. Maybe you're an angel, a figment of my imagination.'

'I'm real. All five foot five of me. Angels don't order chocolate brownies.'

Gabe laughs. 'I think you've done your work on earth here tonight, Alice. Time for you to enjoy the *Correfoc*. You've earned it.'

45

Barcelona's air reeks of gunpowder, and the whole population of the city seems to be packed into a single road. By the time I reach Via Laietana, I can only move when the rest of the crowd does too. I don't feel like an individual anymore. I'm part of something bigger.

It's about fifty per cent terrifying and fifty per cent exhilarating. For the first time I'm excited about the fiesta. What happened with Gabe took me to the edge. I was so frightened history would repeat itself, but now my body is flooded with hope. Tonight feels lucky. And in a couple of hours I might finally find the evidence that could lead me to my sister's murderer, thanks to Zoe.

So maybe I can enjoy this fire run for what it is – a celebration of light.

The grand buildings on either side have clusters of people at almost every window, on the balconies, or even perched (just) on narrow stonework ledges.

The firecrackers sound more distant; we're packed in too tightly for anyone to let them off in the crowd.

Despite everything Zoe said, I hadn't imagined it'd be on this scale. The little kids have the best positions on the shoulders of dads or granddads. Many wear scarves around their faces, like junior bank robbers. A few have full-face screens, like bee-keepers wear masks, with fireproof fabric strips hanging down to protect their hair.

I've stopped shivering and started sweating as I try to make it towards the Metro – that's where Lewis and the others are, according to the text he sent. It's only a few hundred metres but it could take me an hour at this rate. And the fiesta is due to begin any minute now. Even if I didn't know the time, I'd know from the excited faces of the kids that the world is about to explode into flames.

The chatter is almost deafening. I hear Spanish but also German, Chinese, French. And English? It might be Cara and the others, but I can't see anything except the M for Metro sign above the crowd. I try to head towards it.

The lines along the street are already three or four people deep. And on a wide road that must be at least as long and grand as Oxford Street, that's one hell of a gathering.

Then I see him.

'Lewis!'

He's crouching on top of a phone box, along with three more guys with cameras. There's not really room for *any* of them, but they've taken a corner each.

'LEWIS!'

He hears me, but doesn't see me, even though he's scanning the crowd. I try to wave but there isn't room for me to raise my arms. Right now he's like a lighthouse in the sea of people. The angles of his face are lit by the street lights, and his hair has been styled upwards by the breeze so it looks even wilder than usual.

Lewis is one of a kind.

'Alice!' He sees me at last and grins and waves so hard he almost loses his balance on the edge of the box. He grins even wider, laughing at his own near miss.

I don't know what I'd do without him.

Gradually, I manage to move towards the box and he points just beyond it.

Someone grabs my arm suddenly. It's Cara.

'Hey, mystery girl. Where did you get to? We thought you were going to miss it!'

She's wearing Ade's thick blue shirt now, thank goodness. Her legs are still bare from the knees downwards but at least her top half's covered. That was the only thing about the fiesta that was really worrying me, but now I know she'll be OK. She's too close to Ade, but in this crowd, I guess you could just think they were being pushed together by accident.

At first I can't see the other two, but then I spot Sahara skulking next to the wall of a bank, her shoulders hunched over as though the fire's already started and she's trying to protect herself. Her hair hangs in damp strands against her face. I head towards her and when she sees me, she manages a wan smile.

'Thank God you're here, Alice. I thought we'd lost you.'

I can smell her sweat above the musky perfume she wears. The two together make her smell more animal than human.

'No. I just felt the need to be alone for a little while,' I lie. 'Why don't you come a bit closer? I'll help you get out of the way later if it gets too much.'

Sahara doesn't answer but she lets me pull her towards the edge of the parade. When Ade sees her, his face is blank: no pleasure at seeing his girlfriend, and no greeting. He lets go of Cara's hand so suddenly that her arm drops to her side, and she jumps. But then Cara notices Sahara too and I see she understands.

'Where's Zoe?' I ask Sahara.

'Gone to fetch water, I think.'

'I can do better than that.' Ade reaches into his messenger bag and brings out cans of beer he bought earlier, and I hold one up against my forehead. It cools me down straight away.

Everyone's facing the top of the street now. It slopes upwards so we can't really see where it ends.

'Can you hear it?' Cara calls out. 'I think I can hear it beginning.'

'Not yet,' says a voice.

I turn round to see Zoe, holding a thin blue carrier bag with water bottles in it. She pushes back her glove to check her watch. 'The procession starts at the very top of the street in about forty-five seconds' time. It's led by locals from *Correfoc* groups. They make costumes, play the drums. Like Morris dancers on acid.'

Lewis smiles. 'So what do *we* do?'

'Yeah, what happens next?' Cara asks, and this time, Zoe hears the question.

'Run with the dragons and the devils,' she says. 'Try not to get burned.'

'We can just watch them, right?' Sahara asks. 'I hate it when my hair smells of smoke.'

The look Zoe gives her could shatter glass. 'That's pretty much the whole point, Sahara. It's not just smoke. You'll stink of fireworks, too, by the time it's over. And maybe burned flesh.' Now she's staring at Cara's exposed legs. 'The tourists are the worst. They get drunk, then don't realise how badly they've been singed until they wake up next morning covered in blisters.'

'I'm mainly covered up now,' Cara insists.

Sahara shakes her head. 'Cara's not going anywhere near the actual fire. Nor Alice. We promised your parents we'd act in *loco parentis*.' She scowls at Ade. Maybe she's hoping to make Cara sound like a little kid, to put him off.

It's a bit late for that ...

We hear what sounds like thunder in the distance.

'Is that kick-off?' Ade calls out.

Zoe shakes her head. 'Soon. Very soon.'

'LEWIS?' Ade calls up. 'You coming down and into the fray with me? I reckon it's going to be men-only in there.'

'Official photographer, mate. I'm not losing my place,' Lewis tells him.

Cara nudges me and points at where Lewis is gripping the

side of the phone box. 'Nice muscle definition in those arms. I'd say Professor Geek's been working out. Maybe he's trying to impress someone?'

I pretend not to hear.

'The Metro is a good meeting place, if we lose each other,' Zoe says, though I suspect losing us wouldn't be much of a blow to her. 'Now, anyone who's coming in, it's definitely time to get into position.'

I grab her sleeve. 'As soon as this is over, we go to your flat, right?'

She nods. 'I can show you everything I've discovered ...' She hesitates, then leans in closer, 'Wish I'd done it sooner. You were right. We can work faster, the two of us together.'

'We'll get there, Zoe. You've been doing this on your own for too long.'

She smiles at me, the first genuine smile I think I've ever seen on her face. 'Already it feels less of a burden. And safer, even. Sorry I've been such a stubborn cow.'

I'm about to reply but the noises are getting louder: a constant low rumble, together with explosions and screams. So I squeeze her hand instead.

I can't really see what's happening at the start of the procession – too many people in woolly hats and bandannas in my way. Then there's a huge cheer and as I crane my neck to my right, the crowd is silhouetted against a supernatural white glow.

There's nothing supernatural about the smell. Is it gunpowder?

Sahara's eyes are wide now, and she's backing away, pulling the balaclava out of her pocket and squeezing it down over her face. Ade looks almost amused at how ridiculous she looks. He pulls a scarf out of his messenger bag, and a pair of sunglasses, and Zoe repositions *her* scarf so it covers her nose and mouth. Her eyes flash when a firecracker explodes nearby.

'Wish us luck,' Ade says to Cara. I'm still standing next to her, so I see him use the cover of the crowd to reach out and squeeze her waist. It could be nothing more than a friendly gesture, except his hand stays there *just* too long.

Despite the racket, I hear her sigh with pleasure. But she does stay back from the crowd, at least. For once, my best friend seems to have her sensible head on.

There's a new sound coming towards us: drumming. While the firecrackers whine and bang chaotically, the drum beat is rhythmic. Despite the fancy buildings, and the familiar brands being advertised on the store fronts, this feels like a primitive place now.

Then I see the Devil for the first time.

Or *a* devil; there's more than one. Hundreds of them, in fact – a Satanic procession stretching a mile or more up the road. But this devil, my first, ticks all the boxes: red face, black-rimmed eyes, horns growing out of his head and a knife-sharp metal trident that shoots sparks in every direction.

People jump into his path, shrieking with delight or fear or both. I'm just far enough back to feel safe, but I can see his face. He's smiling and I realise that I'm less afraid; he's having too much of a good time to look truly satanic. He's loving the dance, and the crowd is loving him back, as he growls and leaps at them, waving the trident as it lights up in flames. Even the little girl in front of me on her dad's shoulders is reaching out towards him. Well, perhaps they're related; she has her own pair of knitted horns on her head.

It's magnetic. The crazy energy draws me in. On Lewis's phone box, another photographer is climbing up, even though there is no room left on top. They sway like drunks, but two of the guys reach down to pull him up. For a moment, it looks as though they're going to fall off. I hold my breath.

Somehow they manage to stay upright, grabbing each other and twisting and turning.

Ade and Zoe are lost somewhere in this wild crowd, running with the demons and the beasts. Cara's some way ahead of me, too. I can just see her dyed white hair. To my surprise, Sahara's at my side, pushing forward as though she can't help herself.

'That was close. Lewis almost fell off the kiosk, did you see?'

She gives me an odd look. 'It was like they were *dancing*, wasn't it, Alice?' Her voice is muffled by the balaclava.

'Dancing?' I ask, momentarily baffled.

Sahara moves the fabric up off her face. 'Like the tango dancers in the park. Clinging onto each other as though their lives depended on it. Which, in this case, they sort of did.'

'Ah, I see what you ...' and then I realise what she's said. 'The dancers?'

'Don't tell me you didn't see them, Alice,' She's staring at me.

'Who?' Does she mean Ade and Cara?

'The dancers. They were so ... *passionate. Fiery!*'

Oh, God. What if she *did* see them? I can't ask without giving away what I saw myself. Though surely if she did see her boyfriend kissing another girl, she would have confronted him. No one would be able to keep that to themselves, would they? Unless they were planning to get their own back some other way!

Before I can work out what to say, the crowd surges forward. A dragon larger than a racehorse moves towards us, its head tossing and turning, firecrackers bursting from its nose and mouth.

I look for Cara's white hair. She wasn't that far ahead – and I should warn her to be careful. Sahara might not mean what I think she means, but it's better to be safe than sorry.

I can't see my best mate anymore.

'Cara? CARA!'

But it's hopeless. The explosions are too loud for her to hear me, and, even if they weren't, I *know* my best friend too well. I bet she's gone into the fire with Ade. She can't help herself.

46

I try to stay calm. If I can't find Cara, at least I can stay glued to Sahara. No harm done . . .

But when I spin round again, there's no one there. I stare at the bank, but all I can see is a pane of glass reflecting the explosions back at me. The air is foggy with smoke, and firecrackers flash continuously as though press photographers are capturing a movie premiere.

Or the scene of a disaster.

I try not to panic, to think logically. I lost sight of Sahara when we surged forward, but that doesn't mean she's gone after Cara. We've just been separated by the crowd. In a few seconds, there'll be another wave of people and we'll be washed up together again. Human flotsam and jetsam. That's all.

So why can't I breathe? My dark thoughts are as relentless as the drum beats . . .

Sahara argued with my sister just before they died.

Sahara told everyone Tim killed her.

Sahara is the one who keeps insisting she was closer to Meggie than anyone.

Sahara would never let Ade go without a fight.

The smell – no, it's more the *taste* – of gunpowder fills my mouth. I look up at the phone box, try to shout out to Lewis, but he can't hear me, even though he's only metres away. I wave, but he's too busy focusing his stupid phone camera on the action below.

If Sahara was my sister's killer, then she knows she's got

away with it once. Maybe twice, if she killed Tim, too. *What's to stop her doing it a third time?* There's no stronger motive than betrayal.

Thump, thump, thump. Twenty teenagers dressed in red costumes are marking the beat on drums and cymbals, the sound reverberating inside my head. It's so loud it hurts, but I know I must push closer, further forward. A curtain of sparks cascades in front of the drummers. More dragons and devils fill every space.

But there's no Cara. And no Sahara either.

The paraders seem to have an instinctive understanding of how far to go with their torches and their firecrackers. But Sahara was scared of it all. So she can have gone into the parade for one reason and one reason only.

To harm Cara.

Suddenly I am *certain* she saw my friend kissing her boyfriend. And I'm even more certain that the only reason Sahara has kept it to herself is to buy herself time to take revenge.

All it would take would be a blow from one of those tridents, or a firework thrown towards Cara on purpose, and . . .

I'm the only one who can stop this.

I push forward again. There's a clear line between the runners and the spectators. I'm terrified of crossing that line. But Cara's my best friend. She's stuck by me through the highs and lows. I have to do the same for her. I pull my jacket round me, turn the collar up to protect my neck, and launch myself towards the fire.

People spin round as they sense me pushing through, their faces full of suspicion. Perhaps they think I'm trying to steal their wallets. I try to smile. 'Sorry. Sorry.'

Just one more row of people . . .

Now I'm right in the thick of it.

I freeze as everyone dances around me. It's like being

the only sober person at a party, except it's not booze that's intoxicating, it's *fire*.

The drummers pass by, but what's approaching is scarier: an even bigger dragon is bearing down on us. On *me*. I turn away, as the catapults attached to its body send flames hurtling into the air and then sizzling down on top of us.

The dragon seems to be floating above the road, moving of its own accord, but then I notice that there are more devils, using handles to carry it along. They're reloading the bangers as soon as they run out.

'No *PASA! NO PASA!*' the people alongside me have started to chant at the dragon. They sound so angry, though I see delight in their faces. Even as I back away, they sprint towards the dragon, crouching down to attack it from below. But the creature keeps moving, and they keep shouting, and another shower of sparks heads towards me.

It's too fast. I have nowhere to run. I crouch over. Put my hands over my head. Close my eyes. Wait.

The embers hiss as they hit me. I feel nothing for a split second, but then it stings like acid, not just on my hands, but also on my back, despite my clothes. I open my eyes, but the dragon's so close that the lights blind me temporarily. The crackers whizz over my head, louder than an aircraft engine, and I wonder if my eardrums will burst.

'No *PASA!*'

There are loud screams and laughter as the bandits make a last attempt to stop the dragon in its tracks, but the beast is fearless, crashing past. I'm being swept along by the group in its wake.

But it's helping me to move much, much faster than I was. The momentum of the crowd is impossible to resist. We surge forwards in time to the bangs and crashes, like a dangerously fast pulse.

I *must* be gaining on the others now.

Where are you, Cara?

A white hot flash explodes above me, and I can't tell if I've closed my eyes or if the light has blinded me.

Gradually, shapes form again. I look for my best friend, but all I see are more beasts, and manic grins from the few participants who haven't covered their faces. There's one tourist next to me wearing the thinnest cotton shirt, with nothing over his balding head. Already there are burns on his scalp, like pink confetti, but he doesn't seem to have noticed.

As he turns, I smell alcohol: could his breath catch fire, like a dragon's? He tries to take my hands, to dance with me, but I barge past.

I'm looking for Cara in Ade's shirt, or for the black balaclava covering Sahara's face. If I can only find one of them, everything will be OK.

The drumming continues, as though the group wants to exorcise its demons. Or summon them up. The constant bombardment has made the air stink of sulphur and flames. Is this what hell smells like?

Hell?

I'm on a shopping street in a modern city. Ninety-nine per cent of me is sure I'm imagining things. But one per cent ...

When I look to the right, up the centre of the road, all I can see is red and black and orange. Fire colours. What about the lime green of Zoe's head scarf, the pale blue of Ade's shirt, the bright white of Cara's hair?

Please let her be safe. This is *my* fault. If she'd never met Ade, she wouldn't be here. And she'd never have met Ade if it wasn't for me.

'Ali! ALI!'

Am I hearing things? Or is that Cara, calling?

I turn towards the voice, but someone laughs loudly, right in my ear, and I can't hear Cara anymore.

I've come a long way, but when I turn back I can still just

about see the yellow phone kiosk sticking up above the crowd.

Except maybe I'm wrong. Because though the other photographers are twisting around each other to get a shot, there's no sign of Lewis.

I don't have the energy to fight against the crowd anymore. My ears are ringing from the firecrackers and my throat is sore and dry from the smoke. *Where is everyone?* We're moving faster now, sweeping down towards the end of the road, and the harbour beyond.

I try to think rationally. Cara's probably with Ade, snogging in some dark alley. And Sahara's probably gone back towards the hostel, because she's realised this is *so* not her scene.

And she never saw her boyfriend kissing my best mate at all.

I relax and allow the crowd to carry me along. Once this is over, we'll meet back at the Metro station, just like Zoe said, have a drink, a few tapas, and Cara will tell everyone at school about it. 'Yeah. It was a riot,' I'll say. 'Barcelona is full of pyromaniacs. One of the maddest nights of my life.'

Finally, the crush is easing off. There are fewer people ahead, and there aren't as many bangs and flashes. It's as though a sudden cool rain shower has snuffed them out.

Yet it isn't raining. It's still midsummer hot.

A horrible, familiar feeling is overwhelming me, darker and stronger than ever before. The lights are dimming, one by one, till all that's left is night and death and *absence*.

Then the screaming begins.

47

At first it's a single voice – a girl's.

It's horribly familiar.

Cara!

The scream is so piercing, I'm surprised all the windows in the street aren't shattering, sending shards of glass raining down onto our heads.

I push forward towards the scream. I wish I could move faster, but terror is forcing the air out of my lungs, slowing me down.

Another surge of the crowd pushes me the right way. Now, more people are wailing like banshees.

'CARA! Cara, I'm coming!'

Apart from the screaming, the sounds of the fiesta have been silenced. The drumming has stopped, and the fire-crackers too. What am I going to see? Has her hair caught fire? Or could she have been blinded?

'Cara?' I call out, but there's no answer.

'Lewis? Ade? Is anyone here?' I push through, with elbows, knees, head. 'Let me through. Let me through.'

It's not Spanish, but people understand me. They're shouting in a dozen different languages.

'Help her,' a man calls out in English. 'Do *something*.'

'I'm coming, Cara,' I call out.

Am I already too late? The girl's screams have stopped now.

And then the final row of people melts away. There's a tiny figure on the ground.

It's not Cara.

The girl's legs are covered, and she's not wearing Ade's blue shirt.

Definitely not Cara. Thank God.

Then I realise the figure is wrapped in a blanket.

I crouch down, next to a paramedic in a fluorescent jacket, who is shouting into a radio.

'Shit. What's going on, Alice?'

I swing round to see Cara next to me. 'Oh, Jesus, Cara.' I reach up and grab her hand. 'I thought it was you. Where the hell have you been?'

Behind her, Ade appears. For one paranoid moment, I think that they've played some practical joke on me. *Correfoc* hide and seek.

There's a whimper from the person on the ground. And then I *know* why the first voice I heard, the girl screaming, was so familiar.

'Zoe?'

I lean forward and the first aider tries to shield his patient, but not before I catch a glimpse of lime green fabric pulled across her face like a veil.

Oh, God.

Enough of the scarf is still wrapped around her scalp, and I think that at least no one else has seen that she's lost her hair. She'll be relieved about that when she comes round. She fought so hard to keep it a secret.

There's a raw red mark across her right cheek. Her eyes are closed, and the sockets look deeper in the torchlight, as though she's already a skeleton.

'Zoe.' I reach out for her hand, which is lifeless. 'Zoe, what happened? It's me. It's Alice.'

'*Dejala!*' the first aider says. 'Leave her!'

'This is my friend,' I say. 'Please.'

Maybe the first aider recognises the desperation in my voice, because he stops shouting.

'Zoe, what happened to you?'

Her eyelids flicker.

'If you can hear me, Zoe, I need to know if this was an accident, or ...' I'm aware of the others right behind me, so I whisper, 'or if someone *did* this to you.'

Her lips move.

Unless it's a trick of the firelight.

'Try again,' I whisper.

'*Tim.*'

'Tim? But he's dead, Zoe. Tim is dead.'

Her lips purse but nothing comes out this time. Then I'm being pulled away and I realise Ade is behind me when he takes my arm to steady me.

Two paramedics are moving in to treat Zoe. I want to explain but I don't have the words. Lewis could probably manage the odd phrase ...

Lewis! Where is he? And Sahara's missing too.

A siren's getting louder, *closer*. Ade steps forward, but a policeman pushes him back, and it's obvious the officer means business. He's on his radio, and I hear *Ingles*. Maybe they're calling for someone to translate.

'Our friend. Our ... *amigo*,' I say, not knowing if that's the right word or not. 'This is our friend.'

But the circle of emergency staff around Zoe is getting bigger, and I can't see her at all anymore.

None of this seems real. Less than an hour ago, everything felt alive, electric, full of hope. Javier's family were safe, Gabe knew he'd made a difference, and I was almost allowing myself to hope that I could be closing in on my sister's killer.

But now I'm lower than ever.

'What the hell happened?' Ade asks.

'You should know. She went into the fiesta at the same time as you!' I tell him.

'No.' He shakes his head and I see the briefest glimpse of

guilt on his face and I know, then, that he was with Cara, and that they were oblivious to everything but each other.

'What's going on?' It's Sahara, pushing forwards and ripping off her balaclava. Her hair is messy, but she looks calmer than she has done all trip.

'It's Zoe,' I say. 'She's hurt. They're treating her, but ...'

Sahara opens her mouth and I wait for a scream. Instead, she takes a gulp of air, and then another, and begins to fall towards us.

Ade catches her effortlessly, as though it's something he does all the time. And as he pulls her back, the police begin to clear a path so the paramedics can bring Zoe through.

48

Everything seems out of sync and blurry, like a pirate DVD of real life.

Zoe's stretchered away before we can explain to the police that she's with us. We finally find an officer with good English. He arranges for us to be taken to the hospital but, once we get there, no one will talk to us because we're not blood relatives. We're in the dark; we don't know what's wrong with her, or how serious it is, or even exactly where we are, except that we can see the sea from the hospital entrance.

Plus, there's still no sign of Lewis, the only one of us with enough Spanish to talk to the doctors. I've texted him twice but he hasn't answered. I try not to think about the tension between him and Zoe, because that has nothing to do with this. *Does it?*

Tim, she said.

Or was it *him?*

I try to picture the shape her lips made when she tried to speak. But all I can remember is that red slash mark across her face, and the limpness of her body.

Is the killer with me right now?

Sahara's face is colourless, as though she could faint again at any minute. 'How much longer?'

There's no one to ask. The hospital is clean and new and almost empty. No one else seems to have been seriously injured. I guess the locals know how to stay safe.

I stand up. God knows what the police made of us: me and

Ade in our multi-layered *Correfoc* clothes, Sahara dressed like a bank robber, Cara like a sweaty clubber.

'Was she *burned*?' Cara asks.

'I told you, it was difficult to be sure.' I close my eyes. 'But part of her face was red raw. And I could *smell* burning. I thought it was the fireworks, but perhaps that's how *skin* smells when . . .' I feel too nauseous to continue.

'But she was so well wrapped up.' Cara looks down at the bare skin of her own shin: there are a few tiny spots the colour of ripe cherries. She rubs it. 'Ouch.'

Sahara leans over. 'That's what happens when you play with fire.'

'I'm fine,' Cara says. 'And before you have a go at me, look at goody-goody Alice?' She pulls at my jacket and when I look down at my sleeve, I see there are two, three . . . no, at least *ten* little scorches in the fabric.

I remember the first shower of sparks to hit me. 'It was an old jacket.' I could tell her I only went into the fire to protect her, but what's the use?

'But what about your hair?'

I bring my hand up to my head. Cara steps forward, and touches my scalp behind my left ear.

'Ow!'

'It's burned all the way through to the scalp,' she says.

I touch the same place and there's a sore spot the size of a five pence coin. 'I hadn't even realised.'

Cara looks more shocked by that than by anything else that's happened. She tenderly pulls strands of hair from elsewhere to cover the spot. 'It won't show, Alice.'

'Of course, we don't know if she was trampled as well as burned,' Sahara says.

Cara and I gawp at her.

Even Ade, who hasn't spoken since we got here, shakes his head. 'Sahara. The more you speculate, the worse it seems.'

She stands up. 'Well, what are we supposed to do while we wait? There's not even any guarantee they'll let us—'

I see him first. 'Lewis!'

He's running through the hospital doors, towards us. He stares at each of us, as though he's taking a register. 'Zoe? It's Zoe, isn't it?'

I nod.

'What's happened to her?' Lewis demands.

'We don't know yet,' Sahara says. 'You have to try to talk to them. Your Spanish is better than ours.'

He shakes his head. 'If I'm the best we've got, we really are in trouble, but I'll try. Where are the doctors?'

'I'll show you.' I walk with him towards reception. 'Where've you been, Lewis?' I hiss, once we're out of earshot of the others.

'Looking for you lot.'

'Couldn't you see what happened, from up there on the phone box?'

'Don't be ridiculous, Ali. If I'd seen her burning, I'd have helped, wouldn't I?'

'Burning?'

'Or whatever has happened to her.' He turns his back on me and says something to the woman behind the desk, who looks relieved that at last there's someone who might be talking sense. I catch the odd familiar word, and realise she probably can speak English after all, but didn't trust the rest of us.

But that's not the thing that's confusing me right now. *Burning*. How would he know?

'They'll send someone out to see us as soon as they can,' Lewis says.

I look at the floor, instead of at him. Of course it's natural to assume that she's been burned under the circumstances ... and yet he sounded so certain.

261

'You just said you'd have helped if you'd seen her burning. Did you get to talk to her somehow? Did she tell you she was burned? Are you sure you didn't see something?'

His eyes narrow. 'I don't think this is the time for twenty bloody questions, Alice. I assumed she'd been burned, because that's what's most likely to have happened to her in that madness. Plus, it's what people in the crowd told me when I was trying to find you all. They mentioned an English girl being burned and . . .' he hesitates. 'Actually, if you must know, I was terrified it might be you.'

'Oh. Well, I'm fine.'

Lewis sighs. 'I couldn't have lived with myself. I mean . . . I don't know why, but I feel responsible for you.'

'You don't have to. I'm seventeen.'

He laughs strangely. 'Right. Seventeen. Silly me for not realising that makes you indestructible. Anyway, I'm relieved, OK? Not glad about Zoe, but happy you're all right.'

'My anorak's not in the best shape,' I say, pointing at my sleeve.

'I'll buy you a new one. So, what do we know about Zoe?'

I shrug. 'No one is telling us much. I saw her on the ground but I don't know how she got there.'

'Did you speak to her?'

'No,' I lie. 'She was unconscious.'

'Shit.'

We go back to the others.

'I've spoken to a nurse. They'll come and explain soon,' Lewis tells them.

Weird how his presence calms everyone, as though our parents have turned up in the middle of a nightmare, and tucked us back into bed with a glass of hot milk, and told us everything's going to be all right.

Except it's not all right, is it? Zoe's unconscious, and we

don't know what she knows, and I don't know what to believe, or who to trust. Which means I can trust no one.

Almost an hour passes before a doctor appears. He looks younger than me.

'Sorry I could not come earlier, but we were busy with other cases.' His accent is Spanish-American. Maybe he learned English from TV shows. It makes the whole thing feel even more unreal, like being in an episode of *House*.

'How is she?' Sahara and I speak at once.

'None of you are related to her, right?' says the doctor.

'We're friends – the closest she has here,' Sahara says, slightly stroppily.

'As her friends, if there is anything more you can do to contact her family, it would be helpful. It is a matter of urgency.'

'It's that serious?' Lewis asks.

The doctor slumps down into the chair opposite us, with a sigh like an old man's. 'She is stabilised. There is a limit to what I can say, also because the *Mossos* – the police – will want to talk to you. Such an event is very rare here. And, almost without exception, any major injuries at a *Correfoc* involve a tourist.'

'She *lived* here,' I say, feeling the need to defend her. 'She was the one warning *us* that we had to dress up properly before going anywhere near the flames.'

'The flames were not her problem. Aside from a few superficial burns, she was not injured by the fireworks.'

'Has she said how it happened?' Lewis asks.

The doctor hesitates. 'No. It seems probable that she tripped and then was ... trampled by the crowd. Perhaps they did not see her immediately. This would be the most likely cause of the head injuries which are causing us the most concern.'

Lewis frowns. 'She hasn't woken up yet?'

'We are sedating her to keep her unconscious – in a controlled way – while we assess the options and any potential damage.'

Damage. He means *brain* damage.

'No!' I exclaim before I can stop myself.

She can't be. Not Zoe. She kept everything in her head – so many secrets and fears. If her brain is damaged, then the real Zoe will be lost and with her, my best hope of finding out who killed Meggie.

Which, now I come to think of it, must have been exactly what the killer intended.

A soldier would call it collateral damage.

Unfortunate, but inevitable against the backdrop of a wider campaign.

Zoe is tougher than I thought. But then the human body does fight to survive, long after one would assume it would be defeated. Under the circumstances, one has to hope that the mind is less resilient.

There was no time for reflection or certainty, no private moment. Dragons and devils. What a cliché! But she was never the target, whatever she might have believed.

Surely, now, Alice, you realise what you are up against. You are an inspiration, but that does not make you untouchable.

49

The police give nothing away. They take our details and tell us they'll come to the hostel first thing tomorrow to question us. They talk very slowly, and I can tell they think we're idiots.

I don't think it's even crossed their minds that one of us could be a killer.

As we head back towards the beach, there's still a party on the shore. People are laughing and jumping around in the warm waves, not drunk, but exhilarated by the fire run.

No one speaks. Maybe everyone is planning what they'll tell the police. Their 'version of events'. How many of us are planning to lie?

Cara didn't attack Zoe, I am sure of that. But it's not in her interests to tell the truth if she was with Ade during the *Correfoc*.

Sahara seems to be in shock. But she could be pretending. If she was the one who killed my sister, then perhaps she realised Zoe was about to tell me everything she knew. That might have been enough to push her into a third attack.

And then there's Ade: what if he knows Sahara's secrets, or has secrets of his own to protect?

Which only leaves Lewis. My friend. No. My *ally*. Yet I wonder if I can even trust him. The way he turned up at the airport seems a little weird. And is it natural that he was almost as obsessed by Burning Truths as I was?

I try not to let what's happened drive me mad. But here, in the dark, the doubts keep coming, like a shower of firecrackers burning in my head.

We're back by the hostel.

'I am so exhausted,' Sahara says. 'It's the stress.'

Ade nods. Even Cara's yawning.

'I don't know how you can even think about sleeping,' I say, not caring how snappy I sound. 'Not with all that's happened.'

'I'm the same,' Lewis says. 'If you don't think you'll sleep, you can come back to the hotel. There's a mini bar. TV. We might feel better, being together.'

It seems a weird thing to suggest. But then I look at his face. The way he's staring at me, I realise he's trying to tell me something.

Ade shakes his head. 'I'm not in the mood for drinking anymore. It doesn't feel right.'

Sahara grips his hand. 'Exactly.'

'Maybe I have had too much already,' Cara says.

I *want* to go. But should I leave Cara on her own with Sahara and Ade? Except the police are coming in just a few hours – even a truly desperate killer wouldn't risk another attack now.

'It might help, you know, Alice,' Lewis says, 'to talk about what happened.'

Not just to talk, but to plan our next move. This could be our last chance to get answers in Barcelona. 'All right. I'll come back later, if I do get tired. Or definitely in time for when the police come in the morning.'

Sahara and Ade kiss me goodnight, and Cara hugs me tightly. For once she doesn't make any joke about me going off on my own with Lewis.

The two of us walk towards his hotel, but after a few steps, I stop.

'You've got a plan, haven't you?' I say.

'I think we should go to Zoe's flat and get whatever it was she was going to show you.'

267

'You don't think she fell, do you, Lewis?'

'Do *you*, Ali?'

'I can't bear to think that I was only metres away when she was attacked.'

Lewis nods. 'So you *do* think she was attacked.'

'What other explanation is there?'

'That's why we need to go to the flat. Not just because it could help you find information, but because it could help her too. You saw what the police were like. They want to keep this quiet. Pissed tourist falls over. End of story. We're the only ones who care enough to find out what really happened.'

He seems so certain, even though the idea of going through her things makes me feel sick. Of all people, Zoe valued her privacy.

Valued? Why am I thinking about her in the past tense? She's still alive. And maybe there is some clue in the flat that might tell us more about why she's fighting for her life in hospital right now.

'OK. Let's do it.'

Our walk takes us back down the bottom of Via Laietana. It's only a couple of hours since the procession, but everything is normal again. The thousands of spent firecrackers have been cleared up, the barriers and ambulances moved away. The only evidence that any of it happened is the occasional waft of gunpowder, and the odd group of revellers marching down the street, still dressed in their red cloaks and satanic horns.

I can't bear to see where it happened. It makes it worse, somehow, that the signs of what happened to Zoe have been cleaned up so fast. Like erasing a shameful secret from history.

Lewis says nothing, but he takes my hand and holds it firmly. I realise I'm cold again, and his hand warms me up.

We head down cobbled streets, through mazes of alleyways.

He checks the map on his phone: Zoe had given us her address for emergencies and this definitely counts as one. 'Not far now.'

I follow behind him on the pavement, because it's not wide enough for both of us.

'Am I going too fast?' Lewis waits for me. He points down an alleyway where two middle-aged women in very short skirts are leaning against the wall, smoking. 'This is definitely the livelier bit of town.'

'Prostitutes?' I ask.

'Well, it's a funny time of night to admire the view.'

'What great places you take me to,' I say with a half-hearted smile.

'Travel broadens the mind, Ali.'

'But why would Zoe want to live *here*?'

'It's cheap. And real. She was studying digital documentary at uni, wasn't she?'

'Was she?' I realise that I never asked what she did before she dropped out of college.

'Plenty to snap around here,' Lewis says.

He's right. We pass Chinese shops, Polish shops, halal butchers, and stores with signs in lettering that I don't even recognise.

'OK. Here we are,' he says, stopping abruptly by an unlit glass doorway. 'Act normal, right?'

Normal? I don't know if I can remember what that's like. He pushes at the door, which rattles but doesn't open.

My heart's racing. 'Don't you have an app for burglary, Lewis?'

He smiles at me. 'When it comes to breaking into buildings,' he says, taking out a credit card and slipping it into the gap between the door and the frame, 'you just need a little finesse.'

I stare at the open door, not quite believing what he's just done.

'Come on, Ali. Unless you want us to get caught.'

Lewis pulls me into the hallway and uses his phone as a torch, checking the metal mailboxes on the wall. 'Gonzales ... Perrera ... Bingo!'

He reaches into the gap where the post goes, and pulls something out. As we tiptoe up the stone steps, a cockroach scuttles out of our way. There's a ringing in my ears from all the fireworks. Or maybe it's fear.

The stairs are steep and worn with age. I hold on to the banister but parts of it are missing, and there's a slightly rotten smell.

'Almost there. The mailbox says she's got flat four. So the next landing should be her place.' Lewis sounds short of breath. He climbs the last steps, then stops. The apartment door is the same dirty-brown colour as the others, but this is the only one with a spy hole at eye level.

'Lewis, we're never going to get in there. We should go before the neighbours hear.'

'Don't be so defeatist,' he says, and I hear a click, and then the door opens with a whiny squeak. 'Open sesame.'

He pulls me inside and closes the door before switching on the light. 'I'd like to pretend I'm some kind of lock-breaking guru,' he explains, 'but actually, she kept a spare key in the letterbox.' He holds it up.

'How did you know?'

'Lucky guess.'

'But she was so security conscious.'

Lewis nods. 'Yeah, but she'd also only just moved here. And she's not the type to trust people straight away. So she'd have had no one to call if she got locked out.'

My eyes adjust to the light. 'God, what a mess.'

The room is tiny, and both the floor space and the sofa bed

are piled high with paperwork, newspapers and files. The only order is on a small table at the end of the bed, where two laptops sit next to each other. Their power buttons glow orange.

'Not exactly a room with a view, is it?' Lewis says.

There *is* a window, no bigger than an A4 pad, but when I lift the blind, there's a steep drop down to a yard where rubbish has collected. I turn back. Lewis is already switching on the laptops, rifling through the paperwork. I try to imagine Zoe on that bed, working on Burning Truths. I notice the inside of the door has three bolts on it.

'She was really scared, Lewis.' I point at the door.

'So we need to find out why. Keep looking, Ali.'

There's a clothes rail loaded with empty wire hangers that clank together as I brush past it. I open the fridge, but there's nothing inside except two bottles of water and some yogurt. Ahead of me, there's a plywood door, and when I open it, a damp, stale smell hits me.

'I've found the bathroom.'

Except there's no room for a bath, only a loo and directly above that, a showerhead. On the wall there's a mirrored cabinet. My own face reflected in it is unfamiliar, my eyes wide and wired.

And I look even more like Meggie.

I open the cabinet. There's a toothbrush and paste, sun cream, and several brown bottles and boxes labelled with Spanish text. Medicines. I grab them, and take them into Lewis. He's managed to get one of the laptops working, and has attached a memory stick. 'What do you think these are?' I ask.

He examines the boxes, scans their barcodes with his phone camera. Then tuts. 'Sleeping pills.' He takes a second packet. 'Sedatives. Blimey. This would knock out that mammoth in the park.'

'When did you go to the park?'

He shakes his head. 'Yesterday. I didn't spend the whole day with my brother geeks. I did do *some* sightseeing. Anyway, let's focus on what's important. If Zoe was taking even a quarter of this lot, I'm surprised she could remember her own name.'

'Sahara said she couldn't sleep properly; hadn't since Meggie died.'

'The date on these is really recent.' Lewis has opened the packets; more than half the pills are missing from each foil strip. 'You know, this could be another explanation for what happened tonight. If her reactions were slower, she might just have fallen and not been able to get up.'

'Are you saying you think it could have been an accident?'

Lewis sighs. 'No. It's just so shocking: Meggie, Tim, now Zoe.'

It's the first time I've ever seen him upset. But before I can say something, he turns back to the laptop screen. 'OK. Let's focus. What was Tim's second name again?'

'Ashley.'

'I'm downloading Zoe's emails onto the stick. And her internet activity too. But there's so much of it, I want to try to prioritise.' He types in Tim's name. Hundreds of emails pop up. None has a subject line but, as I lean forward, Lewis arranges them in date order. 'The last one was sent on the afternoon of the day Tim died.'

He opens it up.

Hey Zo,

   How's it going?

   Re. leaving, you should follow your heart, and if your heart says Spain, then go. Maybe you need sun, new horizons. Might help your hair, even. Though

**I love you just as much bald as hairy, you know
that.**

'Love? Did he *love* Zoe?'

Lewis shrugs. 'They just sound like mates to me.'

**Don't worry about me, please, Zo. I feel . . . Well,
maybe you won't believe me, but the last few days,
things feel more under control. Not good. Not like
they were when Meggie was alive, but, I dunno.
Like there might still be something to life after all.**
    Might be the daffodils coming out.
    **Re. the site, maybe you should leave it for a bit.
This is my thing. Mine to sort out. And I will sort it
out. But it might be better to wait for things to
settle. That's when the Person will relax. Make
mistakes.**

I read it again: it's exactly what I thought would happen
with the killer. Yet Tim is dead, and now Zoe's unconscious.
Maybe we were wrong.

**You sleeping any better? I've stopped drinking lately
and it's helped me loads. I'd say keep taking the
tablets, but I hate you having to be on them. Maybe
in Spain it'll be better?**
    Hasta la vista, Zo.
    Tim xx

Lewis sighs. 'Ade found him, what, six hours later?'

'And he'd been drinking, but here he says he'd stopped.
What would have made him start again that same day?'

'Unless he was lying to Zoe,' Lewis suggests.

'Why would he—' I stop. 'Did you hear something? Outside.'

'No,' Lewis says, but then his face changes. 'A siren?'

'I think so.'

'Ali, go and check while I finish this.'

I tiptoe out of the flat, into the stairwell. There's a window on the next half landing, facing the street. I have to crane my neck to look through it.

'Shit.' I backtrack, into the flat. 'It's the police. They must be coming here.' My voice is squeaky with fear.

Lewis blinks hard, but that's as near as he comes to showing panic. 'OK. We'll just go to the top of the stairwell. Hide till they're gone. They won't be long. They'll probably be looking for something to help find her parents.'

His hands don't even tremble as he pulls out the memory stick and closes the laptop lid. Then he reaches for the second laptop, the one he couldn't log into, and puts it and the power cable into his backpack.

'What are you doing, Lewis?'

He holds his finger against his lips. 'Shh.'

I follow him out of the flat and up the stairs, my own footsteps sounding as loud as a giant's. We keep climbing, even though I can't breathe.

Finally, just as we reach the top landing, I hear wood split and metal groan as Zoe's front door is forced.

'Now we wait,' says Lewis, as calmly as though we're waiting for a bus.

I have to clamp my jaw together with my hand to stop my teeth chattering.

The police stay less than twenty minutes though it feels like forever. Lewis and I don't speak, though he holds my hand and after a while it stops trembling.

Finally we hear voices in the stairwell – two men and a woman, I think. They're chatting, even laughing, as we hear drilling and clanking metallic sounds. Then the front door closes. Lewis helps me up. My foot's all pins and needles because I haven't moved a muscle while we've been wedged into the corner on the cold floor.

'Let's see what they've done,' he says.

When we get down to her landing, the door is bolted with a huge padlock and chain. We're not getting through there again. We head down the stairs and back through the front door, into the street, where traffic's still passing and the ladies of the night are still chain-smoking, as though nothing's changed.

'That padlock. That's because it's a crime scene, isn't it?' I whisper, once we've gone a whole block.

'You watch too much American telly, Alice Forster. It's because they forced the door, that's all.'

'How can you be so sure? Do you do this kind of thing regularly?'

'Clearly not.' And then he chuckles to himself.

'Why the hell is that funny, Lewis?'

'Because if I really was a career burglar, or spy, or whatever, I definitely wouldn't have broken in and left my bloody fingerprints all over the flat, would I?'

'What?'

'We should have worn gloves, Ali. But never mind, it's too late now and they've got no reason to dust her place for prints.'

As we walk back towards the sea, the moments in Zoe's flat seem completely unreal. So do Lewis's actions. He was so detached, like a burglar or something.

Except for that one moment when he had to admit that Zoe's death couldn't have been an accident.

'I think I should go back to the others,' I say, when we reach the point where we'd turn right for his hotel and left for the hostel. 'Thanks. Like always, I don't know what I'd do without you.'

'Life's never boring with you around, kid,' he says.

I frown.

Lewis hits himself on the forehead. 'Yeah. Mr Insensitive, that's me. But the truth is, Alice, I don't know Zoe. Obviously it's totally bloody awful that she's hurt, but if it's a choice between her being trampled or you, then ... I can't pretend I'm not thankful *you're* OK.'

50

Back in our room, no one is asleep, but we're pretending to be. And at least we're all here: Cara, Sahara, Ade. The way everything else is right now, that feels like something to be grateful for.

At about four in the morning, someone squeezes into my bunk with me.

'I had a bad dream,' Cara whispers. Her skin is damp and she smells of wood smoke. I guess we all must smell the same but it's more noticeable on someone else.

I cling on to her and she clings on to me. Her breathing slows and I catch another smell, of alcohol. A cocktail. Tequila sunrise?

And then I remember: *Javier*.

I freeze. If it's four here, then he may have left the Beach already. How could I have forgotten?

Except I know how I could have forgotten. What happened with Zoe was about the living. I can still have some influence there. What's happening to Javier between dusk and dawn is now beyond my control.

Rest in peace, Javier.

I close my eyes but the tears still escape, running down my cheeks and onto the sheet. I try to sob silently, so I don't wake Cara.

Somehow the night ends and daylight comes. The four of us sit on plastic chairs outside the hostel, waiting for the police to arrive. The beach is busy again, with smart pensioner couples taking the early sun, suave family men with immaculate wives and toddlers, the *chiringuito* owners opening up.

'It was very modern,' Cara says, when no one else seems to be able to find words. 'The hospital. The doctor seemed to know what he was doing. Maybe she's better off in that place than she would have been in a grotty old hospital at home.'

Except none of this would have happened at home.

The city is every bit as beautiful as it was yesterday, but my eyes are raw from crying and lack of sleep and I'm desperate to leave. Though even that's not logical, because if someone *did* attack Zoe, then it must have been one of the people coming home to London with me.

The police are excessively polite, the way teachers are when they secretly want to *scream* at you for driving them mad.

When they call out my name, I have to remind myself to breathe. A male and a female detective show me into a cramped office at the hostel. I'm the last one in.

'Were you drinking before you went to Via Laietana?' the woman asks. I think she's already decided the answer is yes.

'We went to a bar, but I didn't drink. The others had beers. Nothing stronger. And Zoe didn't drink anything there. She arrived late, so we went straight to the festival.'

The man looks sceptical. 'So you are telling us everyone was not drunk when they left the Irish bar?'

'I can't talk for the others, but I was definitely sober. I thought the fireworks would be a buzz ... exciting enough without having to have a drink. Zoe herself said it could be quite edgy.'

'It is perfectly safe,' the woman snaps back, 'or at least it is if you are raised with respect for fire.'

My hand goes up to the burned, raw patch on my scalp. 'I know. Zoe was very insistent about being sensible.'

She sighs. 'Your friends told me that Zoe was covered up.

Yet she has sustained an injury to her face. How would you explain that?'

'I *can't* explain that.'

'There must be a reason, if she wasn't drunk.'

'Look, I just want to go home.'

Except I know they won't let me go yet, will they? There's still Meggie to talk about. There's no way Sahara would have got through her interview without a long, emotional explanation of what we're doing here and how many tragedies have affected *her*.

Unless she kept her mouth shut because she has something to hide . . .

The two detectives exchange a glance. 'We have no reason to make you stay any longer,' says the man. He sounds as though he wishes he could lock us all up and throw away the key.

'I can go?'

'You have a flight this afternoon. You can take it, since none of you appears to have anything useful to tell us about the accident.'

'Incident,' the woman corrects him. But I can tell from their tone that they've already made a decision: drunken, drugged Brit falls over. End of story.

'And Zoe? How is she?'

'That is a matter for her next of kin. There is nothing more we are permitted to tell you.'

'But we can't just go home and leave her with no one to look after her.'

The woman stands up, opens the door to get rid of me. 'Her parents are flying in around now. It's up to them if they'll see you at the hospital. If I was them, I am not certain I would want a reminder of what happened to my daughter when her friends were not looking.'

*

The others have waited for me outside the office with our bags.

'We thought we'd go to the hospital before we head for the airport,' Cara says.

I'd hoped to go onto Soul Beach, to see if Javier has gone, to find out if anyone saw him leave. But it's too late to make a difference there.

Maybe it's too late for Zoe, too.

We're dodging bikes and skateboarders on the boardwalk, pulling our trolley cases behind us. It's hotter than yesterday and already the beach is packed. My skin seems to be burning and my luggage feels heavier, even though I haven't bothered with souvenirs. I don't need plastic castanets or Barcelona mugs to remember *every* detail.

I think of Javier, and Gabe, and there's a lump in my throat.

I'm walking slightly behind the others, watching them. Sahara keeps sighing, and I want to ask her outright: was this you? But I can't, and so with every step, I get angrier and angrier. Halfway along the shore, I realise I'm probably angriest with myself.

I let this happen.

Even if Zoe's parents are willing to let us see her, I'm not sure we deserve it.

'Keep up, Alice,' Cara slows down as we approach the hospital. She reaches for my hand. 'I know this is tough. Especially for you. But it's not our fault, is it? Accidents happen. When we get home, it'll all get back to normal.'

'Not for Zoe.'

'No. That's true. But you can't feel responsible for everyone and everything, hon.'

Except I do, because the rest of the world seems untrustworthy now. The detectives investigating Meggie's murder have two more deaths to answer for. They should have *made* Zoe talk to them, found the photos, searched her emails. It only took Lewis a few seconds to find the one that Tim sent on the day he died, the one where he told Zoe things were getting better.

At least I have Lewis. It's the geek and the teenager against the world. But we care. And maybe caring will be enough to help us succeed where the rest of the world has failed so far.

It's the least Meggie, Tim and Zoe deserve.

51

Lewis is already at the hospital. I hadn't expected him to be there.

'I got here first thing. In case. I'm the only one with any Spanish, after all.' He takes us up to the right floor in a lift. 'Her parents just got here. They're with her at the moment.'

'Have you spoken to them?' Sahara asks.

He shakes his head. 'Thought that could wait.'

'So how did you persuade the staff to tell you where she was?' I ask, when the lift stops and the others get out.

'I told them I was her cousin,' he says, and when I pull a face, he raises his eyebrows. 'You've taught me everything I know about making up stories to get what you want. Remember how you were Triti's *school friend*?'

'That was different.'

'If you say so.'

No one seems in the mood for conversation. I sit down opposite Lewis. Ade and Cara sit next to each other. Sahara paces.

What a mess.

After a few minutes, a couple step into the corridor from a side room. The man carries a holdall. He's tall and as pale as the white walls. She's plump and has bright red hair, but her jutting chin is identical to Zoe's.

Ade walks steadily towards them. They look up, faces frozen, expecting a doctor, perhaps.

'Mr and Mrs Tate, I'm Adrian. A college friend of Zoe's. We were all visiting her this weekend.' He waves at the rest of us, and we stand up, keeping a respectful distance. 'We're so sorry.'

Mr Tate shakes Ade's hand. Mrs Tate doesn't move.

'You were *there?*' Zoe's father asks, and I hear her voice in his. The same brusqueness.

'We didn't see it happen,' Ade says. 'There were a lot of people around and we all got separated and—'

'Not what I'd call friends, then, are you?' Zoe's mother snaps. 'Or maybe this is what counts as friendship these days.'

'Eve, please.' Zoe's father turns back, touches his wife's arm. 'They're not to blame.'

'Her *friends* should have stayed at her side. She's vulnerable.'

'Love, we let Zoe come here because we didn't want to wrap her up in cotton wool.'

'We should have done, though, shouldn't we?' his wife cries.

She looks at us properly for the first time, and her flat grey eyes accuse me. Why does she look so familiar? I've never met her before. Then I realise, it's not *her*, but her desperation I recognise. My parents were the same after Meggie died.

'We should go,' I whisper to Lewis. He nods. Sahara is already halfway to the lift. *It's not like her to avoid a drama,* I think, *so why doesn't she stay?* Unless she's feeling guilty at coming face to face with what she's done.

'We'll go. But we would really, really appreciate it if you could tell us anything about how she is,' Ade says.

Zoe's father sighs. 'She hasn't woken up. They say it's too early to know, that it's better we keep her in this … limbo for now. But they also said that the first twenty-four hours are the most important. Now it's been, what, nineteen hours? She should be responding by now.'

Mrs Tate makes an odd choking noise.

'We'll be thinking of her,' Ade says, and we nod and back away.

The lift is musty, full of stale air and misery. When we get to the ground floor, I have to run outside. The sun shines brightly. A little boy runs past, a yappy dog at his heels, and the kid laughs as he throws the ball and the dog tears after it in a blur.

I'm desperate to be back on *my* Beach. And back home.

In that order.

At the airport, we go from check-in to security to departure lounge like zombies, glad of the tedious queues and rules that stop us thinking.

The security people give Lewis a slightly harder time because he has two laptops, but no one in our group seems to remember that he arrived with just one. Ade and Sahara disappear without saying where they're going. Cara goes shopping, even though she has no money left.

That leaves Lewis and me to find seats in the far end of the departure lounge, where we can talk. He opens up his own laptop straight away.

'Did it work?'

Lewis looks up at me. 'What?'

'The Denial of Service thingy.'

He nods. 'Of course. Can I show you something else?'

'If it's a piano-playing kitten on YouTube then I'm not in the mood.'

Lewis smiles. 'I've been looking at the stuff I downloaded from Zoe's first laptop. There's some interesting information.'

He turns his laptop round to face me. There's a list of hundreds, maybe thousands of files: emails, logs, documents.

'Am I meant to be looking at anything specific?'

He turns it round again. 'Well, it's all potentially useful. This here is the background to Burning Truths: the domain registration, the hosting. But the most interesting stuff is between Tim and Zoe. He keeps talking about an "insurance policy". At first I thought it was life insurance or something, and it made me wonder if Meggie had had a policy he benefited from somehow.'

'She never took out that kind of policy, Lewis. She was only twenty years old.'

'I realised that pretty fast. It's not a policy. It's the photographs Zoe told you about, the ones Tim hid in the locker. I did download some of them off her hard drive, but only the ones she'd already uploaded, or was *about* to upload.'

'*About* to upload? New ones? What do those show?'

He frowns. 'Do you really want to see them now? It's been such an awful twenty-four hours, I thought they could wait till we got home. They're just a couple more odd close-ups of your sister, but I don't want to upset you anymore ...' Lewis looks up at me.

'Now. Please.'

'OK, let me call them up on my laptop. They're fairly heavily encrypted – I thought that was a good idea in view of what's happened – so you'll have to give me a few minutes.' He starts tapping. 'Anyway, I think the other pictures, the thousands she told you about, must be on the other laptop.' He pats the messenger bag that he's keeping tucked under his shoulder.

'Have you cracked the security on it yet?'

'Give me a chance, Ali. I need to try that at home. But there's plenty to keep me busy in the rest of the emails. Zoe set up the site without Tim knowing, and when he found out, he was cross. He asked her to close it down, but she kept insisting it would protect them both.'

I shudder. Tim's dead. Zoe's in a coma. She couldn't have been more wrong. 'Do you think it did the opposite? Incited someone?'

Lewis frowns. 'Impossible to be sure. I did look at the visitor stats for the site. Hardly anyone knew about it. There's you – I can tell your location. There's me – I've hidden my location, but the times fit. And then there are several different locations in Greenwich.'

'Zoe lived in Greenwich, though, before she moved here.'

'True. So one is likely to be her. Another of the visitors is obviously Tim going online to look at the site, the emails he sent to Zoe tie in exactly with when he went online. But there's another regular visitor somewhere near the university . . .' he hesitates.

'*Where* near the university?'

'I don't want to freak you out, but I think it's the halls of residence.'

I stare at him. 'Where Sahara still lives.'

Lewis nods. 'It doesn't automatically mean . . .' he doesn't finish the sentence.

The airport's lights seem to dim and it feels as though the temperature's dropped by ten degrees.

'Are you OK, Ali? Maybe I shouldn't have told you now, not after all the other shocks.'

'I'm pleased you did.'

'Let me get you a coffee. And something sweet,' he says, standing up. Then he adds, 'I'll only be over there by the café. Not far.'

'Lewis. Can I go online from your laptop here?'

He looks at me. 'That was a fast recovery.'

'There's something I need to do before we board the plane.' Or somewhere I need to go – the only place I can ever feel safe.

52

The actions of trying to log on to Soul Beach are automatic now, which is just as well, as all I can think about is Sahara. What I think she's done. Why she did it.

Whether she'll try to do it again.

'Florrie, where have you been?'

My sister is standing on the shoreline. Her eyes are puffy.

'Away, Meggie. I'm sorry. I'm back now, though.'

The airport fades away. My bare feet tingle thanks to the hot sand, and an intense warmth spreads through me like a flame, banishing the chill I felt moments ago.

'You helped Javier.' It's not a question. She knows.

'He's gone?'

'Between dusk and dawn. We'd gone to sleep in a big huddle last night, watching the most fantastic sunset. I woke up cold. Javier had been holding my hand but he wasn't there anymore.' She's trying hard not to cry. 'With Triti, we knew it was coming. But this time, I didn't get a chance to say goodbye.'

'I'm sorry, Meggie.'

Even though I was expecting it, losing Javier hurts like hell.

Without his smartness, his cynicism, the Beach will be a blander place. But of course, the sharpness was armour-plating. Underneath it was a hurt, lost boy who loved his sisters, his mother, and a guy called Gabriel.

Life is change, Alice. One of the last things he said to me. Perhaps it was him telling me he was ready to let go.

'I had so much to tell him, Florrie,' Meggie says. 'About

how much he helped me when I first arrived. He was the only one who never lied about how tough it could be here. I should have thanked him for that.'

'Maybe goodbyes aren't all they're cracked up to be, sis. The important thing is that he knew how you felt about him. But what's happened here in the real world. The things that have allowed Javier to . . . go . . .' I hesitate, 'they're for the best, for the people he left behind.'

'Honestly?'

'I promise you it's true.' Helping Javier is the only thing I feel I did right on this trip, even though losing him forever feels like losing a member of my family.

'We've still got each other, Florrie.'

I look at my sister, and I try to imagine how it'll feel if I manage to set Meggie free. Will I *ever* be able to do that? I take a step forward to hug her, but she holds up her hand.

'I have to ask you something, little sister. I know you have to be careful how you answer, but does Javier going make it more likely that *I'll* be going . . . somewhere else, too? Has it helped you work it out? I don't care either way except I'd like to be prepared, if I can be.'

'I don't know, Meggie. I'll try to warn you before . . . something happens, but it might not be possible.'

She nods. 'I understand. This is hard for you too. Harder, even, because you're the one responsible . . .' her voice breaks, and this time she lets me wrap my arms around her, burying my head in her golden hair.

What the hell?

I'm somewhere else. Not the Beach, not with Meggie. And even though my eyes are closed, I can *see*.

Black gloves. A blue-white flash of light . . . no, not light. Something else.

I open my eyes again. Meggie's backing away. The image disappears.

'What's wrong, Florrie?'

'I saw something when we touched. Like a photograph.'

My sister frowns. '*What* did you see?'

What the hell was it? I know one thing: it scared me.

'Ali? Ali!'

Another voice, a man's, is calling out behind me. I blink, look up from the laptop and see Lewis over by the shop, tapping his watch. 'We need to get to the gate,' he shouts over at me. 'They've already called boarding time.'

'Meggie. I'll be back soon. Tell Danny I ... love him,' I whisper, even though I blush because I'm having to send the message second-hand. 'I'll work it out. I'll work all of it out. Give me time.'

And I close the Beach down, log out of my email, pull my headphones out. I'm about to close the laptop lid when I realise the images of Meggie that Lewis was unencrypting have now opened.

The first shows an extreme close up of her eyes. They're a sludgier, darker blue-grey than I remember, but that's probably the Beach playing tricks by making them look a prettier baby-blue than they ever were in real life.

The eyes in the photo don't show fear, but they do show wariness. Something was wrong, and she knew it.

'ALICE! Come on, we'll miss the plane,' Lewis calls.

I close that window, but a second photo appears behind it. It's another shot of her face, but less close up than the first one.

No. It's not possible!

Those eyes. That girl in the picture. It's not Meggie at all. *It's me.*

By the time we get to the gate, almost everyone else is on board. Ade and Cara are way ahead in the queue and Sahara must be on board already. I climb the steps to the plane, the sun merciless on my back. It makes the tiny burns from last night smart again.

I stumble on the steps. My legs aren't working properly. Lewis takes my hand and helps me into the cabin.

'Almost home,' he says.

The killer has been following me.

The plane's almost full. Lewis is directed into the first free seat by an impatient flight attendant. Ade's in the aisle near the front. Cara's right behind him. I keep walking along the aisle, hanging on to the tops of the seats because I feel unsteady.

'Alice! I've saved you a place!'

Sahara is waving from the centre emergency exit row. She pats the aisle seat. 'I'll buy you a Danish pastry, too. I've saved just enough euros for a treat on the way home.'

I stare at her. It has to be her. Where did she take that picture of me? And why?

She's reaching out for me, her long fingers grasping at the already stale cabin air.

There's something about the shape of her hand.

I blink, and I see the image I saw when I hugged my sister. Those gloves again. Leather. Driving gloves. *Or the kind you'd wear on a motorbike.*

And I realise the flash of light wasn't light at all. It was pale, white fabric. A pillowcase.

'Alice. You're holding up the flight now. Come on, sit down. We'll soon be home. It'll all be over.'

I stumble into the seat, bashing my leg against the arm rest. I can't seem to do up my seatbelt and Sahara leans over to do it for me, like a mother helping her child.

The flash was the pillow coming down onto my sister's face. Probably the last thing she ever saw.

'That's better,' Sahara trills. 'The captain said earlier there might be a few bumps on the way back, due to turbulence. But now you're all safely strapped in.'

Meggie.

Tim.

Zoe.

When will it stop? Am I the end of the line?

I turn to face Sahara, and she's smiling – and so close in these budget airline seats. She's been desperate to get close to me ever since we lost Meggie, and now she's managed it. Even if it does seem to be by eliminating everyone else close to me. 'Thanks, Sahara. I don't know what I'd do without you.'

She beams back at me and I try not to shudder. I know this is more dangerous than anything I've done before, but it's the only way.

To catch the predator, I must become the prey.

When I first heard Meggie sing, it almost made me believe in heaven.

'Twas grace that taught my heart to fear,
And grace my fears reliev'd;
How precious did that grace appear
The hour I first believ'd!'

She made the words of that old hymn so convincing, yet now, somehow, the lyric only works if I substitute Alice for grace ... I believe in Alice, and the idea of a world without her terrifies me.

As time passes, I realise being unmasked is not the most frightening outcome. What scares me most is anonymity. A time when no one cares about the things I've done, when even Alice has moments when she forgets.

The pace is increasing. I know what I have to do to make Alice believe, and I know the time cannot come too soon. She seems almost as impatient as I am.

Acknowledgements

Soul Fire has been edge-of-the-seat stuff – not just for Alice, but for me too.

First and foremost, I have to thank Jenny and especially Amber for helping me to navigate through a challenging maze of deadly secrets, red-hot fire runs and dark gothic alleyways. You're so much better at seeing the (flaming torch) light at the end of the tunnel. I am in awe.

Thanks so much to Nina – top girl and top Twitter guru too – for organising such brilliant publicity for the first book – and to Louise for coming with me to the fab Eternal Twilight.

The team at Orion make up a constellation of superstars. It's been amazing to have Lisa and Fiona championing the book so strongly from the start, Pandora making the audio version so terrific, and Jen, Kate, Louise and Mark doing such a great job to raise awareness online and in the 'real' world.

I'd like to say a special thank-you to the amazing bloggers who work so hard to get books talked about: Amanda from Floor to Ceiling Books, Carly at Writing from the Tub, Emma at Book Angel's Booktopia, Jenny at Wondrous Reads, Karen at Reading Teenage Fiction, Liz, Mark and Sarah at My Favourite Books, Rhiana at Heaven, Hell (now Cosy Books), SJH at A Dream of Books and Viv at Serendipity Reviews. Apologies if I've left anyone off, and tell me for next time!

Hello to so many people who've let me know via Twitter who *they* think killed Meggie. Some of you might just be right . . .

Philippa at LAW is a true book babe, endlessly supportive

and so smart, and Holly makes everything feel fantastically effortless.

My writing friends are such excellent company that I daren't single anyone out. Mwah, darlings, you're all *wonderful*. But it's been great to discover the adventures to be had in the children's book world with SCBWI and SAS folks ... as always, the Board is always a highlight of my day.

The Barça gang helped me survive the ordeal by fire that is the Correfoc – cheers, amigos. Special thanks to Matt and Tina for inspiring us to experience Catalan living in the first place.

A distracted writer isn't always the easiest mate, sister, daughter or girlfriend. So lots of love to Geri and Jenny, Toni, Mum and Dad and Rich for accepting my vagueness.

Last but definitely not least, thanks to *you* for coming on the journey with me to Soul Beach. I'd love to know what you think – you can get in touch with me via my website, www.kate-harrison.com or I'm @katewritesbooks on Twitter.

See you on the Beach ...

Kate xx
Brighton, 2012